Join favourite author

Louise Allen

as she explores the tangled love-lives of

Those Scandalous Ravenhursts

First, you travelled across war-torn Europe
with
THE DANGEROUS MR RYDER

Now you can accompany Mr Ryder's sister,
THE OUTRAGEOUS LADY FELSHAM,
on her quest for a hero.

Coming soon

THE SHOCKING LORD STANDON

THE DISGRACEFUL MR RAVENHURST

THE NOTORIOUS MR HURST

THE PIRATICAL MISS RAVENHURST

Author Note

My exploration of the lives and loves of *Those Scandalous Ravenhurst* cousins began with the story of Jack Ryder and his Grand Duchess Eva in THE DANGEROUS MR RYDER.

At one point Jack's sister Bel intervened in their romance, with almost disastrous results, so I thought it was time for Bel to have her own story. As the widow of a man known as the most boring member of the *ton,* Lady Belinda Felsham knows something has been missing from her life—specifically an exciting, handsome lover—and she knows, too, that she is far too well behaved to ever go out and find one.

But then Major Ashe Reynard, Viscount Dereham, arrives on her hearthrug at one in the morning, and Bel realises she has found the man of her fantasies. Ashe is only too ready to oblige—for, after all, neither of them wants more than a commitment-free *affaire.* Or do they?

I had a great deal of fun, and some heartache, following Bel and Ashe through their tangled path to true love, hindered on the way by a polar bear, a bathing machine and a formidable aunt, and I hope you enjoy the journey too.

Coming next will be THE SHOCKING LORD STANDON—not that Gareth Morant, Earl of Standon, *wants* to be shocking, but sometimes a gentleman just has to make a sacrifice for the ladies in his life.

Dedication

For the wonderful Terry and Peter at the equally wonderful Margate Museum, with grateful thanks for all their kind and generous help and all the information anyone could ever hope to find on the subject of bathing machines.

THE OUTRAGEOUS
LADY FELSHAM

Louise Allen

MILLS & BOON
Pure reading pleasure

First published in Great Britain 2008
Harlequin Mills & Boon Limited,
Eton House, 18-24 Paradise Road, Richmond, Surrey TW9 1SR

© Melanie Hilton 2008

ISBN: 978 0 263 86257 7

Set in Times Roman 10½ on 12¼ pt.
04-0508-79911

Printed and bound in Spain
by Litografia Rosés S.A., Barcelona

Louise Allen has been immersing herself in history, real and fictional, for as long as she can remember, and finds landscapes and places evoke powerful images of the past. Louise lives in Bedfordshire and works as a property manager, but spends as much time as possible with her husband at the cottage they are renovating on the north Norfolk coast, or travelling abroad. Venice, Burgundy and the Greek islands are favourite atmospheric destinations. Please visit Louise's website—www.louiseallenregency.co.uk—for the latest news!

Recent novels by the same author:

RAVENHURST FAMILY TREE

Francis Philip Ravenhurst, 2nd Duke of Allington = Lady Francesca Templeton

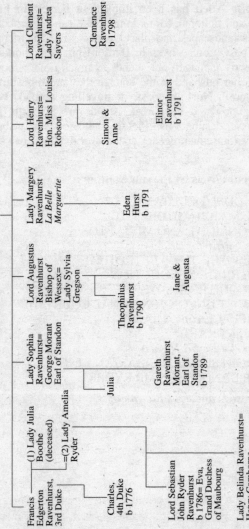

Chapter One

Late July 1815

I want a hero. The words stared blackly off the page into her tired eyes. 'So do I, Lord Byron, so do I.' Bel sighed, pushed her tumbled brown hair back off her face and resumed her reading of the first stanza of *Don Juan*. She and the poet did not want heroes for the same reason, of course. The poet was despairing of finding a suitable hero for his tale; Belinda, Lady Felsham, simply yearned for romance.

No, that was not true either. Bel marked her place with one fingertip and stared into space, brooding. If she could not be honest in her own head, where could she be? Her yearnings were not simple, they were not pure and they certainly were not about knights errant or romance.

Bel rolled over on to her back on the white fur rug and tossed the book aside, narrowly missing one of the candelabra which sat on the hearth and lit her reading. It was well past two in the morning and the candles were beginning to gutter; in a few minutes she would have to get up and tend to them or go to bed and try to sleep.

She stretched out a bare foot, ruffling the silken flounces around the hem of her nightgown, and with her toes stroked the ears of the polar bear whose head snarled towards the door of her bedchamber. 'That's not what I want, Horace,' she informed him. 'I do not yearn for moonlight and soft music and lingering glances. I want a gorgeous, exciting man who will be thrilling in bed. I want a lover. A really good one.'

Horace, unshockable, did not respond, but then he never had, not to any of the confidences that had been poured into his battered and yellowing ears over the years. At the age of nine she had fallen in love with him, wheedled him out of her godfather's study and moved him into her bedchamber. He had stayed with her ever since.

Her late husband—Henry, Viscount Felsham—had protested faintly at the presence of a vast and motheaten bearskin on his wife's chamber floor, but Bel, otherwise biddable and compliant with every stricture and requirement of her new husband, had stuck her heels in and Horace had stayed. Henry had always ostentatiously made a point of sighing heavily and walking around him whenever he made his twice-weekly visitation to her room. Perhaps he sensed that conversation with Horace was more exciting for his young wife than his bedroom attentions had proved.

Bel sat up, braced her arms behind her, and looked round the room with satisfaction. Her bedchamber was just right, even if she was occupying it alone without the lover of her dreams. In fact, she congratulated herself, somewhat smugly, the whole house was perfect.

It was a little gem in Half Moon Street, recently acquired as part of her campaign to emerge from eighteen months of mourning and enjoy herself.

It was still a very masculine house, reflecting the tastes of its last owner. But that was not a problem; it simply gave her another project to work on, and one that was possible to achieve, unlike the acquisition of a suitable lover, which was, as she very well knew, complete fantasy.

Bel was still becoming used to the blissful freedom and independence of widowhood. She would never have wished poor Henry dead, of course not. But if some benevolent genie had swooped down on a magic carpet and removed him to a place where he could lecture the inhabitants at tedious length on their drains, their livestock or the minutiae of tithe law, she would have rejoiced.

Henry had had a knack of being stolidly at her side whenever she wished to be alone and of stating his minutely detailed and worthy opinions upon every subject under the sun. And she had itched to have control of her own money.

But no genie had come for poor Henry, just a ridiculous, apparently trivial, illness carrying him off in what, people unoriginally remarked, was his prime. Her toes were becoming cold. Best to get into bed and hope the soft mattress would help lull her to sleep.

There was a sound from outside the room. Bel tipped her head to one side, listening. Odd. Her butler and his wife, her housekeeper, slept in the basement. The footmen were quartered in the mews and her dresser and the housemaid had rooms on the topmost floor. It came again, a muted thump as though someone had stumbled on the stairs. Swallowing hard, Bel reached out for the poker as her bedchamber door swung open, banging back against the wall.

Framed in the open doorway stood a large figure: long legged, broad shouldered, and dressed, she saw with a shock, in the full glory of military scarlet. The flickering candlelight sparked off a considerable amount of frogging and silver braid, leaving the figure's features in shadow. There was a glint from under his brows, the flash of white teeth. Her fingertips scrabbled nervelessly for the poker and it rolled away from her into the cold hearth.

'Now you are what I call a perfect coming-home gift,' a deep, slurred, very male voice said happily. It resonated in some strange way at the base of her spine as though she was feeling it, not hearing it. 'I don't remember you from before, sweetheart. Still, don't remember a lot about tonight. Thank God,' he added piously.

The man advanced a little further into the room, close enough for his booted toes to be almost touching Horace's snarling jaws. Bel scrabbled a little further back, but her nightgown tangled round her feet. Could she stand up? 'Who moved the bed?' he added indignantly.

He was drunk. It explained the slurred voice, it explained why he was unsteady on his feet and talking nonsense. It did not explain what he was doing in her bedroom.

'Go away,' Bel said clearly, despite her heart being somewhere in the region of her tonsils. Screaming was not going to help, no one would hear her and it might provoke him to sudden action.

'Don't be so unkind, sweet.' His smile was tinged with reproach at her rejection. 'It's not *that* late.' The landing clock struck three. 'See?' he observed, with a grandiloquent gesture that made him sway dangerously. 'The night is but young.' Despite the slurring, the voice was educated and confident. What she appeared to have in her bedchamber was a drunk English officer who could walk through locked doors—unless he was a ghost. But she could smell the brandy from where she was sprawled, and ghosts, surely, did not drink?

'Go away,' she repeated. Somehow standing up did not seem a good idea; she felt it might be like a rabbit starting to run right in front of a lurcher—certain to provoke a reaction. He appeared to be very good looking. Lit by the light of the two candelabra in the hearth his overlong blond hair, well-defined chin and mobile mouth were all the detail she could properly make out, but watching him she was conscious of something stirring deep inside, like the smallest flick of a cat's tail.

'No, don't want to do that. Not friendly, goin' away,' the man said decisively. 'We're goin' to be friendly. Got to get acquainted, ring for a bottle of wine, have a chat first.'

First? Before what, exactly? Suddenly getting up and risking provoking him seemed an attractive option after all. Bel glanced down, realising that not only was she wearing one of her newest and prettiest thin silk nightgowns, but that was all she was wearing. Her négligé—not that it was much more decent—was thrown over the foot of the bed. She inched back as the man took a step forward.

And put one booted foot squarely into Horace's gaping mouth. 'Wha' the hell?' The momentum of his stride took him forward, his trapped foot held him back.

In a welter of long limbs the intruder fell full length on the bearskin rug with Bel flattened neatly between yellowing fur and scarlet broadcloth. Her elbows gave way, her head came down with a thump on Horace's foolish stub of a tail.

'Ough!' He was big. Not fat, though—there was no comfortable belly to cushion the impact. She seemed to be trapped under six foot plus of solid male bone and muscle.

'*There* you are,' he said in a pleased voice, as though she had been hiding. His face was buried in her shoulder and the words rumbled against her skin as he began to nuzzle into it. His night beard rasped, sending shivers down her spine.

'Get off.' Bel wriggled her hands free and shoved up against his shoulders. It had rather less effect than if a wardrobe had fallen on her. At least a wardrobe would not have gone limp like this. There was absolutely nothing to lever on. 'Move, you great lummox!'

The only reply she got was a soft snore, just below her right ear. He had gone to sleep, or fallen into a drunken stupor more like, she decided grimly. This close the smell of brandy and wine was powerful.

Bel wriggled some more but he seemed to have settled over her like a heavily weighted blanket; there was nowhere to wriggle to. Under her there was Horace's fur, the thick felt backing, and, beneath that, the carpet. It all provided some padding, although rather less than her uninvited guest was enjoying. He appeared to be blissfully comfortable.

His knees dug in below her own. That was already becoming painful. With an effort she managed to move her legs apart so he was cradled between her thighs.

'There, that's better.' The answer was another snore, accompanied by a squirming movement of his hips as he readjusted himself to her change of position. At which point Bel realised rather clearly that this was not better. Not at all.

'Oh, my goodness,' she whispered in awe.

Bel had not been sure quite what to expect of marital relations from her mother's veiled hints during the *little talk* they had had just before her wedding day. She had expected it to be uncomfortable and embarrassing at first, and it was certainly all of that. But after the first three weeks of marriage, when the worst of the shyness wore off, she also realised that her marital duties, as well as being sticky and discomforting, were deadly boring. She tried to take an interest, for Henry would be highly affronted if she ever did nod off during his visits to her bed, but it was out of duty, not in the hope of any pleasure for herself.

It was not until the other young matrons with whom she began to mix forgot that she was a very new bride that she got her first inklings that she was missing out on something rather special. One day in particular stuck in her memory.

She had arrived early for Lady Gossington's soirée and found herself in the midst of a group of the very dashing ladies who always filled her with the conviction that she was naïve, gauche and ignorant. They settled round her like so many birds of paradise, fluttered their fans and prepared to subject every arrival to a minute scrutiny and a comprehensive dissection.

'My dears, look who's here,' Mrs Roper whispered. 'Lord Farringdon.'

'Now that,' one of her friends pronounced, 'is what

I call a handsome man.' Bel had studied his lordship. He certainly fitted that description: tall, slim with a clean profile, attractive dark hair and a ready smile.

'And so well endowed,' Lady Lacey purred. In answer, there was a soft ripple of laughter, which had an edge to it Bel did not understand. She felt she was being left out of a secret. 'So I am led to believe,' Lady Lacey added slyly.

Normally Bel would have kept silent, but this time she forced herself to join in; money, at least, was something she understood. 'Is he really?' His clothes were exquisite, but that was not necessarily any indication. 'I did not realise, I thought the Farringdon fortune was lost by his father.'

Their hilarity at this question reduced her to blushing silence. She had obviously said something very foolish. But how to ask for clarification? Lady Lacey took pity on her, leaned across and whispered in her ear. Wide-eyed, Bel discovered in exactly what way the gentleman was well endowed and just how much this characteristic was appreciated by ladies. It left her speechless.

Now she was able to judge precisely what her friends had been referring to. Her uninvited guest was pressed against her in such a way that his male attributes were in perfect conjunction with the point where her tangle of soft brown curls made a dark shadow behind the light silk of her bed gown. And he was drunk and unconscious or asleep and yet he was still...*oh, my heavens*... large. That appeared to be the only word for it. Her previous experience offered no comparison at all. Henry, it was becoming apparent, had *not* been well endowed.

Bel stopped all attempts to wriggle; the *frissons* the

movement produced inside her were just too disquiet-ing. The stirring of sensation she had experienced on first seeing the intruder were as nothing to the warm glow that spread through her from the point where they were so tightly pressed together. It felt as though her insides were turning liquid, but in the most unsettling, interesting way. Her breasts, squashed by his chest with its magnificently frogged dress-uniform jacket, were aching with something that was not solely the result of silver buttons being pressed into flesh. An involuntary moan escaped her lips.

Oh, my... Bel turned her head so she could scruti-nise as much as possible of the stranger. There was not a lot she could see except the top of a tousled blond head and a magnificent pair of shoulders that made her want to flex her fingers on them. This must be sexual attrac-tion! Or was it arousal? She was not very clear about the difference, or how one told. Whatever it was, it seemed alarmingly immodest of her to be feeling it for a man to whom she had not even been introduced. She wished Eva, her new sister-in-law, was in London to ask. But the newly weds were honeymooning in Italy.

Eva—erstwhile Dowager Grand Duchess of Maubourg and now most romantically married to Bel's brother Sebastian—very obviously knew all about sexual attraction. Not only had she been married to one of the most notoriously adept lovers in Europe, she was now passionately attached to Sebastian. Bel had hardly been able to turn a corner in the castle in Maubourg when she had attended the wedding two weeks before, without finding the two of them locked in an embrace, or simply touching fingers, caressing faces, standing close.

There was no one else Bel could trust enough to

discuss such things with; she was on her own with this new sensation. The man seemed nice enough, she brooded. She had observed that drink tended to emphasise any vicious tendencies in a man, so his apparently sunny and friendly nature could probably be relied upon. There was nothing to be done about it but to wait until he woke up and they could have a more civilised conversation. At a safe distance.

It was not easy attempting to sleep while squashed under the body of a large and attractive stranger and prey to one's first stirrings of intimate arousal. The candles began to go out, the room became dark and the only sounds were his heavy, regular breathing and the creaks of the house.

Now it was so dark Bel found her reactions were concentrated on touch and smell. Touch—even the warm caress of his breath against her throat—she tried to ignore, reflecting that if she became any more disturbed by that she would not know how to cope with it. She had heard—probably from one of Henry's pontifications upon the sins of society—that uncontrolled sexual feelings in a woman led to hysteria, and that was definitely to be avoided.

But her nostrils were becoming used to the smell of alcohol and behind it she was catching intriguing whispers of other scents. Soap—a subtle and expensive type—a hint of fresh sweat, which was surprisingly not at all offensive, and man. Henry had smelt just of Henry: rigorously clean and scrubbed at all times. He had used Malcolm's Purifying Tablet Soap, renowned for its health-preserving properties. This man was rather more complex, definitely more earthy and quite unmistakably male. And that, Bel realised, was another source of titillation.

Was this business of sexual attraction more complicated than she had assumed? Did scent and sight and
touch all play a part? And what about the mind? Love
songs and poetry, perhaps? Bel adjusted her head to the
most comfortable angle she could find and resolutely
closed her eyes.

She had not expected to sleep, but she must have
dozed, for when a warm, moist pressure around her ear
woke her, the room was already grey with the earliest
dawn light. Something was nuzzling her ear. Bel froze,
then remembered where she was and who it was. He
was mouthing gently at the sensitive whorls, his tongue
straying up and down them. It was bliss. Her eyelids
drooped again. And then he nipped gently at the lobe.

'Aah!' Bel had never felt so agitated. It should have
hurt; instead, she experienced a jolt of electrifying sensation in a most embarrassing place. Against the un-
yielding pressure of his chest her nipples hardened,
aching.

The lips left her skin instantly and the deep voice
murmured—with only a hint of a slur, 'Mmm…you're
awake. Good morning, sweet.' He settled himself more
comfortably between her legs with a thrilling tilt of his
pelvis and it was obvious that what she had felt before
was as nothing to what was happening now. He was
awake, he was amorously inclined and he thought she
would be receptive to his advances.

For a mad moment Bel thought of simply throwing
her arms around those broad shoulders and waiting to
see what would happen. She wanted a lover—here he
was. Then common sense and her upbringing came to
the rescue. It was one thing to choose as a lover a man

you knew and respected; it was quite another to lie with a complete stranger who appeared to have wandered in off the street, however deliciously tempting he was.

'Yes, I am awake.' She put her palms against his shoulders and shoved, even more annoyed with herself than with him. 'And thank goodness you are, at long last. Now, sir, please get up this instant.'

He did not stand, but at least he rolled off her, landing with a thump on his back. He turned his head and gazed at her with startlingly blue eyes fringed with thick golden lashes. Periwinkles, lapis, the sun on the sea. Bel gazed back, drowning, then pulled herself together and sat up.

'What, sir, are you doing in my house?'

'I was going to ask you the same thing, my sweet. I don't remember ordering you. Don't remember much, truth be told.' He sat up and rubbed both hands through his hair, rumpling it worse than before. 'God, have I got a hangover.'

'Kindly do not blaspheme.' Bel sat up. 'And I am not in your house, you are in mine. And stop calling me *sweet*. My name is—'

He stood up with a sudden lurch, grabbed for the bedpost, missed and looked around, swaying back on his heels. 'Who moved my bed? And what the dev… what on earth is *that*?' He pointed at Horace.

'A polar bear. You fell over him.' Bel got to her feet, her cramped muscles protesting. 'Who are you?'

'Reynard.' He ran a hand over his stubbled chin and grimaced.

'A fox?'

'No, not *reynard*.' His French accent was good, she noted. 'Reynard. Ashe Reynard. Major. Viscount Dereham. Didn't I tell you when I hired you?' He yawned mightily, displaying a healthy set of white teeth. 'I beg your pardon.'

'Dereham.' Of course. It made sense now. 'You sold this house. I live here now.' She had purchased it through his agent, who had told her that Viscount Dereham was on the continent with Wellington's army. That at least explained the way he had got in; she had not thought to change the locks.

'Ah. I sold it, then?' He swayed, sat down on the bed, and blinked at her. Then he looked down at the bearskin, the burnt-out candles, up at her nightgown. 'So you are not a Drury Lane vestal? Not a little ladybird I hired for the night. You are a lady. Oh, hell.' He drove both hands through the mane of golden hair as though to force some focus into his head. 'Have I just spent the night pinning you to the floor?'

Chapter Two

$\mathcal{B}$el glanced at the mantel clock. 'We have spent about two hours of the night on the rug.' He—Lord Dereham, for goodness' sake!—got up, hanging on firmly to the bedpost. His gaze appeared to be riveted on her body. She glanced down and realised all over again just what she was wearing and how the early light was streaming through it. She took two swift steps, caught up the négligé and pulled it on. Reynard rocked back on his heels as she brushed past. He looked as if he truly did have the most crashing hangover.

'My…'pologies…' His eyes were beginning to cross now.

'Come on.' She tugged his arm. Goodness, he was solid. 'Come and get some sleep in the spare bedroom.'

'Haven't got one. Remember that.'

'You did not, I do. I expect it was your study. Come along.' She closed both hands over his arm and tried to drag him like a reluctant child.

'In a minute.' Doggedly he turned round and walked off into her dressing room. Of course, he would know about the up-to-the-minute privy installed in a cupboard in the corner along with the innovative—and unreliable—shower bath. Bel left him to it and went across the landing to turn down the spare bed.

The little house had a basement with the kitchen, store rooms and the set of compact chambers occupied by Hedges and Mrs Hedges. Space on the ground floor was chiefly occupied by the dining room and a salon, with above them her bedchamber, dressing room and what had been a study, now transformed into her spare room by dint of adding a small canopied bed.

'You moved my desk,' Lord Dereham complained from the doorway.

'Never mind that now.' Bel took him by the sleeve again and towed him into the room. He was proving remarkably biddable for such a large man. 'Take off your jacket and your neckcloth.'

'A'right.' The slur was coming back. Those garments shed on to the floor, she gave him a push and he tumbled on to the bed. Which left his boots. Bel seized one and tugged, then the other, and set them at the foot. Reynard was already asleep as she dragged the covers over him, the blue eyes shuttered, the ludicrously long lashes fanning his cheeks.

'What *am* I doing?' Bel wondered aloud, bending to retrieve the jacket and neckcloth from the floor. But what was the alternative? She could hardly push him downstairs and he would probably fall if she made him walk. Rousing Hedges to throw him out seemed unfair to the butler, who would be up and working soon enough, and she could hardly leave him in her own bedroom. 'And I don't expect you will stir until luncheon time either, will you?' she asked the beautiful, unresponsive, profile.

His answer was a gentle snore. Bel hung his clothes over the chair back and took herself off back to bed, feeling that her eyes were beginning to cross quite as much as the major's had.

She was awoken, far too soon, by a female shriek. It seemed to come from the landing. Bel sat up, rubbing her eyes. Silence. Goodness, she was tired. And there was something she should remember; she was puzzling over it as her door burst open. Millie, the housemaid, eyes wide with shocked excitement, rushed in, followed by Philpott, her dresser, and bringing up the rear, Mrs Hedges, red in the face with the effort of running up the stairs.

'My lady,' Philpott pronounced in tones of throbbing horror, 'there is a man in the spare bed!'

A man in the spare bed? A man? Lord! Of course there was. Why had she not thought what her staff would find when they started the day's chores?

'Yes?' Bel enquired, more brightly than she felt. 'I know.'

All three women were staring at her bed, she realised. Staring at the smooth, untouched pillow next to her own, the tightly tucked-in bedding on that side, the perfectly unrumpled coverlet, the chaste order of the whole thing. She could almost see their thought processes, like the bubble above a character's head in a satirical cartoon. Despite the outrageous presence of a man next door, no one, quite obviously, had been in her ladyship's bed, other than her ladyship. She raised her eyebrows in haughty enquiry.

'If I had known your ladyship was expecting a guest—' Mrs Hedges crossed her arms defensively '—I would have aired the sheets.'

'I was not expecting him myself,' Bel said, adopting a brisk tone. 'It is Lord Dereham, from whom I bought the house. He was taken suddenly ill, most fortunately almost upon our doorstep, and, having a key, sought refuge in here.'

'But the front door is bolted, my lady. Hedges bolts it every night.'

'The back-door key, it must have been.' Bel wondered where she had suddenly acquired three such assiduous chaperons from. 'I assume his lordship was passing the mews when he became unwell.'

'Should I send for the doctor, my lady?' the house-keeper asked.

'Er…no. His lordship's indisposition is not medical, it is something that will wear off in the fullness of time.'

'He was drunk?' Philpott was aghast. 'It does not bear contemplating. What is the watch coming to, to allow such a rakehell to roam the streets in that condition? What outrage might he not have inflicted upon a helpless woman!'

'Lord Dereham was perfectly civil, and er…respectful.' If one did not count nuzzling her ear and giving her the prolonged benefit of the intimate proximity of his magnificent body. She stifled a wistful sigh at the thought of just how magnificent it had felt.

'What shall we do with him now, ma'am?' Mrs Hedges, ruffled, made it sound as if Bel had imported an exotic animal into the house.

'Leave him to sleep, I suppose.' Bel wriggled up against the pillows and tried to think. 'When he wakes up, then Hedges can fetch him coffee and hot water. My husband's toilet gear is in the small trunk in the dressing room, if you could find that, please, Millie; no doubt he will wish to have a shave. And then, depending on what time of day it is, it would be only hospitable to offer a meal.'

Her staff scattered, Mrs Hedges to bustle downstairs to update her husband on the situation, Millie to fetch her morning chocolate and Philpott to sweep around the room, tweaking everything into place. 'What shall I put out for you, my lady?' She retrieved the volume of poetry from the hearth, rattled the poker back into its stand and straightened Horace's head with the point of her toe. Bel watched out of the corner of her eye, suddenly incapable of looking Horace in the face.

'The new leaf-green morning dress, please, Philpott. I had intended walking to Hatchard's, but I suppose I had better not go out while his lordship is still here. The brown kid slippers will do for the moment.'

A new gown, her single strand of pearls and an elegant hairstyle would, she hoped, establish a sufficient distance between Lady Belinda Felsham and the scantily clad woman his lordship had crushed beneath him last night. Bel remembered the way his body had lain against hers, the way it had made her feel and the sudden heat in his eyes as they had rested fleetingly on her fragile nightgown.

The unsettling stirrings inside returned, making her feel flushed and uncertain. Was this the effect of desire, or of unsatisfied desire? Would she need to take a lover to stop these feelings disturbing her tranquillity, or, now they had been aroused, was she going to be prey to them for ever?

Bel leaned back on the embroidered linen of her pillows, turning her cheek against the coolness. But the little bumps of the white work embroidery pressed into her skin, reminding her forcibly of the pressure of the major's buttons and frogging against her bosom. She waited until Philpott went into the dressing room and risked a peep under the neckline of the nightgown, expecting to find a perfect pattern imprinted on her skin. Nothing, of course—why then could she fancy she still felt it?

And how was she going to face Lord Dereham when he awoke?

Ashe turned over on to his back and threw one arm across his eyes as light from the uncurtained window hit them. Even through closed lids the effect was painful.

He lay there, waiting patiently as he had done every morning for a month now, waiting for the noise of battle, the shouts and screams, the boom of the cannon and the crack of musket fire to leave his sleep-filled brain. The battle was over. He was alive. The fact continued to take him by surprise every morning. How much longer before he could accept he had not been killed, had not been more than lightly wounded? How much longer would it be before he could start to think like a civilian again and find some purpose in the life he still had, against all the odds?

Eyes remaining closed against the impact of a massive headache, Ashe stretched his legs and came up hard against a footboard. Odd. He did not appear to be in his own bed. Vaguely, through the brandy fumes, his brain produced the memory of a woman. A tall, dark-haired woman with a glorious figure that had fitted against his body as though she had been created to hold him in her arms. A beautiful stranger. And a white bear. A bear? Hell. How much had he drunk last night?

His nostrils flared, seeking her. Wherever the woman

in his memory—or had it been a dream?—had gone, she was not here now. The bed linen smelt fresh and crisp, there was no hint of perfume or that subtle, infinitely erotic, morning scent of warm, sleepy femininity.

Time to open his eyes. Ashe found he was squinting at a very familiar window. His study window, in his house. Only, the desk that always stood in front of it had gone, the bookcases had gone. The room had been transformed into a bedchamber. He threw back the covers and swung his legs out of bed, realising that he was still partly dressed. His boots were standing neatly at the foot of the bed, his dress-uniform jacket hung on the back of a chair. He had not the slightest recollection of taking either off.

The bell pull, thank God, was still where it should be. Ashe made his way across to it, swearing under his breath at the pain behind his eyes, and tugged it, then sat down on the edge of the bed to wait to see who would appear.

The part of his mind that was convinced he was at home expected his valet. The part that was crashingly hungover would not have been surprised to see the door opened by either a white bear or a lovely woman. He had not expected a completely strange, perfectly correct, upper servant in smart morning livery. The butler was bearing a silver salver with a glass upon it filled with a cloudy brown liquid.

'Good morning, my lord. I believe you may find this receipt efficacious for your headache. Would you care for coffee before I bring your shaving water?'

'You know who I am?'

'Major the Viscount Dereham, I understand, my lord.'

'And you are?' Ashe reached for the glass and downed the contents without giving himself time to think about it. Butlers like this one always knew the most repellent, and effective, cures. His stomach revolted wildly, stayed where it was by some miracle, and then stopped churning. He might yet live.

'Hedges, my lord.' The butler retrieved the glass. 'Coffee, my lord? Her ladyship has requested you join her at luncheon, should you feel well enough.'

Her ladyship? 'I am not married, Hedges.'

'As you say, my lord. I refer to Lady Felsham. I understand from her ladyship that you were indisposed last night and sought refuge here, finding it familiar, as it were.'

So he *was* in his own house, and he was not losing his mind. Only he had sold it—he could remember now he had been given a clue. He had written to his agent Grimball from Brussels three months ago. This comfortable little house had proved both too small, and too large, for his needs. He had the family town house—mausoleum though it was—for his mother and sisters on their unpredictable descents upon London, and after selling this house Grimball had taken chambers for him in the Albany for comfortable bachelor living.

But who the devil was Lady Felsham? Surely not the Venus in the translucent silk nightgown he could remember now his head was clearing? She must have been a dream. Women like that only existed in dreams.

The butler was waiting patiently for him to make a decision. 'Coffee would be a good idea, thank you, Hedges, then hot water. And my compliments to her ladyship and I would be delighted to join her for luncheon.'

He frowned at the butler. 'Where is Lord Felsham?' If he remembered correctly, Felsham was older than he—about thirty-five—staid to the point of inertia and widely avoided because of the paralysing dullness of his character and conversation. That did not bode well for an entertaining luncheon, but it was probably all his battered brain could cope with.

'His lordship, I regret to inform you, passed away almost two years ago as the result of a severe chill caught while inspecting the drains at Felsham Hall.' The butler cleared his throat discreetly. 'Her ladyship is only recently out of mourning. If you would care to remove your shirt, my lord, I will do what I can to restore it.'

Stripped to the waist, Ashe shaved himself with the painstaking care of a man who was all too aware that his finer reflexes had a way to go to recover themselves. At least he did not look too much of a wreck, he consoled himself, peering into the mirror after rinsing off the lather. Weeks out of doors drilling his troops had tanned his skin, tightened up his muscles, and one celebratory night of hard drinking did not show—at least not on the outside.

Internally was another matter. He was beginning to wonder what the devil he had consumed, if his memories of last night were so wild. The earlier part was no problem. He had called briefly at his new chambers, changed for the last time into his dress uniform and gone straight to Watier's, leaving Race, his valet, to unpack.

They had all been there, his brothers-in-arms who had survived Waterloo and were fit enough to have made it back to England. And as they had sworn they would the night before the battle, they settled down to a night of eating, drinking and remembering. Remembering the men who were not here to share the brandy and the champagne, remembering their own experiences in the hell that was being acclaimed as one of the greatest battles ever fought—and trying their hardest to forget that they now had to learn all over again to be English gentlemen and pick up the life they had abandoned for the army.

That much was clear. A damned good meal at Watier's, champagne for the toasts, then on through a round of drinking clubs and hells. Not playing at the tables, not more than flirting with the whores and demi-reps who flocked around them, attracted by the uniforms, but drinking and talking into the night. Doing and seeing the things they could do and see because they were alive.

Eventually, about half past two it must have been, he had turned homewards up Piccadilly towards the Albany. And there old habit must have taken control from his fuddled brain and steered his feet into the curve of Half Moon Street, through the mews and up to his own old back door. He could recall none of that, nor how he had got upstairs, nor what had happened next. Because whatever he might expect to find upstairs in the bedroom of the widow of the most boring man in England, a dark-haired Venus and a large white bear were not within the realms of possibility.

'Your shirt, my lord, and your boots.' Hedges materialised with the expressionless efficiency achieved only by the most highly trained English butler. 'And I have taken the liberty of borrowing one of the late master's neckcloths.'

'Thank you.' Ashe dressed in silence, got his hair into some sort of order, submitted to Hedges whisking the clothes brush over his jacket and followed the butler downstairs. In the blaze of silver lace and frogging he felt distinctly overdressed, but sartorial errors were apparently the least of his *faux pas*.

'Luncheon will be served in about twenty minutes, my lord.' Lady Felsham had not changed the function of the downstairs rooms around, he noted as Hedges opened a door, cleared his throat and announced, 'Major the Viscount Dereham, my lady.'

Taking a deep breath Ashe tugged down his cuffs and strode into the drawing room to confront the straitlaced widow whose home he had invaded.

The breath stayed choked in his lungs. He had expected a frowsty middle-aged woman in black. Standing in the middle of the room was his Venus of the night before, regarding him with steady grey eyes, the colour high on her cheekbones.

Only she was now decently dressed in an exquisite green gown that made her elegantly coiffed hair gleam like polished wood. Pearls glowed softly against her flushed skin and the memory of the scent of her almost drove his scattered wits to the four corners of the room.

'Lord Dereham.' Straight-backed, she dropped the very slightest formal curtsy. She could not be a day over twenty-six, surely?

'Lady Felsham.' He managed it without stammering like a callow boy, thank God, and bowed. There was a slight movement at the back of the room and he saw a plainly dressed woman of middle age in the shadows. A chaperon. Where the blazes had *she* been last night when he had needed her?

'Please, sit.' Her ladyship gestured at a chair and sank down on the chaise opposite. The woman at the back sat too. Not a chaperon, then, or she would have been introduced. Her dresser no doubt. 'I am glad you are able to stay for luncheon, Lord Dereham.'

'Thank you, ma'am. I am delighted.' *And I'm gaping at her like a nodcock. Pull yourself together, man!* 'I must apologise for invading your home last night. There is no hiding the fact that I had been celebrating rather too enthusiastically.' A faint smile curled the corner of her lips. The lower lip had the slightest, most provocative, pout. What would it be like to nip gently? He dragged his eyes away from it. 'I am somewhat confused about what then transpired. This is not helped by recollections of a white bear, which leads me to believe I was rather more in my altitudes than I had imagined.'

'Horace.' She might have been naming a relative. 'He is a polar bear skin on the floor in front of the fireplace.'

'Horace.' The damned bear was called Horace. What sort of woman gave her hearthrugs names, for heaven's sake? But at least he was not losing his mind. 'I think I must have tripped and measured my length on your Horace,' he added, the memories coming back now he knew the white bear was not a dream.

Ashe had thought her colour somewhat heightened when he entered the room. Now she flushed to her hairline. What the devil had he said? Lady Felsham could no longer meet his eyes. He closed them, searching the blurred pictures behind his lids. She had been lying on the fur. It was not Horace he had landed full length upon, it was her, and all those tantalising dreams of warm female curves, of the scent of her skin, of, Heaven help him, following the whorls of her ear with his tongue, were accurate memories.

Chapter Three

Ashe stared at his hostess and Lady Felsham gazed back, sitting there, outwardly composed, while inwardly she must be desperately wondering just what he could recall of all this—and whether he was going to gossip about it, or worse. In fact, the more he thought about it, the more anxious he realised she must be—he could ruin her reputation in one minute of indiscreet talk. It was not something he could hint about, and he had no idea to what extent she had confided in her dresser.

'Might I crave a private word, ma'am?' Her polite smile vanished and a shadowed look came into those frank grey eyes.

All she said was, 'Step outside for a few moments, please, Philpott, and close the door behind you.'

Ashe waited for the snick of the catch before speaking. 'I have placed you in a difficult position—'

'Not as difficult as the position in which I found myself at three o'clock this morning,' she interrupted him with some feeling. Ashe almost smiled; she could have been tearful or furious or even hysterical. As it was, her tart tone was refreshing.

'No. I imagine not. I am also aware that there is very little I can do to make things better other than to offer my profound apologies and to give you my word that I will not speak of this to anyone.' She nodded acceptance, her lips still unsmiling. The colour had ebbed from her cheeks somewhat, he was relieved to see; it seemed she trusted him. 'It must have been terrifying for you and I can only wonder at the fact that you did not have me thrown out on to the street the moment you were free to do so. To have given me a comfortable bed and the attention of your servants is charity I am far from deserving.'

'I doubt my nerves would have stood the results of screaming the house down and then being discovered pinned to the floor beneath an unknown gentleman,' she said gravely. 'Once you were on your somewhat unsteady feet I considered what to do and decided that my butler needed his sleep. In any case, the sight of your supine body on the front step would hardly have added to my consequence with the neighbours. I had plenty of time to assess you my lord, and I came to the conclusion that you were harmless enough.'

She was laughing at him now the anxiety was gone. The spark in those fine eyes was not mortification, nor indignation, but amusement. Ashe found an answering bubble of laughter rising and got it firmly under control. Lady Felsham might be prepared to see the funny side of this, but he still felt his own part to have been unforgivable.

'You are too generous, ma'am. I trust I did not injure you.'

'Not at all. Horace has thick fur and the carpet

beneath was also good padding. I have slept more comfortably, I must admit.' She smiled at last, a generous, warm smile that had him yearning to press his lips to it. 'But after almost two years in mourning, living in rural seclusion, a small adventure is not unwelcome.'

There was a discreet tap at the door. 'Come in!'

'Luncheon is served, my lady.'

'Have you an appetite, Lord Dereham?' Lady Felsham rose to her feet with a graceful sway that had him fighting to keep his eyes away from her hips. 'I can promise you that Mrs Hedges is an excellent cook.'

Mrs Hedges had indeed done them proud. Bel was thankful for the distraction the formalities of eating in company provided. Lord Dereham had greatly relieved her mind with his assurances of discretion and the impeccable way in which he was behaving, but even so, the sensations conjured up by even referring to the incident were physically most agitating. Bel shifted uncomfortably on her seat and tried not to fidget.

'Butter, Lord Dereham?' She helped herself to braised ham, then found herself staring at the big, capable hand with its long fingers and the healing scar across the knuckles as he replaced the butter dish on the table. It was the hand of a fighting man, a strong man, and she could not help but contrast it with Henry's white, soft and carefully manicured digits.

'You have not been back in England long?' She tried to imagine that she was presiding over a vicarage luncheon party and not to remember his mischievous twinkle as she had remarked that a *small adventure* was not unwelcome. 'Your agent led me to understand that you were with the army in Belgium.'

'I arrived the night before last from Ostend and reached London late yesterday afternoon.'

'Then no wonder you felt so…unwell yesterday. You must have been exhausted. The Channel crossing alone, I am sure, must be wearisome.'

'You are kind to find an excuse for me.' His smile really was very charming. Bel found herself smiling back. Seduced into smiling. He was dangerous. 'But I have none, in truth. I went out to join fellow officers and we talked and drank—with the result you saw.'

It was on the tip of her tongue to remark that they must have been celebrating when she sensed a shadow. It was not so much that his expression changed, as the light went out behind those remarkable blue eyes. He was sad, she realised with a flash of empathy. On instinct she turned and nodded dismissal to the footman who stood silently by the sideboard. If her visitor was experiencing mental discomfort, he did not need an audience for it.

'It must be so painful to remember all those men who could not be with you last night,' Bel said quietly. 'Is it sometimes hard to believe that you are alive and they are not?'

He had raised his glass to his lips as she spoke, but put it down at her words, untouched. Bel thought she caught the hint of a tremor in his hand, then he was in control again. 'You are the only person I have spoken to who was not there who understands.' He stared at the glass and at his own fingers wrapped around the stem. She waited, expecting him to say something further, but after a moment he lifted the glass again and drank. A sore spot, then, one to avoid. He was going to have a hard time of it though, once he went out into society

again. Everyone would want to lionise another returning Waterloo officer, talk about the battle, demand to
know about Wellington, ask about his experiences.

'We are both going to find our new lives difficult.
You have been in the army, I have been in seclusion,'
she observed. 'Unless you are going back into the army,
Lord Dereham?'

'No. I will go to Horse Guards today and resign my
commission. Quite frankly,' he added with a rueful grin,
'I am strongly tempted to bolt off to the country and rus-
ticate on my much-neglected estate rather than face
certain aspects of London life again.'

'Town is very quiet just now,' Bel reassured him.
'That is why I came up in early June—to replenish my
wardrobe and find my feet again without too many invitations. And then I found myself travelling to the
Grand Duchy of Maubourg, of all places, for my
brother's wedding.'

'Indeed? It sounds an adventure. That is an unusual
place for your brother to be wed, I must confess.'

'Not if you are marrying the Dowager Grand
Duchess of Maubourg.' Bel smiled reminiscently. 'It
was just like a fairy tale—or a Gothic novel, if one con-
siders the castle. Quite ridiculously romantic.'

'I am sorry, I should remember who your brother is,
forgive me.'

'My elder brother is the Duke of Allington. This was
my second brother, Lord Sebastian Ravenhurst.'

'Otherwise known as Jack Ryder! I knew there was
something familiar about you—you have the same
grey eyes.'

So, Lord Dereham knew Sebastian in his secret
persona as spy, investigator and King's Messenger. It

was probably a state secret, but she risked the question. 'Where did you meet him?'

'On the morning of the battle.' There was no need to specify which battle. Bel saw the realisation come over him. 'Then that very handsome woman in man's clothing was the Grand Duchess Eva? No wonder your brother looked ready to call me out when I tried a little mild flirtation with her!'

'Indeed, you were dicing with death, Lord Dereham,' Bel agreed, amused at the daring of a man who would flirt with any woman under Sebastian's protection. 'It is a most incredible story, for he snatched Eva out of Maubourg and back to England in the face of considerable danger.'

'You are a romantic, then?' He poured her more lemonade from the cut-glass jug at his elbow and watched her quizzically for her answer. Bel found herself drowning in that deep azure gaze, rather as she might surrender to the sea. He seemed to be luring her on to confess her innermost yearnings, her need to be loved, her wicked curiosity to experience physical delight. And just like the sea, he was dangerous and full of undercurrents. A completely unknown element. Of course she could reveal nothing. Nothing at all.

'A romantic? I…I hardly know,' Bel confessed, throwing caution overboard and wilfully ignoring the sensation that she might be heading for the reef without an anchor. 'I would not have said so a few weeks ago. I would have said I was in favour of a rational choice of marriage partners, of very conventional behaviour and, of course, of judicious attention to society's norms. And then, when Eva and Sebastian fell in love, I found I would have defied any convention in the world to promote their happiness. I virtually gatecrashed a Carlton House reception, in fact, then kidnapped poor Eva to harangue her for breaking Sebastian's heart.'

'Passionate, romantic and daring, then.' He sounded admiring.

Bel knew she was blushing and could only be grateful that she had dismissed the footman earlier. 'In the cause of other people's happiness, Lord Dereham,' she said, attempting a repressive tone.

'Will you not call me Ashe?' He picked up an apple and began to peel it, his attention apparently fixed on the task.

'Certainly not!' Bel softened the instinctive response with an explanation. 'We have not even been introduced, ridiculous though that seems.'

'I am sure Horace did the honours last night,' Ashe suggested. 'He strikes me as a bear of the old school. A stickler for formality and the correct mode.'

'Even so.' Bel allowed herself the hint of a smile for his whimsy, but she was not going to be lured into impropriety—her own thoughts were quite sufficiently unseemly as it was. And she was not going to rise to his teasing about her silly rug. Goodness knows what familiarity she might be tempted into if they became any more intimate than they were already.

'Reynard, then?' He was not exactly wheedling, but there was something devilishly coaxing about the expression in the blue eyes that were fixed on her face.

'I should not.' She hesitated, then, tempted, fell. After all, it was only such a very minor infringement of propriety and who was going to call her to account for it? Only herself. 'No, why should I be missish! Reynard, then.'

'Thank you, Lady Belinda.' The peel curled in an uninterrupted ribbon over his fingers as he slowly used the knife. 'Now, tell me, why are you such an advocate of passion for other people, but not yourself?'

'You forget, I am a widow,' Bel said sharply. That was far too near the knuckle.

'I apologise for my insensitivity. Yours was a love match, I collect.' The red peel fell complete on to his plate and formed, to her distracted gaze, a perfect heart.

'Good heavens, no! I mean—' She glared at him. 'You have muddled me, Lord…Reynard. Mine was a marriage much like any other, not some…' She struggled to find the proper, dignified words.

'Not some irrational, unconventional, injudicious—do I have your list of *un*desirable attributes correctly?—storm of passion, romance and love, then?'

'Of course not. What a very unsettling state of affairs that would be, to be sure, to exist in such a turmoil of emotions.' *How wonderful, exciting, thrillingly delicious it sounds.* 'No lasting marriage could be built upon such irrational feelings.'

'But that is the state true lovers aspire to, is it not? Your brother and his new wife, from what you say, feel these things. It is not all so alarming.'

'And you would know?' she enquired, curious. Surely, if there was some blighted romance in his life, he would not speak so lightly; she might safely probe in return.

'The storms of passion? Yes, I have felt those on occasion. The more tender emotions, no, not yet.' He quartered the apple and set down his knife, watching her slantwise. 'Respectable matrons would warn you that I am a rake, Lady Belinda. We are immune to romance, although passion may be a familiar friend.'

'Are you attempting to alarm me, sir?' She had never knowingly met a rake before and she was not at all certain she had met one now; Reynard could very well be teasing her. Upon her come-out she had been strictly guarded by her mama, for the daughter of a duke was not to be left prey to the attentions of fortune hunters— or worse—for a moment. On her marriage there had been Henry to direct all her social intercourse and, as he would not dream of frequenting any place likely to attract the dissolute, or even the frivolous and fun-loving, such perilous men had not crossed her path.

'Not at all. If I was dangerous to you, that would be a foolish tactic for me to adopt.'

'Or perhaps a very cunning one?' she suggested, folding her hands demurely in her lap while he cut his apple into smaller segments and ate it, each piece severed by a decisive bite.

'Lady Belinda, I am too befuddled by last night's excesses and too bemused by your beauty to manage such clever scheming.'

'My beauty? Why, I do believe you are flirting with me, Reynard!' He *was*. How extraordinary to be flirted with again. She could hardly remember how it had felt and certainly not how to deal with it.

Lord Dereham wiped his fingers on his napkin and dropped it beside his plate. 'I was attempting to, I did warn you.' Before she could respond he was on his feet, standing to pull back her chair for her. 'That was a delicious meal, ma'am; you have heaped coals of fire on my unworthy head with your generous hospitality in the face of my out-rageous invasion in the early hours. And now I will remove myself off to Horse Guards and leave you in peace.'

'I hope your business goes well.' Bel held out her hand. There went her adventure, her glimpse into the world of excitement, scandal and loose living. And all it had left her were some very disconcerting sensations, which she could only hope would subside once a certain tall blond gentleman removed himself from her sight. Somehow she doubted it. Somehow she knew that Lord Byron's verse was going to be accompanied by some very vivid pictures from now on.

'Lady Belinda.' He shook her hand, his cool fingers not remaining for a fraction longer than was strictly proper. It was most disappointing, although doubtless the best thing, considering Hedges was hovering attentively in the background.

'Your hat and gloves, my lord. I found them upon the chest on the landing.'

The door closed behind Reynard and Bel found herself standing in the hallway, gazing rather blankly at the back of it. The sound of Hedges clearing his throat brought to herself with a start.

'I hope his lordship remembered to return his backdoor key to you, my lady. I understand from Mrs Hedges that that was how he obtained entry last night.

'His key? Oh, yes. Of course,' Bel said brightly. 'Please ask James to be ready to accompany me to Hatchard's in fifteen minutes, Hedges, and send Philpott to my room directly.'

As she climbed the stairs, Bel realised that she had just lied to her butler without hesitation. Without, in fact, the slightest qualm. Of course Lord Dereham had not given her back the key. Had he forgotten it, as she had done up to the moment the butler asked about it, or was he deliberately keeping it? And was he really a dangerous rake, or was he just teasing her? Whatever it was that was fluttering inside her it was not fear, but it was a decidedly unsettling feeling.

* * *

Ashe walked briskly away from Lady Belinda's front door, reached Piccadilly, raised his hand to summon a hackney carriage and then, abruptly changing his mind, strode diagonally across the crowded road and into Green Park by the Reservoir Gate.

He needed, he found, space to think—which surprised him, for he had thought he had the next few days clearly planned out in his head. Horse Guards to resign his commission, then back to the Albany to settle in comfortably. There was the town house to check out for Mama, shopping to be done to fit himself out as a civilian gentleman once again, and letters to write. He had intended to stay in London for at least a fortnight before venturing west to Hertfordshire and Coppergate, his country estate.

He had been home on leave a mere six weeks ago, shortly before the battle. His family knew he was safe, where he was and that he had business which would keep him in London for a week or so. That would give him time to get accustomed to his new circumstances, allow him to mentally rehearse the stories he was prepared to tell his family about his experiences. If he told them the truth about the great battle, they would be appalled; he needed some distance from his recent past and space to create the comfortable fictions in order to shield them.

At Coppergate he would interview his estate manager, sort out his affairs and come back to town as soon as he decently could. Ashe loved his family, had missed them while he was away, but in the country he felt purposeless, empty and restless. Why, he had no idea. He enjoyed country sports, he was deeply attached to the estate and the strange old house at the heart of it. And there was certainly plenty he could be doing there, as his steward would tactfully hint.

And now, unexpectedly, he felt the same way here. It must be the hangover. He strolled around the perimeter of the Reservoir amidst the small groups of gossiping ladies with servants patient at their heels, the nursemaids and shrieking children and the occasional elderly gentleman, chin on chest, deep in scholarly thought as he walked off his luncheon.

The fresh air finished the work of Hedges's potion and a good lunch on his headache, but it did not cure his restlessness. Ashe struck off away from the water and headed for St James's Park, abandoning the idea of taking a hackney. He found he was avoiding thinking about last night, about Lady Belinda and about his reaction to her. He made himself do so.

It was a relief to realise that he had behaved with at least some restraint, although the feelings of a respectable lady on finding a drunken, amorous officer in her bedchamber defied his imagination, even if he had confined his assault on her person to falling full length upon her, licking her ear and then falling asleep for hours. He grimaced at himself. *Even!* He had treated Lady Belinda like a lightskirt and he was fortunate she was not even now summoning an outraged brother to demand satisfaction.

The dangerous Mr Ryder was safely out of the country, and the duke was where he always was, reclusive on his northern estates. Ashe wrestled with the conundrum of whether honourable behaviour required that he write to the duke, account for himself and make assurances about his behaviour, or rest upon the lady's remarkable forbearance. He decided, with relief, that he was under no such obligation to frankness. Nothing irretrievable had, after all, occurred.

Lady Belinda did seem to have forgiven him. Her straitlaced late husband could hardly have given her much cause to become used to gentlemen overindulging, so he supposed she must simply be a very understanding woman.

She had been embarrassed, though, he mused, kicking at daisies in the cropped grass as he walked. It was not as though she was one of those dashing widows who would greet the unexpected arrival of a man in their bedroom with opportunistic enthusiasm. Which was a good thing, he thought with a self-deprecating grin; he had been far too drunk to have performed to any lady's satisfaction, let alone his own.

Lady Belinda had been tolerant, sensible and pragmatic, he concluded, which was more than he deserved. The thought struck him like a punch in the gut that if she had chosen to be difficult she could, very easily, put him in a position where he would have had to marry her. And marriage was absolutely not in his plans. Not for another five years or so, by which time his mother's gentle nagging would become strident and she would cease merely hinting that Cousin Adrian would make a terrible viscount and order him to do something about the succession before his thirty-sixth birthday dawned.

He had almost succeeded in coaxing Lady Belinda into flirting, which had been agreeable. Ashe began to feel better. Flirting with pretty women was a cliché for the returning warrior, but it was certainly a good way to keep your mind off blood, death and destruction.

Ashe returned the sentry's salute and ran up the steps into Horse Guards. Perhaps civilian life in London, even out of Season, would not be so bad after all.

Chapter Four

Bel too, was contemplating her sojourn in London with rather more attention than she had previously given it. She had moved simply to assert to herself and her in-laws that she was an independent woman about to start a new life. Her lovely little house was a gem, she was enjoying the walks and the shopping and now she began to wonder if perhaps there was not some social life she could comfortably indulge in.

The fact that the extremely attractive Lord Dereham might form part of that social life was undeniably an incentive. Bel found she was gazing sightlessly at a row of the very latest sensation novels, plucked a volume off the shelf at random and went to sit in one of the velvet chairs Hatchard's thoughtfully provided for their browsing customers.

In place of her vague, innocent and completely uninformed dreams of a lover, of passion and excitement, her night-time visitor had presented her with a flesh-and-blood model of perfection. And some valuable, if highly disturbing, practical information about the male animal. Daydreaming about Ashe Reynard would doubtless be frustrating but…delicious. She flicked over the pages and read at random.

Alfonso, tell me I am yours, do not betray me to the dark evil of my uncle's plans! Amarantia pleaded, her *eyes shimmering with unshed tears. Her lover strained her to his breast, his heart beating in tumultuous acknowledgement of her…*

Bel gave a little shiver of anticipation and forced herself to consider the realities. She might see Reynard again. He might flirt with her. She might learn to flirt in return. That was, of course, as far as it could go. Actually taking a lover was a fantasy, for she would never dare to go any further than mild flirtation and he showed no sign of wanting to do so, in any case. Why should he? London was full of sprightly and sophisticated feminine company and Lord Dereham no doubt knew exactly where to find it.

No, it was just a game for her to play in the sleepless night hours. A fantasy. Lord Dereham was never again going to strain her to his breast, his heart beating hard against hers as it had last night. She sighed.

'Belinda!'

Bel gave a guilty start and dropped her book. The spine bent alarmingly. She would have to buy it now. 'Aunt Louisa!' Lady James Ravenhurst was fixing her with a disapproving stare over the top of the lorgnette she was holding up. 'And Cousin Elinor. How delightful to see you both.' She got to her feet, feeling like a gawky schoolgirl as Elinor retrieved the novel from the floor.

'The Venetian Tower,' she read from the spine. 'Is that a work of architecture, Cousin Belinda?'

'Er…no.' Bel almost snatched it back. 'Just a novel

I was wondering about buying.' Aunt Louisa seemed about to deliver a diatribe on the evils of novel reading. Bel hurried on, knowing she was prattling. 'I had no idea you were both in London.'

'As The Corsican Monster chose to escape from Elba at precisely the moment I had intended leaving on a study tour of French Romanesque cathedrals, my plans for the entire year have been thrown into disarray,' her aunt replied irritably. Her expression indicated that Bonaparte must add upsetting her travel arrangements to the list of his deliberate infamies. 'I had plans for a book on the subject.'

'Romanesque? Indeed?' What on earth did that mean? Surely nothing to do with the Romans? They did not build cathedrals. Or did they? Aunt Louisa was a fearsome bluestocking and her turn for scholarship had become an obsession after the death of Lord James ten years previously. 'How fascinating,' Bel added hastily and untruthfully. 'And you are in town to buy gowns?' After one glance at Cousin Elinor's drab grey excuse for a walking dress, that was the only possible explanation.

'Gowns? Certainly not.' Lady James trained her eyeglass on the surrounding shelves. 'I am here to buy books. Our expedition will have to be postponed until next year, so I will continue my researches here. Elinor, find where they have moved the architecture volumes to. I cannot comprehend why they keep moving sections around, so inconsiderate. You have the list?'

'Yes, Mama,' Elinor responded colourlessly. 'Britton's *Cathedral Antiquities of England* in five parts and Parkyns's *Monastic and Baronial Remains*. Two volumes.' She drifted off, clutching her notebook. Bel frowned after her. She could never quite fathom her cousin. Elinor, drab and always at the beck and call of her mother, was only two years younger than Bel. At twenty-four she was firmly on the shelf and certain to remain there, yet she neither seemed exactly resigned to this fate, nor distressed by it. She simply appeared detached. What was going on behind those meekly lowered eyes and obedient murmurs? Bel wondered.

'Belinda.'

'Yes, Aunt Louisa?' Bel reminded herself that she was a grown-up woman, a widow who was independent of her family, and she had no need to react to her formidable relative as she had when she was a shy girl at her come-out. It did not help much, especially when one had a guilty conscience.

'I hear you have purchased a London house of your own. What is wrong with Cambourn House, might I ask?'

What business it was of hers Bel could not say, but she schooled her expression to a pleasant smile. 'Why, Lord Felsham has it now.'

'I trust your late husband's cousin does not forbid you the use of it!' Lady James clutched her furled parasol aggressively.

'Certainly not, Aunt. I just do not choose to be beholden to him by asking to borrow it.' The new Lord Felsham was a pleasant enough nonentity, but his wife was a sharp-tongued shrew and the less Bel had to do with them, the happier she was.

'Then you have engaged a respectable companion, I trust?'

Bel moved further back towards the theology section, away from any interested ears browsing amidst the novels. 'I have a mature dresser and a most respectable married couple managing the house.' *And what would you have said if you could have seen me last night, I wonder?* The thought of the formidable Lady James beating a drunken Lord Dereham over the head with her parasol while he lay slumped on the scantily clad body of her niece almost provoked Bel into an unseemly fit of the giggles. She had the sudden wish that she could share the image with Reynard. He would laugh, those startling eyes creasing with amusement. His laugh, she just knew, would be deep and rich and wholehearted. 'I am very well looked after, Aunt, I assure you.'

Elinor drifted back, an elderly shop assistant with his arms full of octavo volumes at her heels. 'I have them all, Mama. I do like that gown, Cousin Belinda. Such a pretty colour.'

'Thank you. I must say, I am rather pleased with it myself; it is from Mrs Bell in Charlotte Street. Have you visited her?'

Lady James ran a disapproving eye over the leaf-green skirts and the deep brown pelisse with golden brown frogging. 'A most impractical colour, in my opinion. Well, get along, man, and have those wrapped, I do not have all day! Come, Elinor. And you, Niece— you find yourself some respectable chaperonage, and quickly. Such independence from so young a gel! I do not know what the world is coming to.'

'Good afternoon, Aunt,' Bel said to her retreating back, exchanging a fleeting smile with her cousin as she hurried in the wake of her mother. Lord! She did hope that Aunt Louisa retained her fixed distaste for social occasions and did not decide it was her duty to supervise her widowed niece's visits now that she was in London.

* * *

The afternoon post had brought another flurry of invitation cards. It seemed, Bel mused, as she spread them out on her desk, that she was not the only person remaining in London well into July this year. Perhaps the attraction of the officers returning from the Continent had something to do with it.

She took out her appointments book, turning the pages that had remained virtually pristine for the past eighteen months, and studied the invitations that had arrived in the past few days. Her return to town after the Maubourg wedding had been mentioned in the society pages of several journals and it seemed her acquaintances had not forgotten her now her mourning period was over.

Lady Lacey was holding an evening reception in two days' time. That would be a good place to start. No dancing to worry about, familiar faces, the chance to catch up on the gossip. Bel lifted her pen, drew her new-headed paper towards her and began to write.

'Belinda, my dear! Welcome back to London.' Lucinda Lacey enveloped Bel in a warm hug, a rustle of silken frills and a waft of *chypre* perfume. 'We have so missed you.'

'I have missed you too.' Lucinda had not written, not after the first formal note of condolence, but then Bel had not expected her to. Lady Lacey's world was one of personal contact, of whispered gossip and endless parties and diversions. She would not have forgotten Bel exactly, but she would never have the patience for regular correspondence with someone who could not provide titillating news in return.

'All your old acquaintances are here.' Lucinda wafted her fan in the general direction of the noise swelling from the reception rooms. 'We will talk later, there is so much to catch up upon.'

As her hostess turned her attention to the next arrivals, Bel took a steadying breath and walked into the party. At least her new jonquil-silk gown was acceptable, she congratulated herself, sending a quick, assessing, look around the room. The bodice was cut in a V front and back and the hem had a double row of white ruffles connected to the high waist by the thinnest gold ribbon. The length, just grazing her ankle bones, and the detail of the bodice and sleeves were exactly in the mode. It seemed strange to be wearing pale colours again after so many months.

She glanced down at the three deep yellow rosebuds she had tucked into the neckline. They had come from the bouquet of roses that had arrived the day after her encounter with Ashe Reynard, accompanied by a very proper note of thanks and apology. Bel had tucked the note into her appointments book, marking the day they had met. It was an absurdly romantic thing to do—just as absurd as her new habit of flicking back through the pages to look at it.

'Belinda!' The descent of three of her old acquaintances, fans fluttering, ribbons streaming, drove all thoughts of Lord Dereham from her mind. Therese Roper, Therese's cheerfully plump cousin Lady Bradford and Maria Wilson, a golden-haired widow with a sprightly air.

'Come and sit with us,' Therese commanded, issuing the familiar invitation to join the circle of bright-eyed ladies as they gossiped, criticised and admired the other guests. This was the forum that had convinced Bel that her husband's attentions in the bedroom fell far short of the bliss to be expected. She wondered what they would say if they knew their sheltered friend had been severely tempted by an intimate encounter with a handsome man on her bedchamber hearthrug and wished she could trust any of them enough to talk about it.

'Now that is a truly lovely gown,' Annabelle Bradford declared as they settled themselves on a group of chairs. 'I swear I am green with envy—divulge the modiste this instant!'

Obligingly Bel explained where she had purchased the gown, submitted to a close interrogation about the total lack of excitement in her rural retreat, agreed that Lady Franleigh's new crop was a disaster on a woman with a nose of such prominence and exclaimed with indignation at the revelation that Therese's husband had taken up with a new mistress only a month after promising to reform his habits and become a model of domestic rectitude.

'What will you do?' Bel was shocked and intrigued. Imagine Henry carrying on like that! It would have been unthinkable. Therese sounded far more annoyed than upset by the current state of affairs, but then she had had six years to become accustomed to Mr Roper's tomcat tendencies.

'I shall abandon my own resolution to be faithful, for a start.' Her friend lowered her voice to a conspiratorial tone. 'I have not yet decided who the lucky man is to be, for I am greatly tempted by two gentlemen, either of whom would be perfect. Let me tell you—oh, my—' She broke off, raising her gilt quizzing glass to her eye. 'My dears, just when I thought I had passed all the available gentlemen under review, yet another gorgeous creature arrives to distract me!'

'Where?' They turned like a small flock of birds, following the direction of Mrs Roper's interested gaze.

'Oh, my, indeed,' Mrs Wilson exclaimed. 'Now that is what I call a very handsome man. A positive Adonis. Where has he sprung from, I wonder?'

Elegant in corbeau-blue superfine, his legs appearing to go on for ever in tight black evening breeches and with the crisp white of immaculate linen reflecting light on his chiselled jaw, Lord Dereham strolled negligently into the room, deep in conversation with a man in scarlet regimentals. There was a collective sigh from the ladies, masking Bel's little gasp of alarm.

It was one thing daydreaming about meeting Ashe Reynard again, it was quite another to come across him in the company of three hawk-eyed ladies bent on either flirting with him, seducing him or observing who did.

'It is Dereham,' Lady Bradford decided after a minute scrutiny. 'I thought he was an attractive man last time I saw him, but a few years in the army have definitely added a certain something.'

Muscles like an athlete, an air of quiet authority that make goose bumps run up and down my spine and a gaze that seems to be scanning the far horizon, that is most definitely 'a certain something', Bel thought ruefully, wondering if she could find an excuse and slip out now, before he saw her.

Too late. The officer he was speaking to clapped him on the shoulder and strode off, leaving Reynard in the centre of the room. He turned slowly, scanning it, and Bel made a rapid decision.

'It is Lord Dereham's house in Half Moon Street that

I have purchased,' she confided, apparently intent upon the twisted cord of her reticule. 'He called the other day. A very pleasant man, I thought.'

'*Pleasant!* Is that the best you can find to say about him?' Therese stared at her. 'Is there something wrong with your eyesight, Belinda?'

Bel wrinkled her nose in disdain, searching for something to explain her faint praise. 'I find that blond hair rather obvious.' The others regarded her as though she had remarked that she was about to become a nun, then turned their collective gaze back on his lordship who was, Bel saw with a sinking heart, making his way over to her.

Sinking heart *and* racing pulse and fluttering insides would be more accurate, she realised, despairingly cataloguing her physical reaction to Reynard's approach even as she fought to attain some mental coherence.

'Lady Belinda, Lady Bradford, Mrs Roper, Mrs Wilson.' His bow was a masterpiece of graceful restraint. The ladies were bowing and simpering, returning the courtesy with a chorus of murmured greetings. He had scrupulously addressed them in order of precedence, Bel realised, getting her alarm that he had spoken her name first under control. There would be nothing there for the others to pounce and speculate upon.

Then his eyes fell on the rosebuds at her bosom and she saw a gleam come into them. What was it? Had he recognised the flowers he had sent? Perhaps he had just ordered his butler to see to a suitable bouquet and had no idea what had been delivered. His lips parted as though to speak.

'I must thank you again for calling the other day,' she said, cutting across Mrs Wilson who had begun to remark on how unexpectedly crowded London was.

Reynard's eyebrows started to lift and she hurried on. 'I was so grateful for someone to explain the idiosyncrasies of the plumbing on the first floor. Your agent seemed completely baffled.' Around her she could sense the amusement of her sophisticated acquaintances. *Poor little Belinda, she has this gorgeous man in the house and all he has come about is the plumbing!*

'It was my pleasure.' His eyebrows had returned to their normal level, but the gleam—the *wicked* gleam—was more intense as his voice slurred slightly over *pleasure*. Something wicked in her flickered into being in response and she could tell he had recognised it in her eyes. 'After all, the shower bath in the dressing room was put in at my insistence, but I fear the plumber had never come across such a thing before and it still works only intermittently.'

There was a flutter of interest. A shower bath was so novel, and the act of discussing bathing with a man so *risqué*, that the ladies fell to exclaiming and laughing. Reynard stooped to pick up the handkerchief that had fallen from her reticule and murmured, 'Clever.'

'You too,' Bel murmured back.

'A good team.' He pressed the scrap of lace-trimmed nonsense into her gloved hand, his fingers closing for a moment around hers, then his attention was back on the others. 'You were saying that London is very full of society, Mrs Wilson?'

'Quite amazingly so for July, do you not agree?' She batted her eyelashes at him. 'I think it is because all you wonderfully brave officers are coming back home and everyone wants to meet you.'

There it was again, that shutter descending, closing down the animation in Reynard's startling blue eyes.

'And all the *wonderfully brave* men as well,' Bel said abruptly, remembering something she had read in the newssheet only the other day about the wounded men still straggling back from Belgium. 'But they are not receiving so much positive attention, are they? After all, scars and missing limbs are not so glamorous shielded only by homespuns as they are beneath a scarlet dress coat.'

There was a collective gasp, but Reynard turned to her, a smile lurking behind his grave countenance. 'Indeed, that is very true, Lady Belinda. But doubtless society ladies are already rallying to form charitable organisations to help the men and their families, and urging their husbands to find them work.'

'One can only hope so,' she responded seriously.

'If you will excuse me, ladies? I am promised to Lord Telford for a hand of cards.' Reynard bowed again and left them to turn on Bel in a flurry of indignation.

'How could you drive him away like that? Honestly, Belinda, the most handsome man in the room comes to talk to us and you start prosing on about plumbing and amputations!' Annabelle Bradford scolded.

Bel schooled her face to meekness. 'I am sorry, I did not think.' Reynard did not want to speak about his experiences, and she was not going to let these feather-brained women torment him with them, not if she could help it. *A good team.* The words warmed her inside, adding to the strange hollow feeling that she was beginning to recognise as anticipation and the low, pulsing ache that she supposed was desire.

She turned her face resolutely to the opposite end of the room from where the card room door was. 'Tell me all about the other attractive men you wicked things have in your sights.' There could not have been a better choice of subject to distract them. In a ruffle of gorgeous plumage the group settled down in their chairs again.

'*Well,*' Therese began conspiratorially, 'have you met Lord Betteridge? Just back from the Congress, and I swear…'

Chapter Five

That had not been so bad, Bel told herself as she was driven home that evening. She had survived meeting Lord Dereham again without betraying herself in front of the sharpest eyes for scandal in town, she had mingled comfortably with any number of old acquaintances and met several congenial new people and she found herself more confident and poised than she had ever been in society before.

Age, she supposed, did have its benefits in bestowing some confidence. One came to realise that not every eye in the room was upon you, that you could make little mistakes without the world coming to an end and there was neither a strict father, nor a critical husband, to remind you constantly how much you needed to improve yourself.

Bel recalled with a smile how last month she had even brazenly broken her last days of mourning and taken herself off to the Prince Regent's reception for the Grand Duchess Eva with the sole intention of getting her Serene Highness to herself to upbraid her for breaking her brother Sebastian's heart.

She had cast every tenet of polite behaviour to the winds when she had done that, and, although she suspected her well-intentioned meddling had actually made things worse for a while between the two lovers, she now had a friend for life in her new sister-in-law.

Lucky things, she mused wistfully. How must it feel to have a man look at you the way Sebastian looked at Eva when he thought himself unobserved, his very soul in his eyes?

'My lady?' They were home, the groom was holding the door of the carriage for her, and had probably been standing there patiently for some minutes.

'Thank you, James.' She gathered up her things and stepped out. Yes, all in all, this evening had been a success and she felt confident about repeating it. Tomorrow night was the Steppingleys' dancing party, an opportunity, she had been informed by Mrs Steppingley that evening, of giving her daughter and her friends some experience before their come-out next Season. Lady Belinda need not fear a juvenile party, she had been assured, her hostess had invited a mixture of *interesting* people and there would be cards for those not wishing to dance.

It would be fun to dance again, although she would avoid the waltz, of course, and perhaps meeting all those interesting people she had been promised would help keep her mind off a certain broad-shouldered gentleman with a sinfully tempting curve to his mobile mouth. If only he did not make her feel so *wicked*.

Philpott glided about in her usual stately fashion, unpinning Bel's hair, locking away her jewellery, stuffing the tissue paper into the toes of her evening slippers before coming back to unfasten her gown.

Bel unclasped the *diamanté* brooch that had been holding the rosebuds in place. They were beginning to lose their firmness, the delicate petals felt like limp velvet under her fingers.

'Will you fetch me a box of salt, please?' she asked the dresser. 'About so big?' She gestured with her hands six inches apart.

'Now, my lady?'

'Yes, please. These are so pretty, I intend to preserve them as a memory of the first social engagement of my new life.'

'Very well, my lady.' Expressionless, Philpott helped her into her robe, handed her the hairbrush and went out. Did she guess the real reason Bel wanted to keep the flowers? If she did, she was far too well trained to let a flicker cross her face.

Bel pulled the bristles through her hair in a steady rhythm, contemplating her aunt's demand that she engage a companion, then shook her head, sending the heavy fall of hair swishing back and forth against the silk of her robe. Privacy was difficult enough with a houseful of servants, let alone with some stranger, obsessed with propriety and convinced her employer required her company at all times.

No, life like this might be a trifle lonely, but she had grown used to that, even when Henry had been alive. In fact, loneliness was a welcome space of peace and privacy. Those things were more important than satisfying the conventions.

The guests at Mrs Steppingley's party proved every bit as entertaining as she had promised. After an hour Bel had met a colonel from one of the Brunswick regiments, a gentleman pursuing researches into hot-air balloons as a means of transport for freight, several charming young girls, wide-eyed with excitement at their first 'proper' dancing party, a poetess and an alarmingly masculine bluestocking who, on hearing who she was, delivered a diatribe on the mistaken opinions of her Aunt Louisa on the evolution of English church architecture.

As Bel was just about capable of differentiating between a font and a water stoop and had not the slightest understanding of the vital importance of rood screens, she was greatly relieved to be rescued by the poetess, Miss Layne, who tactfully removed her with the entirely specious excuse that Bel had promised Miss Layne her escort into the room where the dancing was about to begin.

'Phew! At least Miss Farrington despises dancing, so she will not pursue us in here.' Miss Layne found them seats halfway along the wall and sank down with a hunted look back at the doorway. She fanned herself vigorously, giving Bel a chance to study her. She supposed she must be about forty, a slender woman with soft mouse-brown hair, amused hazel eyes and an air of being interested in everything. 'What a bore she is.' She suddenly whipped a notebook out of her reticule, jotted a note and stuffed it back again.

Bel blinked. 'Inspiration?' she enquired.

'Yes! See that young couple over there, pretending not to look at each other. So sweet, and so gauche. It gave me an idea. I have a fancy to write a really romantic verse story.'

'Will I find your work at Hatchard's?' Bel enquired. 'I am afraid I am very ignorant about poetry. My husband considered it frivolous, so I never used to buy it, although I have to confess to reading my way through Lord Byron's works at the moment.'

'Yes, you will find mine there, I have several volumes in print. But you must allow me to send you one as a gift. Some are frivolous, some are serious. But I see no harm in occasional frivolity—' Miss Layne broke off, her gaze fixed at something over Bel's shoulder. 'And speaking of frivolity, what a very beautiful man. Lord Byron would give his eye teeth for such a hero.'

Bel did not have to turn around to know who it was out of all the handsome men in London at the moment. The very air seemed to carry the awareness of Reynard to her, as intensely as if he was running his hands over her quivering skin.

'Really?' she made herself say lightly, stamping on that unsettling image. 'I am all agog, Miss Layne, I do hope he passes by us so I can see, for I can hardly turn round and stare—'

'Lady Belinda. Madam.' Yes, it was Reynard and her pulse was all over the place. Miss Layne was looking up at him with the air of a lepidopterist who has just found a rare species of butterfly and was wondering where her net had gone. Bel pulled herself together. A surge of lust, for she supposed that was what was afflicting her, was no excuse for a lady to forget her manners.

'Lord Dereham, good evening. Miss Layne, may I introduce Lord Dereham?'

They shook hands. 'Miss Layne—not the author of *Thoughts on an English Riverbank*?'

'Why, yes. It was published at the end of last year,' she explained to Bel. 'You have read it, Lord Dereham?'

'On the eve of the battle of Quatre Bras, Miss Layne. It was a lovely contrast to the scenes around me, and I must thank you for it.'

The poetess beamed up at him. 'I am delighted to have been able to provide a distraction at such a time.'

'More than that: a reminder of what we were fighting for.'

Bel bit her lip at the undercurrent of emotion in the controlled voice, then he was smiling again. 'May I have the honour of a dance, Miss Layne?'

'I do not dance, Lord Dereham, Lady Belinda kindly rescued me from an importunate acquaintance and we took refuge in here.'

'Lady Belinda is a notable rescuer of all her friends,' Reynard observed seriously. 'If you are merely hiding in here and the other gentlemen have not yet found you, then perhaps your dance card has a vacancy for me, Lady Belinda?'

Bel laughed, flipping open the fold of embossed card that hung from a cord around her wrist to show him. 'Quite empty, Lord Dereham. I have been talking too much to look for partners, I fear.' She liked the way he had asked the older woman first instead of simply assuming she would not be dancing. It was thoughtful, but done without the slightest suggestion of patronage.

'May I?' He lifted the card, his fingers brushing against hers. Even through the thickness of two pairs of evening gloves Bel seemed to feel the warmth. She made herself sit still while he took the tiny pencil and stared at the list of dances. The noise of the orchestra carrying out its final tuning faded as she looked at his bent head. She knew what that thick golden hair felt like against her cheek, she knew what it looked like, tousled from sleep, and her free hand strained against her will-power to lift and touch it.

'There. I hope that is acceptable.' He had put down a waltz as well as a country dance. Bel opened her mouth to tell him that she would not be waltzing, then threw her resolution overboard with an almost audible splash. This was Reynard; she wanted to be in his arms and she could admit to herself a disgraceful impulse to make other women envious.

'May I fetch you ladies some lemonade?' They shook their heads with a murmur of thanks. 'Then I will see you for the second country dance, Lady Belinda.'

'That man has lovely manners,' Miss Layne remarked as they watched Reynard's retreating back. 'Oh, good! There is my brother now, I was not certain if he was coming tonight.' She waved and a slender, brown-haired man who was just passing Reynard waved back and began to make his way across to them.

'Kate, fancy finding you in the ballroom!' Mr Layne was considerably younger than his sister, but he had her soft brown hair and quizzical hazel eyes. He smiled at her affectionately and bowed to Bel. 'Ma'am.'

'Lady Belinda, may I introduce my brother, Mr Layne. Patrick, Lady Belinda Felsham.'

Bel shook hands and gestured to the vacant chair beside her. 'Mr Layne?'

'Thank you, Lady Belinda, but I am promised for the next dance. Might I ask if you can spare me one later? Although I expect your card is filled already.'

'Not at all, I would be delighted.' She showed him the virtually empty card and smiled acceptance as he indicated the first waltz.

'Very daring of him,' Miss Layne observed as her

brother went in search of his next partner. 'I do hope he has learned the steps.' They both observed in anxious silence as Mr Layne went down the first measure of the country dance without error. 'Thank goodness. He must have been taking lessons. He has been rather preoccupied learning to manage our uncle's estate for the last two years; I was beginning to despair of him ever getting out into society.'

'And meeting a nice young lady, perhaps?' Bel teased.

'Indeed. Our uncle is Lord Hinckliffe and Patrick is his heir—he is taking that all rather seriously. I was worrying that he would end up an elderly bachelor like our relative at this rate.'

Mr Layne was a long way from that condition, Bel realised a little later, as he swept her competently into the waltz. Far from having to temper her steps to a learner, she found he was testing her own rusty technique to the limit. They were laughing as they whirled to a stop and well on the way to being very well pleased with each other's company. He was coaxing her into allowing him another dance when Bel saw Reynard making his way towards them.

Patrick Layne's voice faded and the air seemed to shimmer as the crowded room became a mere background to the man in front of her. Bel wondered dazedly if she was about to swoon.

She blinked and the illusion of faintness vanished, leaving her startled and confused. It was not simply that Reynard was a handsome, personable man. She had just spent five minutes, very pleasantly, in the arms of another man who could fairly be described in the same way. This was different. This was something she could only try to understand.

With an effort she kept her voice normal as she agreed to dance the cotillion with Mr Layne later in the evening. Then she turned, smiling, to take Reynard's outstretched hand with a sense of surrender that filled her with nervous delight. The deep-sea eyes smiled at her and she stopped fighting the apprehension. A die had been cast; the problem was, she did not know what game they were playing.

The steps of the country dance were intricate enough to keep Bel's full attention on her moves. After the first circle she found herself standing next to her partner. His soft chuckle had her glancing up at him, disconcerted.

'What is it?'

'You are frowning Lady Belinda. If I was a nervous man, I would think I had displeased you; as it is, I am hoping you are concentrating on your steps.'

'I do beg your pardon,' Bel said hastily, then saw the skin at the corner of his eyes crease in amusement. 'Oh! You are teasing me. I was not frowning at all, was I?'

'Not at all,' Ashe confessed. 'But you were concentrating very hard and I was rather hoping for some of the stimulating conversation one usually indulges in during these dances. We are off again.' He took her hand, twirled her and began to promenade down the double line. Army life had allowed for numerous scratch balls in the most unlikely places and with the most unconventional partners. Now he did not even have to think about the steps.

'Unless things have changed a great deal while I have been in mourning,' she retorted, 'that means exchanging platitudes about the music, the temperature and what a crush it is this evening. Surely you do not find that stimulating?'

Ashe steered her into place and grinned. 'It depends on the company. I suspect your view of the social scene may be a little more entertaining than most, Lady Belinda.' He had her attention now; she was not anxious about her steps or smiling over that lad she had just been dancing with. He was conscious of an unfamiliar twinge of jealousy. The young man, whoever he was, had made her laugh, had brought colour to her cheeks and she had seemed very relaxed in his company.

He had nothing to feel jealous about, for heaven's sake. The first time they had met he had embarrassed himself and escaped considerably more lightly than he deserved. The second time had been a mere social exchange, although he had applauded the fierce indignation that had made her defend the wounded soldiers and the quick wits that had provided a plausible excuse for their previous meeting. Now they were nothing more to each other than casual acquaintances.

Only…there were none of his casual acquaintances whose back-door keys were in his possession. His valet had found the key in his pocket and wordlessly placed it on his dressing table amidst the litter of cards and notes. Whenever he picked up his cologne, or replaced his brushes, the metal clinked. There was no excuse for leaving it there. He should have wrapped it up and sent it back with the roses, he knew that. Why he had kept it, why he had not mentioned it, he was carefully not examining.

But Lady Belinda had not asked for the key back. Obviously she had not thought about it, forgotten it, or perhaps she had taken the precaution of having the locks changed. He stepped into the circle and took the hands of the lady opposite, twirled her round and restored her to her new place in the set, watching while Belinda was twirled in her turn.

Not a conventional beauty, Ashe told himself, trying to look at her dispassionately. It was difficult to be objective for some reason. He did his best. Speaking grey eyes, glossy dark hair, those were admirable—but a connoisseur would say her nose was a little too long, her chin rather too decided and her mouth too mobile. He watched it now, intrigued. A polite smile for the man who had just turned her became serious, her full underlip caught between white teeth as she thought about the next moves. Then she gave a secret smile of relief when she remembered what she had to do next.

A dancer moved too energetically, knocking against Belinda, and the smile became a fleeting wince, then she caught his eye and smiled and he found himself smiling back as uninhibitedly as though they were alone on a hillside with no one for miles around. It shook him, and it seemed to have surprised her too, as though she had shared the feeling.

Her expression was serious again in an instant, although he was conscious of her glancing at him sideways from under the sweep of her lashes, a feminine trick that always amused him in other women. Now, he felt the urge to whirl her out of the set, catch her face between his palms and lock eyes with her, to read what was going on in her mind.

Ashe gave himself a brisk mental shake. This was not how he had ever felt about a woman before, and he could not account for it. But then, he knew he was not feeling quite himself somehow. Perhaps he would be back to normal when he had bitten the bullet and gone home for a while.

The lines of dancers were facing each other now, men on one side, women the other. The ladies advanced, bringing them together, so close that the provoking swell of Belinda's breasts was almost against his waistcoat. She glanced up, saw goodness knows what in his expression, blushed and retreated. When it was his turn to come forward she did not raise her eyes to his, suddenly endearingly shy.

It was the effect of living with a dull man, no doubt. She was unused to other men, unused to even the mildest flirtation. It was rare in a married woman to see maturity combined with such an air of innocence. Why that made him feel both aroused and protective, both at the same time, was the mystery.

The music came to a crashing finale, everyone clapped politely and left the floor. Ashe returned Belinda to her seat and nodded coolly to the young man who had been dancing with her earlier, noting his likeness to Miss Layne. Her brother, no doubt. Young whelp, Ashe thought with a sudden burst of irritation, striding off to find his partner for the next dance. London was definitely not what it was.

Chapter Six

'Hmm. His lordship does not like me, I fancy.' Patrick Layne stood to position her chair so that Bel could see the dance floor more easily.

'Why do you say that?' She was pleased with herself for not letting her gaze stray after her partner's retreating back. Miss Layne was chatting to a chaperon on her other side, so no one could overhear their low-voiced exchange.

'If looks could kill, I would be laid out at your feet,' he said dramatically, grinning.

'Why on earth should Lord Dereham take a dislike to you?' Bel demanded, genuinely puzzled.

'Need you ask?' Patrick stooped to pick up the fan that had slipped from her fingers. 'I was waltzing with you, and now I am sitting with you. All his lordship gets is a country dance and the privilege of returning you to my company.'

'But…that would mean he was jealous, and he has not the slightest reason to be.' Bel was aghast that anyone might think such a thing, with its implication that she and Reynard were in some way involved.

Which they were not. Not in the slightest. 'I hardly know him. And in any case, he chose which dances to ask me for, and we have a waltz later.'

She was protesting too much, she saw it in the amused quirk of Mr Layne's mouth. The truth was that he too was flirting with her, in a rather roundabout manner. It was all very disconcerting; somehow she had not expected such a thing when she had contemplated her return to society. As a widow she had imagined her attractiveness to men would automatically have ceased. Apparently she was mistaken.

She was saved from any more badinage by Miss Layne returning her attention to her brother and declaring that she was faint from hunger and he must give them his escort to the supper room. Bel was not feeling particularly like eating, but their departure did at least remove her from the sight of Lord Dereham's elegant progression down the floor with a vivacious redhead.

By the time he came to claim her for their waltz Bel was feeling far from happy. 'What is it, Lady Belinda? Are you cross with me?'

'Cross? No, goodness gracious, of course not.' She was so flurried that he might think it that she was in his arms and waltzing before she could be apprehensive about his touch. 'I very foolishly let myself be persuaded into eating a crab patty I did not really want, I have just had my toes trodden on by a very clumsy young man in the last dance and I am wondering if my ambition to establish myself in London was an awful mistake and I should have stayed in the country where at least I know what I am doing.'

Reynard swept her competently around a corner and

Bel found she had settled into his embrace as though they had danced a hundred times before. For a tall and very masculine man he was surprisingly graceful. Bel had never been quite so masterfully partnered before and she was well aware that for the duration of this dance she was going to go precisely where he intended. She realised that, far from feeling overpowered by this, or resentful, she could relax and simply enjoy the dance, confident that he was in control.

'You are feeling as I do at the moment about London, I think.' He gathered her a little closer as an unskilled young couple blundered past, laughing immoderately at their own clumsiness. 'We have been away, living very different lives. Perhaps it will take a little while to get back into the swing of things.' Somehow he kept her just that little bit closer to his body, although the danger of collision was past.

'Yes, you may well be right. No doubt that is all it is.' Comforted, Bel let herself go as he executed a complicated turn. 'Oh!' Her skirts swung, tangled for a moment in his long legs, and then they were gliding down the floor again. 'You are a very good dancer, Ashe.'

The name was out of her mouth before she realised it. 'I beg your pardon, Reynard, I…'

'But I asked you to use my first name.' She could hear the smile in his voice.

'That does not mean I should do so, however.' Bel fixed her gaze on the top button of his waistcoat, which seemed the safest place to look.

'I like it when you do. Do not stop.' His voice was a coaxing rumble close to her ear. Far too close.

'That is all the more reason for not using it!' Bel's

vehement retort make him chuckle. 'Do not laugh at me,' she added crossly. 'Just because I try to behave as convention demands, there is no need to mock.'

'I am not mocking,' Ashe said seriously. 'I enjoy being with you, I do not find your modest demeanour at all amusing. But I do relish the serious way you keep reminding yourself to behave. It makes me sense some tendency to mischief beneath that very elegant exterior.'

Bel was not at all sure how to take that, it was a positive layer cake of a remark. There was some flattery, a somewhat backhanded compliment and a strong hint that Ashe would very much enjoy it if she were to give her mischief free rein. With him. It seemed he had seen the new wickedness that lurked within her. She contented herself with a sound which was supposed to be a disdainful *humpf!* and emerged regrettably like a giggle.

The dance ended and she stepped back out of his arms. Ashe bowed slightly, then, as his eyes met hers, she saw in them quite unmistakable desire. It was gone in an instant, his lashes sweeping it away to reveal nothing more than polite admiration. But it had been there, fierce, thrilling and utterly dangerous, and she had recognised it, even though she had never had a man look at her like that in her life before.

The sudden heat she had glimpsed called up an answering warmth in her. The disturbing pulse she was aware of, fluttering low in her belly whenever she was close to him, became insistent, flurrying her. Just that exchange of glances and they were both aware of his desire and her knowledge of it. In her inexperience it seemed incredible that such a thing was possible.

Then her glance flickered lower and hastily away. Her instincts were palpably correct.

The Dowager Duchess of Malmsbury, an outrageous old harridan, had once announced loudly in her hearing that the fashion for skintight, fine-knit, evening knee breeches was excellent as it allowed one to tell precisely what a young man was thinking. Bel had retreated blushing and had hardly dared look at a man below the waist for weeks after that. Now she knew exactly what her Grace had meant and even more exactly what Ashe was thinking about.

'Th…thank you. That was a delightful dance.' She sketched a curtsy and turned to walk off the floor. The sets were already beginning to form for the next dance.

'Lady Belinda?'

'Yes?' She hardly dared turn round. She had fantasised about physical desire. Now she was so acutely aware of it vibrating between them that it terrified her.

'Might I have one word in private?'

'Um. Yes…of course.'

Ashe guided her towards the loggia overlooking the lawns. It had been opened up as a cooling promenade for the dancers, away from the heat of the ballroom. There was nothing to worry about, Bel assured herself. With so many young and inexperienced girls in the company, Mrs Steppingley had made sure all the curtains were pulled back and the arcaded walk was well lit. Several couples were already strolling up and down its marble floor amidst potted palms and baskets of orchids.

'This is most pleasant.' Bel unfurled her spangled fan, realised she was positively flapping it, and began to wave it languidly to and fro. *What is he going to ask me?*

'Indeed, yes.' Ashe took her free hand and placed it

on his forearm. 'I simply wanted to tell you that I should have returned your key, and I did not want to mention it where we might be overheard. I apologise for not having dealt with it sooner.'

'My key.' Bel stared at him blankly. Despite the relative cool of the loggia, she could sense the heat of his body as he walked so close beside her. And surely he could feel the hammering of her pulse where her wrist lay on his forearm? Of course, the key. She made herself say something sensible before he thought her a complete lackwit. 'You overlooked it, no doubt. An easy thing to do under the circumstances.'

'No. I did not forget.' The denial took her completely by surprise. They had reached the end of the arcade and she turned to face him, her back against the balustrade as he stood close in front of her, one arm raised so his hand rested on the column, effectively cutting her off from the rest of the company.

'I do not understand.'

Ashe nodded. 'No, neither do I.' He grimaced. 'It has been lying on my dressing table in full view ever since that day, being pointedly ignored by my valet. I cannot pretend to have forgotten.' He moved away from her as though he was uncomfortable with their conversation and went to lean on the balustrade. Bel glanced down at the strong ungloved hands as they curled over the carved stone, then up at his profile as he looked out over the garden: classical, handsome, unreadable. Vulnerable.

She blinked and looked again. Whatever it was she had glimpsed, it had gone, leaving only a sense of aloofness.

'I will have it sent round tomorrow.' Ashe turned to face her again, his hands at his back bracing him against the stonework, his long, lean body making an elegant black line against the grey background. 'In a package so it is not obvious what it is.'

Thank you, that would be very thoughtful of you. The right words formed in her mind, polite and cool and correct. Bel opened her lips to articulate them. 'Please keep it,' she said.

What? Ashe almost said the word out loud. He must have misheard her. *Keep her door key?* 'I beg your pardon, Lady Belinda. I thought you said—'

'I said, *keep it*. The key.' There was colour flushed across her cheekbones and her eyes were wide, apparently in shocked disbelief at her own words, but Lady Belinda's voice was quite steady. 'You may like to drop in one evening on your way home. For a nightcap.' She might have been inviting him to afternoon tea. He saw her throat work as she swallowed, hardly able to believe what he was hearing, surprised that he could focus on such tiny details while he was being so amazed.

'A nightcap?'

'To drink, I mean.' Ashe nodded, fascinated. 'Not to wear,' she clarified. Belinda's slender fingers flew up to seal in what sounded like a gasp of horrified laughter at the image she had conjured up. Her wide grey eyes became serious again in a second. 'My staff will always be in bed by one. There is no need to knock and, er… disturb anyone. Just let yourself in as you did the other night.'

This was not an hallucination. This was proper, respectable Lady Belinda Felsham, the widow of a man of paralysing respectability, suggesting that he come to her home at one in the morning—for a *nightcap*?

It was not unknown for married ladies or widows to

make it clear to gentlemen that they would not be averse to an *affaire*. It had happened to him in the past on occasion and he was equally skilled at pretending not to understand what was being hinted at, or at taking advantage of the opportunity for some mutual pleasure, depending on how he felt about the lady, and how territorial her husband appeared to be.

But was *this* sheltered lady really suggesting what he thought she was? Perhaps Belinda genuinely expected him to drop in for a glass of brandy and a chat on his way home from the clubs. She did not appear to sleep very well, if it was her habit to be reading on the hearthrug at two in the morning. And she was most certainly inexperienced with men. It must be his own desire for her that was making him believe she was offering her body, not her company.

'Lady Belinda.' He paused to choose his words with care. 'I should point out that however innocent a late-night drink between two friends might be, it would not be seen in that light by a third party. It would be regarded in the worst possible light. It simply is not done.'

'Oh, dear!' Bel regarded him in dismay. 'I am making such a mull of this. You see, I am not in the habit…that is to say, I am not used to inviting gentlemen to… Oh, dear. I should have asked Ther—I mean, a friend—how it is done.'

'How what is done?' Ashe asked bluntly, wondering if there was something wrong with the champagne. He was not accustomed to feeling this light-headed. Not after a mere three glasses of good wine.

'How one asks a man if he will become your lover.'

'Ah.' Ashe took a deep, steadying breath. It occurred to him, distractingly, that the last time he had found it necessary to do so he had been standing up to his ankles in mud, a sword clenched in his fist while the French cavalry had been advancing towards him at a gallop. He was not certain that this was not more terrifying. 'I was not sure that was what you meant.'

'That I was asking if you would be my lover?' She repeated the noun as though trying to become used to it. 'Of course, if you do not want to…please, do say so.' It sounded as though she was offering him a plate of macaroons. 'I mean, I would feel awful if you felt you had to say *yes*, just to be polite.'

'Polite? No, politeness is not a consideration, I assure you. Nor, believe me, is desire, or lack of it. I find you highly desirable.' Ashe strained his ears for the sound of footsteps behind them. He had moved into this position for discretion; now they were discussing matters so sensitive they should be at the bottom of the garden, not in the middle of a popular promenade.

'Thank you.' She looked up at him from under her lashes, suddenly shy again.

He found his lips curving into a smile. Belinda was so deliciously serious as she accepted as a compliment what he had intended as a simple statement of fact. She should not have needed telling; he was still chastising himself for his loss of control back there on the dance floor. But the rhythms of the music, the sway of her body in his arms, her trusting surrender to his lead just made him want to sweep her away into a bedchamber and continue to explore those rhythms, that yielding, until they reached the ultimate conclusion.

If only he did not keep getting memory flashes of her lying on that damned bearskin rug, her hair tousled, her feet bare beneath a fluttering silken hem, he would find it easier to control himself. But it seemed he did not need to. It seemed, improbably, that the well-behaved widow of the most boring and conventional man in society wanted to take him to her bed.

'Ashe?' She was biting the fullness of her under lip; the idea of his own teeth just there made his loins throb. 'You are frowning. I should not have asked, should I? I expect men always prefer to do the asking. Only, I did not think that you ever would and I have no idea how to flirt so that you would understand it would be all right.'

He wanted to touch her, lift his hand and touch the smooth curve of her cheek, run the pad of his thumb over the line of the enticing red swell of her mouth, but there were people all around them and preserving her reputation had to be paramount.

Ashe did not answer the anxious questions at once. 'Let us walk. I do not want to attract attention.' He turned, offering her his arm again; after a moment's hesitation she took it. He had thought her almost un-naturally composed, now he could feel the tremor running through her, transmitting itself through silk and broadcloth into him. She was as scared of herself, of what she had just done, as she was of him.

'It is not a question of preference, of the man wanting to ask,' he tried to explain, returning to her anxious question. 'Only, with you, it would never occur to me that the question would meet with anything but a stinging box to my ears. My mild attempts at flirtation so far have not been wildly successful.'

Belinda gave a little gurgle of amusement, but her voice retained its anxiety as she probed. 'So, before, you thought me too respectable for such things, and now you think me—what? All the words are so horrible. The reality of doing this is not at all the fantasy I had of it.'

'I think that you owe no one an explanation of your behaviour other than yourself,' Ashe said, meaning it, trying not to speculate about her fantasies. 'You are not contemplating betraying your marriage vows, you have no children to shelter, no great public position to protect. You are discreet, you have honoured me with your trust—and believe me, I will not betray it. I have no attachments or commitments that I would be breaking. That makes you a private woman with private needs who is able to satisfy them. Nothing more.'

He would never have dreamed he would be having such a measured, serious, discussion with a would-be lover, but it seemed Belinda needed that reasoning. She was not doing it lightly, this was no whim. It made him reassess his opinion of the late Lord Felsham. Had the man been such a superlative lover that his wife was pining for a man in her bed? And yet, if he had not known better, he would have thought her a virgin, her responses were so innocent. The effect of knowing one man only, he supposed.

'Then you will?' she asked, looking up suddenly. 'Be my lover?' The intensity in her eyes, even in the shadow of the loggia, shook him. No, she was no natural lightskirt like her frivolous friends, who were separated from their sisters in the muslin company only by wealth and breeding, not by temperament.

'I would be honoured,' Ashe said, meaning it. That Layne fellow was strolling towards them, a very young blonde chattering animatedly at his side. Time to draw this to a conclusion before anyone commented on how long they had spent together. 'Lady Belinda, may I call tomorrow?' He dropped his voice to a murmur as the other couple came up to them. 'Soon after one.'

Not tonight, then. The strength of her disappointment shook Bel. She was shocked at herself. What had she wanted? That Ashe sweep her up in his arms and take her to bed immediately? Find a bedchamber here and lock the door? *Yes, of course that is what I want!*

'Certainly.' Bel produced her best social smile. 'And that time tomorrow would be most convenient. Thank you, my lord.' With a nod to Patrick Layne and his partner, Ashe was gone, cutting easily through the congestion at the entrance to the loggia.

'Lady Felsham, may I introduce Miss Steppingley?' She dragged her attention back and smiled at the blonde girl. She was very young, very pretty, wide-eyed with shy excitement.

Bel shook hands and listened with half an ear to Miss Steppingley's effusions about how thrilling it was that Mama had held this dance party and was letting her and her cousins attend, even though they were not out until the new Season. She caught Mr Layne's eye and he grinned at her over Miss Steppingley's head, obviously amused by the naïve chatter.

'Shall we go back? I am not sure your mama would wish you to be promenading with a gentleman unchaperoned.' Bel began to stroll towards the ballroom. If Lady Steppingley knew what her guest had just done, she would be far more shocked by her daughter talking to Bel than she would by her walking alone for a little while with the respectable Mr Layne. *I am a scarlet woman,* Bel thought. *Almost.* She shot Mr Layne a look that she hoped indicated that she was not suggesting he was an unsafe companion, and was reassured by a slight nod of his head.

Miss Steppingley soon found a friend to chatter to, leaving Bel alone with him. 'That was probably very wise of you,' he said, following the giggling pair with a tolerant eye. 'She's far too young and trusting to know the ropes yet. Not at all up to snuff. Very dangerous.'

'For her to be with you, Mr Layne? Surely not.'

'For me.' Patrick Layne grinned. 'The next thing you know with girls that age, they have decided that a little mild flirtation behind the potted palm indicates lifelong devotion and you're in Papa's study explaining your intentions.'

'And have you ever been in that position?' Bel looked round the room as though watching the party. Ashe had vanished.

'No, I am glad to say. I prefer ladies closer to my own age.' As she guessed he was twenty-six, her age exactly, Bel wondered if this was another of his indirectly flirtatious remarks.

'There is your sister.' It was better, she decided, to ignore it. Her brain was spinning too much to worry about Mr Layne's intentions. 'I must say goodbye.'

'Do call.' The poetess slipped a card into her hand as Bel explained she was about to leave. 'I would be delighted if you would call and take tea.'

'Thank you.' Bel put it carefully into her reticule. This was precisely what she had hoped for in coming to London, to make new friends, to build a pleasant social life for herself. It was not, whatever she had fantasised, to take a lover. But she had—almost.

If Ashe Reynard had not had too much to drink the other evening, this would not be happening, Bel thought, settling back in the corner of her carriage and ignoring how badly her new evening slippers pinched. But Ashe had ended up on his old, familiar doorstep, and they had met, and something inside her could not stop yearning for him.

She had danced with several attractive gentlemen that evening. Patrick Layne was good looking, good company and, she was certain, discreet. But it would never cross her mind, not for a single moment, that she might want an *affaire* with him.

But with Ashe she had met the man of her fantasies, it was the only explanation. And if she did not follow her instincts now, she would never have the chance, or the courage, again.

Chapter Seven

'Did you have a pleasant nap, my lady?' Philpott placed a cup of tea by the bedside and went to draw back the curtains at the window, letting in the late afternoon sunshine.

'No, not really,' Bel said vaguely, pushing her hair back out of her eyes. Philpott, studying her with professional frankness, sniffed.

'You will have bags under your eyes, my lady, if you do not get some sleep. London life does not appear to suit you. You look as though you did not get a wink last night either. You are quite pale.' She leaned closer, frowning, convincing Bel that she must look such a hag that Ashe would retreat in alarm after one look at her.

'Yes, there are smudges under your eyes, my lady, even if there are no bags. Yet.' The dresser turned away, leaving her mistress to digest this ominous lecture, and began to tidy the dressing table. 'Once a lady reaches a certain age, she has to take extra care,' she added. 'In my last position, try what I might, I could not persuade my lady to use Denmark Lotion. And look what happened.'

'What did happen?' Bel slid her arms into her wrapper and got up. Perhaps if she got dressed and had a walk before dinner, she could manage a short sleep after it.

'Crows' feet,' Philpott confided bleakly.

Bel sat on the dressing-table stool and regarded herself in the mirror. Even if the ultimate horror of crows' feet had not yet arrived, she certainly looked like a woman short of sleep. And that was hardly the way to appear to a sophisticated, experienced gentleman who was used, she had no doubt, to lovely, assured and vibrant lovers. Not to inexperienced ones who were too nervous to sleep and consequently were wan and heavy-eyed. To say nothing of utterly ignorant on the subject of pleasuring a man in bed.

The thought of pleasuring Ashe in bed, whatever it involved, had Bel closing her eyes with a breathless sigh of anticipation. Then she opened them again and stared at her pale reflection.

She tried to find consolation in the glossiness of her hair, which she had washed that morning. Philpott began to style it again and Bel was seized with a new worry. How should she dress to receive Ashe? Would he expect her to be in evening dress and for them to have a conversation first? Or would he expect her to be in bed? Or up, but *en négligé*? How on earth was one supposed to know these things? Bel worried, distractedly buffing her nails. There ought to be a book on the subject. Perhaps there was, and she was too ignorant to know how to find it. Poor Lord Dereham.

Ashe slid the key carefully into the lock and eased the back door open. The night was quiet, moonless, and here, at the rear of the house, almost totally dark. As he had passed the front façade on to Half Moon Street he had seen the candlelight flickering through a gap in Belinda's bedchamber curtains. She was awake and waiting for him.

His lips curved in a smile of pleasurable anticipation, unclouded by nothing more than two glasses of claret with his dinner. He had returned to his chambers for a shave and to check there was no last-minute message cancelling their rendezvous and now he was conscious of the steady pulse of his blood, of a certain tightness low in his belly and the slight, pleasurable, *frisson* of nerves.

He expected it before battle, welcomed it to keep him sharp and alert. It amused him to feel it now, before the start of a new *affaire*. It was novel, that feeling in these circumstances, but then Belinda was different somehow. He had never been a careless or thoughtless lover, he reassured himself as he made his way unerringly through the familiar house. But this was important to get right.

He paused halfway up the stairs, frowning into the darkness. Why was that? Then he shrugged. The lady was not going to thank him for keeping her waiting while he brooded on the philosophy of relationships. As soundlessly as he had moved operating behind enemy lines Ashe drifted upstairs, turned right on to the landing and scratched lightly on the door panel.

She opened the door to him on to a room lit by a candelabrum on a side table and another by the bedside. As he stepped inside, Bel closed the door and moved wordlessly to stand by the table. It looked as though she had been sitting there reading.

The flickering light struck rich reflections off her unbound hair, as though amber had been threaded through its brown length. Ashe wanted to lift it, run his fingers through it. *All in good time. Patience: she is worth it.* 'Lady Belinda.'

'My friends call me Bel,' she confided, her voice husky with nerves.

'Bel.' He tried it and smiled, pleased with the sound on his tongue. A small word, but sweet and rounded, like her. 'Lovely. It suits you.' She was wearing a long robe of amber silk tied with ribbons that fluttered as she moved. Under it he could see a nightgown in a deeper hue. With her hair heavy on her shoulders and her bare toes peeping out, she was the woman he remembered from that first night.

Only he did not recall her being this pale, nor her eyes looking so enormous in the oval of her face. Last night, at the dance, she had not seemed so fragile. 'Are you all right, Bel?' He moved to come to her and stopped, his toe stubbing against something. He looked down. Malevolent green-glass eyes glinted up from a massive furry head. His toes were against a set of savage teeth. That ridiculous bear again. 'Good evening, Horace,' he said, sidestepping the thing.

Bel gave a little gasp of laughter. 'I am all right. I am just…nervous, I suppose.'

'So am I,' Ashe said easily, closing the distance between them. Hell, she looked as though she had not slept at all, and the hem of her gown was vibrating as though she was shivering. He had the sudden thought that if he clapped his hands she would faint out of sheer alarm. Now was not the time to stand around talking, she needed sweeping off her feet.

Ashe lifted his hands to her shoulders, feeling the slender bones and his breath hitched in his throat. She stood watching him, grey eyes wide so he saw his own reflection as he lowered his mouth to hers.

The shock jolted through him as their lips touched. What was it? The scent of her, faintly floral, wholly feminine—or the taste of her? Even at that light touch he could sense sweetness. But he had touched his lips to her skin before, held her close. Perhaps that familiarity accounted for the sense of rightness as he angled his mouth to slide questing over hers.

Bel gave a little gasp against his lips, but her hands came up to press against his upper chest as though she did not know whether to hold on or push him away. He let his tongue explore along the seam of her lips, wondering how easily she would open to him, how she would taste as he slid inside. Surely she understood what he was doing, what he wanted? He sucked gently on that deliciously pouting lower lip and felt her jolt of surprise.

It seemed she did not understand. Ashe did not try to force it, but eased the pressure, letting his tongue slide over the swell of her lower lip. Her hands crept up to curve over his shoulders and she moved a little closer. Encouraged, he let his own hands slide down to hold her against him, supple, yielding as she had been in the waltz, letting him lead.

He sucked her lower lip into his own mouth and she came up on tiptoe, pressed against him so that the urge to cup her buttocks and crush her against his swelling groin was almost painful. At last her mouth was opening to his gentle assault. Ashe slid his tongue between her lips, into the warm, moist sweetness and her own tongue moved to touch his in a shyly tentative caress. He did not think he had ever felt anything so touching as that innocently trusting gesture.

It seemed her husband was not a magnificent lover who had left his wife bereft after all. But how could a man be married to Bel and not want to lavish every art of seduction and eroticism upon her? How could she be this innocent?

She was clinging to his shoulders now and he sensed it was only that grip that was keeping her standing. Gently Ashe lifted his mouth and smiled down at her. The colour was animating her face now, a little smile tugged at the corner of her mouth. Already it seemed fuller, more swollen from his assiduous kisses.

'Hello,' he murmured, as though she had been away.

'Hello.' Her lashes fluttered down to hide her eyes and he opened his hands to release her. Those frivolous ribbons fluttered with the movement and he began to undo the bows, slowly, indulgently, letting the sensual slide of the silk satin through his fingers tantalise him with the thought of how her skin would feel when he caressed her.

'I can do that,' she said uncertainly, her hands fluttering above his as he worked with slow concentration.

'I enjoy it. This is a very lovely garment; the colour is perfect against your skin, your hair.' The last bow yielded and the robe fell open to reveal the low-cut neckline of the nightgown. Ashe had seen the lovely swell of her breasts before—this was no lower cut than the fashionable gown she had worn last night, but this time it was for him alone, and he could touch her. Holding his breath, he trailed the back of his fingers across the exposed skin.

Bel gasped, stepped back, but he simply stepped forward, matching her retreat, caught the edges of the robe and pushed it off her shoulders. Long, slim arms, bare now without gloves, the light glinting on her skin, turning it to ivory, and shoulders, naked except for slim ribbon straps, sloping elegantly up to the column of her neck. The pulse there was beating wildly, he could see it, was immeasurably aroused by it. Low down, where he ached for her, his echoing pulse throbbed with urgent need.

'*Belle*.' He gave it a lingering French intonation, laying his fingers gently against the betraying pulse. 'Belle. You are so lovely, so lovely.'

'Should I…should I get into bed?'

He had planned to kiss her almost insensible there where they stood, then scoop her up and enjoy the sight of her sprawled on the deep green satin of the bed cover. But all his instincts told him to go slowly, let her do what seemed comfortable to her. 'If you like.'

She edged backwards, lifted the side of the covers. 'With the candles lit?'

'Why, yes. I want to see you.'

'You do?' She slid into bed and sat watching him, the covers up to her chin.

'Definitely!' Ashe sat down with caution on the delicate bergère armchair, took off his shoes, undid the buckles at the knee of his evening breeches and began to roll down the silk stockings. With his feet bare he stood up and shed his coat, letting it fall with a carelessness that would have wrung a moan from his valet's lips.

As he began to unbutton his waistcoat, Bel stammered, 'What are you doing?'

'Undressing.' He dropped the garment on to the coat and pulled the knot of his neckcloth free.

'But…don't you want to do that in the dressing room?'

Ashe stared at her. 'No. No, I would like to undress here, where I can watch you.'

'Oh.' Bel shut her eyes. 'Oh, dear.'

'Bel.' They stayed shut. 'Bel, I know you have seen a naked man before—'

'No, I have not.'

'What?' Ashe sat down, heedless of the crushed garments on the chair. *No, do not tell me you are a virgin. Please!* You heard about it. Marriages that stayed unconsummated for one reason or another. He had never made love to a virgin in his life, and he was most certainly not going to start now.

'I have never seen a naked man because Henry always used to come to my chamber in his nightgown and then snuff out the candles,' Bel explained prosaically, eyes still screwed firmly shut. Ashe let out a tightly held breath and felt the sweat cooling on his brow.

'And then he would take his nightshirt off?'

'Oh, no. He would get into bed and kiss me on the cheek and then he would…you know.'

'With his nightshirt on?'

'Of course.' Bel opened her eyes cautiously as though expecting to see him standing there indecently naked and rampant. She seemed relieved to find him still in shirt and breeches.

'And you still in your nightgown?' She nodded. 'And then he would make love to you?' Another nod.

'And then he would kiss me on the cheek again and say "Thank you dear. Goodnight", and off he would go until Wednesday. Or Saturday.'

'He would visit your room twice a week on set days?' Ashe knew he was staring, but couldn't help himself. His mouth was probably open. The man must have either had ice water in his veins or have been blind. Or both.

Bel yawned, hugely, clapping both hands over her mouth. 'Oh, I am so sorry. I didn't sleep very well last night.'

Ashe ignored the yawn. 'Forgive me, but may I ask…was your husband a very passionate man? I mean, did you find his lovemaking, er…?'

'Dull. I found it very, very dull. But Henry did not seem to think I ought to be enjoying it, you see. He was always rather apologetic about doing it at all, so I assumed it was expected to be horrid.' Ashe blinked at her frankness. *Poor bloody Henry. You idiot.* 'So I had no idea that there was more to it, or that I might enjoy it. Not for a long while. But then there were things people said—when I stopped being a new bride—and things I read. I guessed that perhaps it can be more than just sticky and boring and embarrassing.'

Bel regarded him hopefully. 'It is, isn't it? More? I mean, I began to feel there was something I *needed*.' She frowned over the word, then gave her head a little shake as though she could not think of a better one.

'Yes. I promise it is. So much more. So much that will satisfy that need.' She looked so fragile, sitting up in that big bed. And so nervous and so tired. 'Bel, you have not considered simply getting married again? It would have been a more conventional way of finding affection. Safer, perhaps.'

'Goodness, no. No, I am *absolutely* determined never to marry again. You do not know what a husband is really going to be like—look at Henry. I mean, he was a decent, honest, respectable man. He was kind. But he was so dull and he made me be dull—yet I never guessed how it would be until I married him.

'And even if he is not dull, a husband rules his wife and now I know what it is like to be able to think for myself I could not bear it. And then, if by some miracle he did *not* try to dominate me—imagine how awful it must be to be married to the sort of man who did not care what you did and positively encouraged you to take lovers. How do you respect a man like that?'

'And unlike a husband, you can change a lover if he does not please you? Like a library book?' Ashe asked, only half-jesting.

'No! You should not treat people like that.' Bel wriggled up against the pillows, forgetting to be shy in her indignation. 'That is why I thought it could only be a daydream, a fantasy. I never intended to take a lover, not really. I had no idea how to find one. And then you came that night and I thought you were attractive. I was tempted, when you woke up on top of me, to say nothing, but to kiss you and see what happened. I did not, of course.' She blushed. 'But I thought you were safe.'

'*Safe?*' Never in his life had Ashe been called safe. *Dangerous flirt* was the term that careful mamas had applied to him in the course of the last Season he had spent in London. *Amorous devil* was the description not a few society ladies had used, not without a secret smile as they said it. But *safe*? He rather thought he had just been insulted. 'I was drunk, for goodness' sake!'

'I think that drink shows what people are really like. It makes bullies worse and cruel people violent. You were gentle and funny and polite. And you seemed to want me, but you did not take advantage of me.'

'I did want you. I do.' And if he did not have her soon

he was going to be in agony. Every word she said made him want her more, made him ache to teach her just how sweet love making could be. There was so much to explore together.

'So you see?' Bel's lips curved into a smile. 'You are safe, and you said you are a rake, so you understand about not wanting entanglements, and I will not have to worry about toying with your affections or breaking your heart or anything like that. But you do want to make love to me—even I can tell that. I quite understand if it is only once—I do not expect I will be any good at it. But then at least I'll know what I have been missing.'

'Close your eyes,' Ashe said, returning that smile. 'I can promise to be safe. And gentle. And to show you what you have been missing. But I am not sure I can promise to be funny, not all the time.'

'All right.' Reassured, still smiling, Bel closed her eyes and waited, trying to follow what Ashe was doing. There was some rustling, then his footsteps padding round to the other side of the bed.

'You close your eyes, too, Horace,' she heard him order, and stifled a gasp of nervous laughter. The covers lifted, cooler air fanned over her body for a moment as the bed dipped with his weight, then she felt the length of him against her side. Long, hard, warm. 'You can look now,' Ashe said as he put an arm under her shoulders and pulled her against him.

'Oh.' Instead of the bare skin she was prepared for, there was the soft linen of a dress shirt. 'I thought…'

'And I thought you might be more comfortable like this for a little while. Now, relax, snuggle up, put your arm here and just lie with me. We do not have to hurry.'

It was not at all what she had expected, but Bel did

as she was told, awkwardly putting her left arm over
Ashe's chest and letting herself be gathered in against
his ribcage.

He was as big as she remembered, his chest broad
as she spanned it, the shoulder her head was cushioned
against as solid as only hard-won muscle could make
it. Her own breathing was all over the place, Ashe's was
steady, deep and easy.

And the scent of him was the same, too, only without
the tang of sweat from a hard night's revelry or the
strong smell of brandy. There was a hint of a subtle
citrus that she guessed was his soap, the laundry smell
of clean linen, fresh from the iron, and, underneath it,
man. Ashe's own, personal scent, his skin.

Bel rubbed her cheek against his shirt, wishing she
could feel the texture of that skin. Their feet touched,
bare, and Ashe hooked his right ankle over to capture
her feet. It felt secure, warm, as though she was special.
Her eyes drifted closed as his hand began to stroke her
head. The span of his fingers could have encircled her
throat, had wielded a weapon, could master a horse, and
yet his touch was so gentle that she sighed with content.
The thought drifted through her mind that already he
had spent almost as much time in her bed as Henry ever
did in one visit.

She had expected almost any emotion, any sensation
other than this peaceful drift, this warmth moving
gently to the rhythm of his breathing. So peaceful, so
safe…

Chapter Eight

‘Good morning, my lady. You had a proper night's sleep at last, I am glad to see.’

Bel opened her eyes on to bright sunlight and the sounds of Philpott in the next room briskly organising her wardrobe for the day.

She scrambled up into a sitting position and stared wildly round the room. Where was Ashe? Beside her the bed was neat, the far side tucked in tight as she tugged on the covers. The pillows were smooth. There was no litter of male garments across the floor, her poetry book sat chastely on the table where she had put it last night and the candles had been carefully pinched out, not left to gutter and burn away.

It had all been a dream? It must have been. No man would accept an offer to a lady's bed and then simply cuddle her, make the bed again and silently slip away while she slept. Which meant that she had dreamt a safe ending to her fantasy. Had she even dreamed asking Ashe to be her lover?

Confused, Bel turned to run her hand over the pillow

beside her and saw it. On the embroidered linen was a single blond hair. She picked it up and it curled in her fingers, the one strong filament conjuring up the image of a whole head of hair: golden, thick, curving over-long into his nape.

Ashe was here last night. I did not dream it. And he had come to bed in his shirt because she was shy, and he had let her sleep in his arms because she was tired and he had made the bed, quietly, so as not to disturb her or betray that he had been there. Behind her eyes something prickled. Bel scrubbed the back of her hand across them as her dresser came back into the room, her arms full of petticoats.

'Are you quite well, my lady?' Philpott frowned, anxious. 'You look a trifle emotional.'

'No, I am quite well. My eyes are watering, that is all. Just the after-effects of such a long sleep, I expect.' Ashe had been gentle and kind and tolerant. But he was not going to come back, that was certain. Male pride, she knew from observing every male of her acquaintance, did not take kindly to rejection, and rejection did not come in more comprehensive form than a woman falling asleep in a man's arms when he was intending to make love to her.

She felt fidgety, unsettled and sad. A strange combination of emotions. She was going to have to write and apologise. What on earth could she say to excuse her behaviour? But at least she could do something about the fidgets and perhaps later she would know what to say in her note. And there was that kiss to remember, always.

Bel threw back the covers and went to her little desk in her bare feet. 'I will drive in the park this morning, Philpott. Please have this note taken round to Lady

James Ravenhurst's London residence immediately and tell the footman to wait for the reply.'

There was only one woman in London she felt she could safely be with at the moment without betraying some clue as to her inner turmoil and that was Cousin Elinor. Elinor would not notice anything amiss unless a Greek charioteer drove through Hyde Park, or St Paul's Cathedral sprouted minarets, she was certain of it.

Miss Ravenhurst's note gratefully accepting the offer of a drive and luncheon was returned promptly and Elinor was equally prompt when the barouche drew up outside the house. When Bel thanked her for not keeping the horses standing, she brushed it away with a shake of her head in its plain straw bonnet. 'I did not want to dally, believe me! Mama is sure to have thought of some piece she wants me to transcribe after all and really, this is far too lovely a morning to be shut inside.'

'You help my aunt a great deal with her researches, then? It must be fascinating,' Bel added mendaciously, thinking that, unless Elinor was as committed as her mother, it must actually be quite ghastly.

'It has a certain interest. Anything does if you come to know enough about it.' Elinor folded her hands neatly in her lap, the tight buttoned gloves precisely the wrong shade of tan to go with the mouse-brown skirt and pelisse she wore. Either she was colour blind or her mother insisted she dress to repel men. Knowing Aunt Louisa, Bel strongly suspected the latter.

'Besides,' her cousin added, with the air of making her position quite clear, 'I have to do something with my time. Fortunately there are no elderly aunts who require a companion and I may be thankful that neither Simon nor Anne expect me to dance attention on their offspring. I am not at all good with children and I make a dreadful aunt. So, if one must be on the shelf, this at least has the advantage of being intellectually stimulating.'

It was the longest speech Bel had ever heard Elinor make, and certainly the first time she had ever volunteered her thoughts on her own situation. 'I do not understand why you should be on the shelf,' she ventured, choosing her words with caution. 'You are very pretty, well connected...'

'I am too tall and I have red hair,' Elinor contradicted. 'You are lucky, Cousin Belinda, you are one of the brown-haired Ravenhursts. I am one of the redheads.'

'Auburn,' Bel corrected. 'It is lovely, like conkers.' Poor Elinor. At least, whatever other problems she had, Bel had never been made to feel plain. 'Cousin Theophilus has much redder hair than you do.'

Elinor smiled. 'You are very kind, but I know I have no charm and *that* is essential to attract gentlemen. I am too practical, I expect. And I have not met Cousin Theophilus for years: Mama says he is a loose fish and a wastrel. Where are we going to drive?' She craned around inelegantly to see where they had got to, one hand firmly clamped on the crown of her awful hat. 'Hyde Park?'

'I thought so. And then shall we go to Gunter's for ices?' Eating ice cream in the morning was decidedly self-indulgent, but she felt she needed it.

The carriage made several turns, Bel pointing out the exotic sight of a lady with a pair of elegant long-haired hounds on a leash. Elinor twisted again in her seat to watch them, unconcerned about creasing her gown. 'I think those are saluki hounds, from Arabia. Cousin Belinda…' she frowned as she turned back '…there is a man following us in a curricle.'

'How can you tell? The streets are jammed.'

'I saw the curricle behind you when you picked me up, and he was there again when I looked to see where we were and now he is still behind us. He is driving a striking pair of match greys—I cannot be mistaken.'

'I expect he is going to the park as we are and our ways just happen to coincide.' Elinor looked dubious, but Bel was not going to scramble about in the carriage, peering out at the traffic behind them. 'Why should anyone want to follow us? I do believe you are a secret novel reader, Cousin! I can assure you, I am not being pursued by a wicked duke for some evil end. Perhaps he is after you.'

Elinor blushed so furiously at the suggestion of novel reading that Bel decided that not only must she consume the productions of the Minerva Press avidly, but that Aunt Louisa had no idea and would not approve. 'I have just borrowed *The Abbess of Voltiera* from the circulating library, if you would like to have it as I finish each volume,' she offered. 'It is quite blood curdling.'

'That would be very nice,' Elinor said primly as they entered the park. 'Oh look, there's a gentleman waving to you. See? On that horse close to the grove of chestnuts.'

Ashe. Bel followed the direction of her cousin's gaze and saw Mr Layne approaching them on a good-looking bay hack. 'Pull up,' she called to the coachman as her treacherous pulse returned to normal. 'Mr Layne, good morning. Cousin Elinor, may I make known to you Mr Layne, the brother of the renowned poetess? Mr Layne, my cousin, Miss Ravenhurst.'

He brought his horse alongside the carriage and leaned down to shake hands. 'A lovely morning for a drive, is it not?'

'Delightful,' Elinor agreed. 'Are you also a poet, Mr Layne?'

'Not at all, I fear. I can hardly rhyme moon and spoon.' Patrick laughed, shaking his head in self-deprecation. 'All the talent in the family is with my sister. I manage my uncle's estates.'

'That requires talent also,' Elinor observed.

Now he would be perfect for her, Bel thought, suddenly struck as she watched them chatting easily. Mr Layne showed no sign of alarm at either Elinor's despised auburn hair, nor her appalling dress sense. He was a young man with his way to make in the world and, with her connections and excellent common sense, she was just the sort of woman to…

'Oh, look, Cousin Belinda, that man who was following us has just driven past.' Elinor pointed.

'What?' Mr Layne stood in his stirrups to observe the rear of the curricle that was sweeping away down the carriage drive. 'Has someone been annoying you ladies? Shall I catch up to him and demand his business?'

'No! I am certain it was just coincidence that he was behind us for such a way. Please, do not concern yourself Mr Layne. See—he has gone now.'

'Then let me ride beside you as escort in case he comes back.' He reined back to one side and matched his pace to the barouche as it moved off, keeping far enough away so as not to appear to be with them.

'A very gentlemanlike young man, I think,' Bel observed quietly.

'Indeed, he is.' Elinor glanced sideways to observe Mr Layne from under the brim of her bonnet. 'You are fortunate in your admirers, Cousin.'

'Goodness, he is no such thing. I must tell you, Elinor, I am firmly resolved against a second marriage and to encourage anyone to have expectations—not that Mr Layne has any, I am sure—would be most unfair.' No more husbands. And no lover either. Bel repressed a wistful sigh. There was no point in repining; she had daringly given herself an opportunity and it was all her fault it had ended as it had. Lord Dereham could not have acted more chivalrously, poor man.

They trotted along as far as the Knightsbridge gate without further incident. When they reached it Mr Layne came up and touched his hat. 'Your mysterious follower has gone, it seems, ma'am.'

'I am sure it was simply a coincidence, but thank you for your escort. We are going to Gunter's for some refreshment—would you care to join us?' Bel had hoped for some peace and quiet with Elinor to recover the tone of her mind a little, but she had the notion that perhaps she could matchmake here. After all, she had never heard her cousin utter a single opinion about a man before.

'Thank you, but I regret that I have an appointment shortly. Do enjoy your ices, ladies.'

Bel and Elinor watched him canter away, Elinor's face unreadable. *Bother*—perhaps she was indifferent after all.

'Gunter's next, please,' Bel called up to the coachman and settled back against the squabs. Rescuing Elinor from Aunt Louisa was a worthwhile project, she felt. But how to get her into new clothes? She was never going to attract gentlemen dressed like that, even the amiable Mr Layne. This needed some planning. 'I am so pleased you could drive with me,' she remarked as they turned into Charles Street. 'Do you think Aunt Louisa would spare you again?'

'I should think so.' An unexpected twinkle showed in her cousin's green eyes. 'I am sure she would think it a sacrifice well worth while if I can provide some chaperonage for you.'

They were still smiling over plans for further expeditions as they walked into the confectioner's, securing a place in a corner with a good view of the room. Elinor ordered a vanilla ice and chocolate, and, despite her resolution to have only a small lemon ice and a cup of tea, Bel succumbed to the same choices.

'It is delicious if you chase a spoonful of ice with a sip of chocolate,' Bel was observing when Elinor sat bolt upright and said in a penetrating whisper, strongly reminiscent of her mother,

'It's that man again!'

'What man?' Bel had her back to the door.

'The one who was following us into the park. He is coming over, the presumptuous wretch. Oh, dear, and I do not have a hatpin!'

'We are in the middle of Gunter's, Elinor, nothing can happen to us here, you have no need to spear him—'

'Lady Felsham, good morning.'

Bel dropped her spoon into the saucer with a clatter. 'Lord Dereham!' It was Ashe, standing there, large as life, smiling blandly as though he had not seen her since the dancing party. Elinor cleared her throat and Bel realised she was gaping at him in complete shock. *Please*, she prayed, *please don't let me be blushing like a peony*. 'Good morning. May I introduce my cousin, Miss Ravenhurst? Elinor, Lord Dereham.' They shook hands. 'Will you join us?' *He is here, he is smiling, he has forgiven me…*

Elinor's eyebrows rose as Ashe took the third seat at their small round table and clicked his fingers for the waiter. Her lips narrowed. 'Do you know, my lord, I am convinced that I have seen you before today, several times. In fact, I could have sworn you were following us.'

Bel tried to kick her under the table, missed and made contact with Ashe's ankle. It was a very small table. 'Oh, yes,' Ashe admitted, wincing. 'I followed you into Hyde Park. Amazing how easy it is to bump into acquaintances, even at this time of year.' He smiled. 'I would have stopped to chat, but you were talking to Mr Layne and I did not want to interrupt.'

'How fortunate you were able to find us here then,' Elinor observed severely, obviously not believing a word of it. Bel shook her head at her slightly. This was not the time for her cousin to take her pretend role as chaperon so seriously.

'Was it not?' Ashe beamed at her as the waiter produced a pot of coffee for him. 'I could have sent a note, of course, but I wanted to make sure that the problem Lady Felsham is having with the plumbing is now corrected. I could send my own man round if it is not.' Elinor was looking baffled. 'Lady Felsham bought her house from me,' he explained. 'I feel responsible for the problem she is having with it.'

'Oh. I see.' Elinor took a sip of chocolate and subsided, obviously disappointed that this was neither a Gothic horror story nor a case of over-amorous pursuit for her to foil.

'Or I could have called later, but I am going to be visiting old Mr Horace this evening. Do you know him?'

'Old Mr Horace?' Did he mean what he appeared to mean? Bel opened her mouth, shut it rapidly and tried to get her tumbling thoughts into some sort of order. 'The, um…northern gentleman? The one with the snowy white hair and the problem with his teeth?' Ashe nodded. 'And you are going to visit him again?' Another nod. 'That is very kind of you, Lord Dereham. I had understood that your previous experiences with the old gentleman were not encouraging.'

'He is somewhat eccentric,' Ashe agreed. 'And a very poor conversationalist. But I derive a great deal of, um…*satisfaction* from the relationship. And hope to obtain more.'

Now she *must* be blushing. How could he be so brazen? But it seemed that *she* was forgiven for falling asleep: she just hoped that he would not be disappointed tonight. She was very certain that she would not be.

'Virtue,' Elinor pronounced piously, 'is its own reward.' She looked somewhat taken aback when both of her companions collapsed into peels of laughter.

Bel sat in front of her dressing table mirror, brushing her hair. It shone in the candle light, picking up the auburn highlights that all the Ravenhursts had in their hair, even if they were not redheads like Elinor and their cousin Theophilus.

She was quite pleased with her appearance tonight, she concluded dispassionately, studying her reflection.

That was a good thing, considering that she had spent the whole evening fretting over it. The good night's sleep and the fresh air that morning had restored her colour and the smudges had gone from under her eyes. Around her on the stool pooled the silken folds of a new aquamarine nightgown with ribbon ties on the shoulders and at the bosom and not a great deal of substance to its layers of skirt. As for the bodice, Bel was careful not to breathe too deeply. Ashe, she was hopeful, would like it.

She twiddled the earrings in her ears and then removed them, her fingers hesitating over her jewel box before lifting a long, thin, gold chain. She fastened it, observing the way it slithered down into the valley between her breasts. Was she trying too hard? What would he expect? She bit her lip in indecision, then touched a tiny dab of jasmine scent where the chain vanished into shadowed curves.

There. Enough. When she found out what pleased Ashe, then she could be more daring. The thought of what that voyage of discovery might entail sent a shiver up and down her spine as the landing clock chimed the three-quarter hour. Soon he would be here.

The minutes dragged as she sat waiting, elegantly disposed in the armchair, her volume of Byron open and unread in her lap. When the scratch on the door came she was so tense that the book fell to the carpet as she jerked upright and she was scrabbling on the floor behind the bed for it when the door opened and she heard Ashe come in.

'Hello, Horace old chap. Where has Bel gone?'

'Here.' She popped up from the other side of the bed, painfully aware that her hard-won pose of seductive sophistication was completely ruined. 'I dropped my book.'

'Not playing hide and seek, then?' Ashe smiled. 'A pity—I can think of some entertaining forfeits.'

Bel felt hopelessly gauche. Ashe seemed to regard this lovemaking thing, which she had always assumed was a rather serious business, as a game, as fun. 'I am sorry about last night,' she said, eager to get that over with. 'I was so nervous I could not sleep the night before and then when you were so gentle and soothing I could not help myself drifting off. You must have been so angry with me. It is very kind of you to come back.'

'Don't apologise, Bel,' Ashe said shortly, something very like the anger she feared flickering in his eyes. 'Don't you dare. Do you think I would expect you to make love when you were tired and apprehensive? I am not your husband, I do not expect anything as my due. We give each other only what we are able to, what we want to. Do you understand?'

'Yes,' Bel lied, unable to believe it. Men made demands in bed, women obeyed them, that was the way things were. The only difference was that some men made those demands more nicely than others and would take the trouble to ensure the woman enjoyed the experience.

He smiled, the warmth chasing away the spark of anger. 'Tell me what you would like? Shall we read poetry together?'

'I would like you to kiss me,' she said, boldness masking the fact she could not stand the tension of waiting any longer. He was probably teasing about the poetry in any case.

'Very well, my lady. I feel a trifle overdressed.' Ashe had come in pantaloons and long-tailed coat, not in the formality of knee breeches. As she watched, he heeled off his shoes and shed coat and waistcoat on to a chair, then turned and held out his arms.

Bel walked into them, sliding her palms up his chest, feeling the heat under the fine cotton, catching her breath as they passed over his nipples, hardening under her touch. As she looked up, his lids lowered in sensual pleasure and his arms came round her.

Chapter Nine

T he caress of Ashe's mouth was as gentle as it had
been the first time he had kissed her, but this time it was
surprisingly undemanding. Gradually Bel began to feel
impatient with the respectful slide of closed lips over
hers. She wanted his heat again, the taste of him, the
hard thrust of his tongue, the indecent way he had
sucked her lip between his.

Greatly daring, she parted her lips and ran her own
tongue along the join of his, feeling them curve into a
smile before he opened to her. Hazily Bel was aware that
he had lured her into taking the initiative, but she was too
engrossed in exploration now to feel resentful at his tactics.

She let her tongue slide languorously over his, then
answered a sudden thrust with one of her own, duelling,
teasing and being teased while the taste and the scent
and the feel of him swept over her, until she felt she was
melting into his body.

Ashe lowered his hands until they cupped her
buttocks and pulled her up against him so she could feel
the hard ridge of his erection against the curve of her

stomach. It was a blatantly sexual display of desire and the intensity of the response it provoked in her was outrageous. She wanted him, now, desperately.

Heat seemed to pool low inside her, and she wriggled against him, seeking relief for the ache that was building, just where he pressed. Arousal, desire, sheer physical yearning—all the things she had not realised existed, had now only hazily began to suspect, could be hers with this man.

Shockingly she felt Ashe grow harder as she clung close, and deep in his throat he growled softly, the sound vibrating against her lips, a masculine signal of need that should have terrified her. Instead she felt powerful, amazed that she could have this effect upon him despite her ignorance and his experience.

Bel slid her fingers between their bodies and began to unbutton his shirt. Impatient with the mother-of-pearl buttons, she tugged and pulled and then, as her fingertips met skin and the rasp of hair, she froze. 'Go on,' he said huskily in her ear. 'Touch me Bel. I want your hands on me.'

'I do not know what to do,' she whispered. But it seemed her hands did know, sliding under the parted front of the shirt. She felt the tickle of hair on her palms and then hot, satiny skin as they slid over his ribs. Back to the centre, then down over ridges of muscle to the flatness of his stomach where the hair seemed to focus. Her thumb found his navel and dipped in, wiggled experimentally, provoking a gasp of laughter.

He was moving his hips against her as he held her, signalling his need, yet he controlled it for her. It seemed impossible that this big, powerful man would let her explore like this, would seem content for her to set the pace.

Ashe lowered his face into the angle of her neck and began to lick slowly up until the tip of his tongue found her ear. The caress brought back memories of lying crushed beneath him on the floor, his mouth hot and moist as he explored her, and all she could think about was feeling his body over hers again, his heart against hers, his mouth taking hers.

Bel's fingers slipped lower, into the waistband of Ashe's trousers where the tantalising trail of dark hair vanished. '*Yes*. Bel, yes.' The fastenings were tight; he sucked in his breath so she could twist her fingers round and open them, then her hand was curling round the hard, hot, terrifying length of him. A moment later and she was on her back on the bed, Ashe was shedding the remains of his clothes and she was staring wide-eyed at the first naked man she had ever seen in the flesh.

And what flesh. Bel swallowed. He was beautifully made, the candlelight flickering over smooth muscle and long limbs and… Suddenly she was nervous, her eyes closed tight. She was very aware of how flimsy her own garment was, how she must look to him, sprawled wantonly on the bed.

'It's all right, Bel, don't be frightened.' His weight dipped the bed beside her and Ashe began to stroke her quivering body, his hand running softly over the fine silk. It whispered against her skin. 'I won't do anything until you want me to, I promise.'

'I do want you to. To do everything. Anything. But I do not know what those things are that I want.' Bel opened her eyes and smiled ruefully. 'That is what is so scary.'

'Then, Bel, let's find them together.' He smiled back, then bent to kiss her breast just where the edge of the nightgown ended. '*Belle, bella, bellissima.*' His lips fastened over one nipple and he began to suck it gently through the gossamer fabric, sending shock waves of sensation through her. She writhed, gasped, clutched his head, uncertain whether she wanted him to stop at once or never stop at all. It seemed he intended never to stop. Perhaps she would simply die of the sensation. Tongue, teeth, lips combined to send her into a fever, reduced her to a helpless, panting puddle of longing and desire.

Just when she was certain she could bear it no longer she felt his hand caress up under her skirts, his fingers slide into the secret folds that were hot and wet for him, slip between them to find the entrance to her body and then, as she arched in shock against his mouth, into the heat. Bel sensed her muscles clasp around the intrusion as his thumb found the single aching focus of her straining body and she felt his weight over her, his mouth on hers as she screamed in agonised delight and collapsed, shuddering, under him.

She wondered hazily if she had lost consciousness for, as she regained her senses enough to differentiate between the parts of her own body and his, she found the nightgown was gone and she was moulded, flesh to flesh, heartbeat to heartbeat with Ashe.

'Let me take you, *Belle*,' he murmured and surged into her on one powerful thrust. Always before she had lain rigid under such an onslaught, enduring the meaningless, effortful, mercifully short male striving towards release. Only now Ashe seemed quite as concerned to bring her to that peak of ecstasy again as to reach his own, and it seemed that the beautiful body dominating hers was quite capable of going on for as long as it took. She wanted it to last for ever because it was so wonderful, and yet to be over at once, because she wanted to share that storm of completion with him.

She felt the tension twisting into unimaginable heights, felt a change in his body, heard his breath rasp in his throat and curled her legs around his hips, pulling him in. 'Ashe! Ashe, please…' He gave one more thrust as she lost herself, then she was conscious—just—of him leaving her, holding her tight, gasping into her hair as they fell together, down into darkness.

Ashe rolled on to his back, bringing Bel with him to lie cradled against his chest in the curve of his arm. She gave a soft whimper of pleasure and snuggled close as his groping hand found the corner of the sheet and pulled it over their damp bodies.

He gazed up at the underside of the curtains as he let the aftershocks of their lovemaking shudder through his body. It had been beyond anything he had imagined and he could not understand why. Bel was lovely, sweet, eager. But she had come to him completely untutored and repressed—as close to a virgin as a woman could be after sleeping with a man. She had none of the tricks to pleasure him his mistresses had known—and yet the tentative wonder of her hands on his body, the awe in her eyes, the total trust with which she had given herself to him were powerfully erotic. And humbling, he realised.

'Bel?'

'Mmm?' She snuggled in closer, rubbed her cheek against his pectorals and found his nipple with her lips. 'Mmm.'

'Stop it, wicked woman. Let a man catch his breath.' She released the tense flesh and he saw her ear go pink at what she must have thought was a reproof. 'I like it too much,' he explained, mentally cursing her husband again, and she relaxed. 'Are you—are you all right?'

He had expected her to be shy at the question, to answer hesitantly. Instead she wriggled up until she was sitting, her knees curved into his hips, and smiled at him, the sheet pooling around her. Glowing, that was the only way to describe her. Her skin was flushed pink, deeper across her breasts. Her hair tumbled wantonly around her shoulders and her eyes, fixed on him, were wide and wondering. 'All right?' She shook her head, the curling locks shifting in the candlelight. 'That phrase hardly seems adequate. I had no idea it was like that. Is it always like that?'

It seemed he had not disappointed her. Ashe felt himself relax. He had not been conscious of a tension, but now he saw what a responsibility he had accepted and how hurt Bel could have been if she had chosen a man who did not live up to the trust she had placed in him.

'I find it hard to believe that it would ever be like that for me again,' he said seriously. 'It can be as good—it will be—but that was special.'

'Oh.' Bel considered this, equally serious. 'But I did not know what I was doing.'

'You didn't need to; you did what came naturally and that was…wonderful.'

'Oh,' she said again, dropping her lashes. 'May we do it again? Soon? I mean, of course, when it is a convenient evening for you.'

'It is very convenient now,' he said smiling.

'But—' She glanced down to where her wriggling had pulled the sheet away from his loins, and her mouth opened slightly in surprise as her gaze had the predictable effect on him.

'You see what you can do just by looking? If you would like to explore,' Ashe suggested, lifting her hand and placing it on the flat plane of his stomach, 'we can see just how soon that convenient moment will arrive.'

Bel was woken by the pressure of Ashe's lips against her temple. 'Sweetheart, I must go now. What do you want to do about the bed?'

She struggled back to consciousness through what seemed to be a drift of rose petals, swansdown and fluffy clouds and found him sitting on the edge of the bed, fully dressed and smiling at her. 'What time is it?'

'Four.' It was not a dream this time either, then. He had been there, he had made love to her—*three times*— he seemed pleased with her and she, she was still floating. *Three times, each time different, each time blissful...* 'The bed?' he prompted, grinning at her befuddlement.

Bel pushed back her hair with both hands and looked around at the tangle of bedclothes and the tumbled pillows. 'We will never make it look as it did before,' she concluded. 'If you can arrange the covers so it looks as though I was restless and pushed them right off, and pass me that copy of Byron...' She heaped up the pillows and snuggled back into them, half-sitting, half-lying, then remembered her nightgown, found it on the floor and dragged it on. 'There. I could not sleep, sat up half the night reading and fell asleep with my book.'

Ashe straightened up from arranging the covers artistically and grinned at her. 'Very convincing. But I think next time I had better wake up in time to make the bed—or we strip it first.' He came round to the side of the bed, then bent and kissed her. Bel put up a hand, cupping his stubble-shadowed cheek and enjoyed the rasp of whiskers as she rubbed gently.

'Thank you,' she whispered. *Next time, there is going to be a next time.*

'No, *ma belle*, thank *you*.' Then he was gone, shoes in hand, slipping out of the room. The door snicked shut and she was alone. Bel tossed the volume of poetry carelessly on the covers as though it had fallen from her hand, reached out to pinch the wick of the remaining candle and lay back against the heaped pillows.

Her body thrummed, lighter than air, yet so heavily relaxed it felt she might sink through the mattress. She felt wonderful, although she knew that in the morning she was going to be stiff and perhaps a little sore. It had been a miracle. Ashe had been a miracle. Bel's lids drooped. As sleep took her again she thought hazily, *This is so perfect. So perfect...*

Bel floated, blissful, through the next morning. The fluffy pink clouds still enveloped her, the sun shone, just for her, the birds were singing, just because Ashe had made love to her. At lunchtime she received a bouquet of yellow roses with a note that said simply, 'One? A.' and rushed out to purchase two new nightgowns, a pair of utterly frivolous backless boudoir slippers, a cut-glass vase for the roses and pink silk stockings. She then went and took refuge in Ackermann's, browsing through the latest fashion plates until her maid was nodding with boredom and she could hand a note and a coin to the doorman without being noticed.

'Please see this is delivered,' she said brightly, without any appearance of secrecy. 'I should have left it with my footman and quite forgot.'

The man touched his hat respectfully and snapped his fingers for an errand boy. The note, hurried away in the lad's firm grip said only, 'Yes. B.'

She, Bel Cambourn, respectable widow, was having an *affaire*. She had a lover. She was living out her fantasy and it was utterly perfect. Bel drifted round the end of a rack of maps, wondering vaguely whether she was going to exist in this happy blur for the duration of the affair or whether it would wear off. There were doubtless all kinds of things she should be doing, calls she should make, business she should attend to, but she could not concentrate on a single thing other than the image of Ashe, nakedly magnificent—

'Ouch!' The pained voice was familiar.

She found herself almost nose to nose with her Cousin Elinor, who had been browsing through a stack of small classical prints. Elinor's right foot was under Bel's left. She hastily removed it and apologised for her abstraction.

'I have decided to create a print room in my small closet,' Elinor explained, once they had finished apologising to each other for not looking where they were going. 'I think I have enough now. Do you?' She regarded a pile of prints doubtfully.

'How big is the room? I would take a few more if I were you. And you will need borders,' Bel pointed out, wrenching her mind away from erotic thoughts. 'I did the same thing at Felsham Hall and bought everything here. They sell borders by the yard.' She picked up the top print, discovered it was a scantily clad Roman athlete with a physique almost as good as Ashe's and hastily returned it to the pile. Ashe did not have a fig leaf.

Elinor had found a shop assistant while Bel was recovering her composure and he returned with a selection of borders for the ladies to chose from. 'You look very well, Cousin.' Elinor glanced up from fitting a length of black-and-white paper against a print of the Forum. 'Excited,' she added, rejecting that border and trying another.

'I do? Oh.' Bel bit her lip; she had no idea that her inner state would be obvious. 'How?'

'Your colour is better and—I do not know quite how to describe it—you are glowing somehow.' Elinor put her head on one side and frowned at her cousin.

'It's the lovely weather, and I am enjoying being back in London. I did a lot of shopping this morning.' Although shopping was not a reason for excitement that Elinor would recognise.

'I wish I could have come with you.' Unaware she had startled her cousin, Elinor made a decision on the borders and handed her choice to the assistant.

'Really?' Thank goodness, her cousin was taking an interest in clothes at last.

'Yes, I need some stout walking shoes, some large handkerchiefs and tooth powder,' Elinor said prosaically, dashing Bel's hopes of fashionable frivolity. 'Mama is meeting me with the carriage—would you care for a lift home?'

Bel sat on one of the stools at the green-draped counter. 'No, thank you, I will walk, I need the exercise.' If truth were told, she was more than a little stiff from last night's exertions and would have welcomed the ride, but the thought of enduring Aunt Louisa's close scrutiny was too alarming. If Elinor could tell something was changed, Aunt Louisa most certainly could.

She walked out with Elinor, the porter hastening behind with the packed prints. Sure enough, drawn up at the kerb side in front of the shop, was Aunt Louisa's carriage with the top down, and there, walking towards her along the pavement, a willowy lady on his arm, was Ashe.

'Belinda!' Aunt Louisa.

'Lady Belinda.' Ashe. 'Miss Ravenhurst.'

'Lord Dereham.' That was Elinor. Her mama, startled by the novelty of her daughter addressing a man in the street, turned with majestic slowness and raised her eyeglass. Ashe bowed gracefully.

'Lady James, Lady Belinda, Miss Ravenhurst.' Ashe raised his hat. 'Are you acquainted with Lady Pamela Darlington?'

'No, I am not. Good afternoon, Lady Pamela.' Bel shook hands with a politeness she was far from feeling. What she did feel, shockingly, was the urge to push Lady Pamela into the nearby horse trough. The pink clouds of happiness vanished.

'Ha! I remember you.' Aunt Louisa was regarding the very lovely young woman severely.

Bel found she could not speak. Lady Pamela was pretty, beautifully dressed, totally confident. She shook hands with Lady James without showing any alarm at her ferocious scowl, smiled at Elinor and Bel and chatted pleasantly while, all the time, keeping her hand firmly on Ashe's arm. From time to time she glanced up at him with a proprietorial little smile that widened as he smiled back. He had all the hallmarks of a man receiving the attentions of a lovely woman, damn him, Bel thought savagely, smiling until her cheeks ached. Behind Lady Pamela stood a maid and a footman laden with packages.

Bel did not know where to look. She did not dare meet Ashe's eye, terrified of showing some emotion her aunt could read. With her insides churning with what she had not the slightest difficulty in recognising as violent and quite unreasonable jealousy, she did not want to look at Lady Pamela and all the time she knew that simply by standing there, dumbstruck and awkward, she risked making herself conspicuous.

'We have been purchasing prints for a print room,' she said suddenly, into a lull in the conversation. Lady Pamela smoothed an invisible thread off Ashe's sleeve with a little pout of concentration on her face. Bel gritted her teeth.

'How very artistic of you, Lady Belinda,' Ashe remarked, the first words he had addressed to her since his greeting.

'Miss Ravenhurst is the artistic one, my lord, I am merely helping her choose some images,' Bel replied, her lips stiff. She made herself meet his eyes. There was not the slightest sign in his expression of anything other than good-mannered interest in what she was saying. How could that be? Bel had felt it would be obvious to everyone who passed—let alone her aunt— that the two of them were lovers; she felt as though it must be emblazoned across her face. But no one seemed in any way suspicious and all Aunt Louisa's attention appeared to be focused upon Lady Pamela and Ashe.

And just what was he doing with the lovely Lady Pamela? Why were they smiling at each other like that? Pamela was hanging on to his arm in a manner that was positively clinging and Ashe was doing nothing to distance himself. He seemed to know her well. Very well.

'Belinda!' She jumped. Aunt Louisa was gesturing

to the open carriage door and the groom waiting patiently beside it.

'No, thank you, Aunt, I will walk back, I have my maid with me.'

'Join us, Lady Belinda,' Ashe suggested, proffering his other arm. Lady Pamela's smiling lips compressed into a thin line. 'We are going to Hatchard's bookshop, so I imagine our ways lie together.'

'Thank you, no, my lord,' she said coolly. 'I have more than enough foolish romance to be going on with, just at the present, without buying any to read.' She bowed slightly to Lady Pamela, smiled at her relatives and set off briskly westwards.

'My lady?' Millie scurried to keep up. 'Are you all right, my lady?'

'Yes, of course I am.' Bel blew her nose fiercely but slowed her pace for the girl's shorter legs. The smoke and the dust must have got into her eyes, there was no other explanation for the way they were watering.

How could Ashe be so…? She wrestled for the word. Deceitful. That was it, horrid as it was. He had told her he had no attachments, no commitments, yet there he was, strolling along, giving every indication that he was on the very best of terms with one of the most eligible young ladies in the Marriage Mart. And that was a highly risky thing to be doing if a man was not serious. It led to gossip at best and to interviews with enraged fathers at worst.

If she had known he was on the look-out for a bride, nothing would have led her to make her outrageous proposition, Bel thought angrily, the low heels of her shoes clicking on the pavement with the force of her steps. He had only needed to pretend to misunderstand her, as he had done at first, and there the matter would have ended. She would have been embarrassed, yet probably relieved once she had time to think things over, and Ashe would have neatly extricated himself from a tricky encounter, as doubtless he had many a time before.

But he had not extricated himself, and she had slept with him. They had made love and while it probably meant nothing to him, Bel told herself, piling on the misery, she was never going to be the same again.

Half an hour ago she had thought her life was perfect. *Perfect.*

Chapter Ten

'It is very nice, my lady. Will you be going in to see if they have it in a different colour?'

'What?' Bel found she was standing in front of a milliner's shop, regarding a hat on a stand, and Millie was waiting patiently at her side.

'You said it was perfect, my lady. But I don't think you usually wear that shade of blue, do you, ma'am?'

Now she was talking to herself. Bel took a long, steadying breath. She was a grown-up woman, if a naïve and inexperienced one. Now she knew about Lady Pamela Ashe would not come to her again, not after having found himself in public between his lover and the object of his more permanent attentions. One just had to put it all down to experience. And at least she had experienced physical pleasure. She knew what all the fuss was about now.

All she had to do was to stop aching with desire for Ashe. Surely that would happen naturally after a few days? One simply could not exist as she was now, feeling like this, not without going mad.

Bel pushed open the shop door and stepped in. Shopping as a cure for misery was shallow, but she did not care. Tomorrow she would find something worthwhile to do. Today she was going to buy a hat.

The soothing qualities of a new hat, even an outrageously frivolous one that an unmarried girl like Lady Pamela would not be allowed to wear, were predictably short lived. Bel knew perfectly well that she could shop until she dropped, dance her slippers through, read the most frivolous journals and gossip until she was hoarse—but the empty ache would still be there. It did not help to tell herself that by the very nature of their relationship there could be no emotional commitment. Ashe had made none. What she felt now was too close to that for either safety or comfort—perhaps it was better that it was ending now.

Bel found herself at half past midnight unable to sleep again. She sat up in bed, her arms wrapped round her knees, her books discarded on the table and tried to think.

She was twenty-six. She was never going to marry again and she would never dare entangle herself with another man. That left a considerable number of years stretching into the future to be filled with something other than domestic duties or passion. Bel knew that while she was perfectly intelligent she would never be a bluestocking like her cousin, so retreating into some form of intellectual study was out of the question. Parties and shopping were fun, but hardly the basis of a fulfilling life.

Which left good works. Bel contemplated the idea. When she had been married she had undertaken charitable activities on the estate and in the surrounding parishes as a matter of course, but now there was no estate to provide her with a ready-made supply of children to educate, elderly and infirm persons to support or fathers of large families to find work for. She was going to have to find a cause of her own.

Throwing back the covers, Bel slid out of bed and padded across to the table, the voluminous skirts of the plain cotton nightgown she had chosen flapping about her ankles. She found paper and ink and settled down to make a list of causes. It would need to be something engrossing and worthwhile—she was not going to play with this like so many society ladies did.

Children, widows, animals, the elderly, she wrote, biting the end of her quill. *Education? Employ...*

The door opened. Bel swung round on her chair and stared. *'Ashe?'*

'You were expecting someone else, Bel, my sweet?' He strolled in and dropped his hat and gloves on a chair. Tonight he was elegant in evening dress. 'Lord, my great-aunt's parties are a bore, bless her. I love the old darling, but her entourage of geriatric swains is quite another matter. I have just sat through at least six elderly gentlemen telling me how Wellington should have deployed his troops at Waterloo and one who was confused enough to think he had been at Quatre Bras personally.'

'I was not expecting *you*,' Bel said, her pen dropping unheeded and spattering ink spots across her list.

'Why not?' Ashe shed his jacket and waistcoat and began to deconstruct his elaborate neckcloth. 'You sent me a reply to my note.' He walked towards her, the ends in his hands, then stopped, frowning. 'Aren't you well, sweetheart? Do you have a headache? I'll go, of course.'

'No, I do not have a headache and I am quite well. Don't *sweetheart* me.' Bel stood up and saw his expression change as he took in the exceedingly chaste nightgown and the sharp tone of her voice. 'And I replied to your note *before* I saw you with Lady Pamela. If I had had any notion that you were involved with someone else, I would never have embarked on this…liaison.'

He looked as tempting as sin itself standing there, those gorgeous blue eyes fixed intently on her, the thick gilt of his hair slightly tousled, the neck of his shirt open just enough to give her a glimpse of the skin beneath. And that was precisely what Ashe was: sin. Highly experienced, completely unprincipled sin.

'Lady Pamela? You think I am in some way committed to Lady Pamela Darlington?'

'Yes, Lady Pamela. Is there anyone else I have missed? So far she is the only one I have seen hanging on your arm, exchanging little smiles with you, generally behaving as though she has proprietorial rights over you and getting doting looks in return. And as Lady Pamela is a well-bred, single young lady and the leading light of this year's Marriage Mart, there is but one conclusion to be drawn from such behaviour.'

'You are jealous.' Ashe said it with a hint of a smile. She glared and the smile vanished. 'But that's ridiculous Bel.'

Bel took two rapid steps forward and jabbed him in the chest with one sharp finger. Ashe swayed backwards a trifle, but did not retreat. 'Yes, I am jealous, and do not tell me I have no right to be because I know that perfectly well. But don't you dare tell me I am being ridiculous either; you told me you had no commitments and I would not have dreamed of…of…' she waved a hand towards the bed '…*that* if I had known.'

'Ah.' Bel narrowed her eyes at him. He did not look the slightest bit chastened, not the remotest bit guilty. 'I have known Lady Pamela since she was six. She is a minx and as much of a hussy as a well-bred girl can be and, despite her father's adamant refusal to consider the suit, she is head over heels in love with a very good friend of mine.'

'That makes it worse!'

'Head over heels,' Ashe persisted, removing himself to the relative safety of the fireside. 'And set on persuading me to invite both him and her to a house party.'

'Which house party?'

'The one she expects me to host for the sole purpose of allowing her and George to moon about in the shrubbery out of sight of her chaperon.'

'If that is the case, why was she spreading herself all over you like butter?' Bel demanded, provoking a grin from Ashe at her language.

'Because she is one of the prettiest girls in London, used to being the acknowledged star in any firmament and, when she comes face to face with another lovely woman, her instincts are to lay claim to any male in the vicinity between the ages of sixteen and seventy. I happened to be handy.'

'Oh.' Bel swallowed, clenching her hands. *Lovely woman? Her?* 'I have made a fool of myself, haven't I?'

'A bit.' He smiled affectionately. 'I suppose I helped. But, given the basilisk eye of your Aunt Ravenhurst, I thought it best to play up to Pamela and to treat you with polite indifference.' Bel bit her lip and focused her gaze on the point where his shirt opened over golden skin. 'Were you truly jealous? That is very flattering.'

'Flattering? It was horrible. Jealousy was a thoroughly reprehensible reaction in the first place, and I know I have absolutely no right to feel it. I felt mean and miserable.' Bel sifted through her emotions, then added honestly, 'But it hurt, and I do not like you telling me I am being ridiculous.'

'I am sorry.' Ashe stepped over Horace and gathered her in against his chest. Bel gave a little sigh and clung to as much of him as she could get her arms around. 'I forget you are very new to these intrigues. It is not in your nature to dissemble, but we cannot afford to look at each other and have our closeness show, you know that.'

'I know.' Bel nodded, rubbing her cheek against the warmth of his shirt front. 'It is all right now.' She had dissembled for all the years of her marriage, feigning interest and obedience. But that was a very different thing to hiding desire and the intimate knowledge of another person.

'I am not sure that it is all right,' Ashe said gravely, running his hands up and down her back. 'What on earth are you wearing, Bel? I thought I had strayed into a nunnery.'

'I did not think you would be coming and this is the most boringly respectable nightgown I have. I didn't want to think about you, you see.'

He gave a snort of laughter and stepped back to study her. Then he frowned. 'We have a problem. You want to make love, I imagine, but I am very much afraid that garment has killed my passion quite dead, which was obviously the intention of the designer. There is only one thing for it, unless you wish me to leave or to spend the night reading poetry with you.'

'What?' Bel enquired, heat pooling inside her. Ashe was teasing her, of course. No man wearing thin skin-tight knit breeches could pretend he was not aroused when he was.

'You will just have to seduce me.' He looked rueful.

'Seduce you?' Bel heard her voice squeak. *Me? How?*

'Yes, seduce me. On the bearskin rug, I think. The novelty will, perhaps, arouse my jaded appetites.' Ashe leaned negligently against the bedpost and waited for her reaction.

Jaded appetites, indeed! This was a game. Bel suppressed her immediate reaction, which was to blush and stammer that she did not know how. He probably expected her to do that, but she would not. The sight of him, elegant and hard and all of him—every inch—hers, made her blood sing and her breath come short. She wanted him desperately, she wanted to learn more about lovemaking, she wanted to please him, and herself.

'Very well, but you must promise to do as I say,' she ordered boldly. She waited for his nod, noticing with interest the effect her agreement had on him. The pulse under the sharp line of his jaw was very visible, the skin at the base of his throat was flushed and his pupils had begun to dilate, turning the deep sea blue a darker, stormier purple.

Very deliberately Bel undid the top two buttons on her nightgown, but that was all. Then she folded her arms, knowing the action pushed up her breasts, and stood there, considering. If Ashe thought she was going to drape herself all over him like a cat begging for caresses, he was mistaken. 'Take off your shirt.'

He pulled it over his head, giving her a view of the

muscles of his back rippling as he bent right over, then stretched upright, magnificently unselfconscious. Bel stood looking, studying the way his muscles strapped over his ribs, the way his chest hair changed texture as it narrowed down towards his navel. She saw his nipples harden under the caress of her gaze. Power. Such power.

'And now the rest of your clothes,' she said, making her voice indifferent. He kept his eyes locked with hers as he undressed and Bel toyed with one more button on her gown. He was so beautiful she found it desperately hard to keep her hands off him. Her own nipples were peaking painfully against the thick cotton, her breasts ached into heaviness; the intensity of his gaze seemed to bore through her to hit at the base of her spine.

'Now lie down,' she ordered, gesturing towards the thick white fur at her feet. *Seduce him? As if he needs it! If he becomes any more aroused, I will refuse to believe it physically possible.*

Ashe stretched out on the great pelt of fur, a magnificent barbarian in his shameless nudity. He moved sensuously on it, his broad shoulders shrugging into the softness, the movement of his hips a demonstration of lithe masculinity.

'Am I arousing your interest yet?' Bel enquired huskily.

'Mmm? This is very comfortable, I may go to sleep.' He was watching her like a hawk from beneath hooded lids, his very focus a contradiction to his words.

Bel moved to stand at his feet and let her gaze wander up the length of him from the high arches, up the straight shin bones, up the trained muscles of his thighs, up—lingeringly—past the slim hips. She let her tongue tip run over her lower lip and saw him shift restlessly as she did so. Bel stepped forward so her feet were either side of Ashe's knees and started to undo the rest of her buttons.

Despite the expression of languid uninterest he was maintaining the heavy lids rose, dragged up to follow her slowly moving hands. Bel fought her own eagerness as she made herself free each button with finicking care until the entire gown to below her waist was open. Then she shrugged one shoulder free. Ashe's tongue slid between his lips and she saw his hands fist into the fur at his sides. Another shoulder, then she let go and the entire garment slipped down to pool around her feet.

She kicked it aside as Ashe came up on to his elbows. 'No, my lord, I am sorry if you are bored, but I must insist you lie down. Do try to sleep if you wish.'

He fell back with a growl as Bel knelt, her knees either side of his hips. The power of what she was doing felt incredible. It was like sitting astride a thoroughbred horse; she could feel the leashed strength beneath her, knew she could not control it, that only his will was keeping him tame, biddable to her.

Her hand slipped between her thighs, found him, hot, hard, impossibly aroused, and positioned herself. 'Now,' she whispered and slowly sank down, taking him within her, stroking every inch of him with her heat and her slickness and her desire.

He growled, reached for her and she caught his wrists, leaning into him so she pressed them to the ground on either side of his head and the tips of her breasts caressed his chest. 'Awake yet?' she teased, her lips hovering an inch above his.

'Ride me.' And he surged up against her. Bel heard herself cry out, knew her body was responding, plunging, demanding, but it all became a blur, a wonderful, intense, heated blur with the only reality the deep blue-black eyes holding hers, the beat of his pulse under her fingers, the musk of their lovemaking as potent as drugged incense in her nostrils.

Ashe bucked beneath her, then she was beneath him, her own wrists trapped, and she cried out again and again as she fell into a whirlpool of velvet darkness and he finally left her body.

Some incalculable time later Bel felt Ashe roll away from her and reached for him. He was back in a moment, carrying pillows and the bedcover. 'I like it on this fur. Here, these will make us more comfortable and preserve your chaste bed from disturbance.'

Bel snuggled up against his chest again. Horace's soft fur was warm and sensual beneath her, Ashe's body was hot and smooth under her hand. 'This is nice.' *This is Heaven.*

'You are addictive Bel,' Ashe said ruefully, gathering her snugly against himself. Other women had curled against him like this, but none had ever seemed to fit so well. 'But I am going to have to leave you for a few days.'

'Leave? Why?' Bel wriggled free and sat up, shaking her head at her own vehemence. 'No, I am sorry, I did not mean to sound so demanding, or to pry. Will you be away long?'

'Ten days, perhaps.' He reached up and traced a finger round the curve of her jaw, enjoying the way she turned her head into his hand for more caresses. Bel was so sweet, so formal somehow—when she wasn't in the throes of passion. She had even managed to be jealous in a polite manner. Ashe could recall mistresses and lovers who would have thrown ornaments at his head for less provocation than he had given her that morning. 'I am going home. I should have gone at once, but somehow—' How to explain to her?

'Somehow what you had just experienced abroad was too raw?' Bel suggested.

'Yes.' She understood what he sometimes had difficulty articulating to himself. Ashe lifted her hand and kissed the knuckles, then turned them against his cheek. 'Exactly. But if I stay away any longer, they will start worrying that I am hiding something after all.'

'And you can make arrangements for the house party you are going to give,' Bel suggested slyly.

'I had no intention of doing any such thing, although if you would come to it, I might be persuaded to change my mind.'

Bel looked deliciously ruffled by the suggestion. 'I could not bear to be so close to you and have to behave properly all the time.'

'Who said anything about behaving? That is the whole point of house parties—camouflage for misbehaviour.'

'I…I find I am shocked.' She shook her head in wonderment at her own reaction. 'How very hypocritical of me!'

'You are not being uniquely wicked in taking a lover, you know, *ma belle*, other people have liaisons too.' But in a way she was unique, Ashe realised. Bel would not move from him to another lover when this was over. This was an experience for her that she would sample because she had needed so badly to understand physical love, then put aside, never to be repeated.

'What are you frowning about?' She reached out and massaged the crease between his brows with the pads of two fingers. Ashe fought not to close his eyes and simply purr.

'I'm not sure,' he confessed, smiling at her anxiety. But he knew, all the same. He did not want to envisage life without Bel, he did not want to imagine her alone, chaste, unkissed and uncaressed and he could not imagine having another woman in her place, in his arms. But *affaires* ran their course, it would happen one day and they would move on. He would find someone else.

'Tell me about your home,' she suggested, snuggling down again, her hand drifting slowly up and down his chest in a way that predicted any conversation would be short.

'Coppergate? Well, it is in Hertfordshire, out beyond St Albans in the hills. It was built in the seventeenth century by a Mr Copper, a merchant who made his fortune, bought by my ancestor when Mr Copper's luck ran out and it has been with us ever since. There is a lake…'

Chapter Eleven

The lake was still as a reflecting mirror under the August sunshine as Ashe tooled the team through the gates and up the long curving sweep of carriage drive towards the old house.

Home. And by some miracle he was approaching it unscathed, with all his limbs intact and not even a romantic scar for his sisters to exclaim over. No scars that showed on the outside at least and those that were hidden were far from romantic. But the nightmares were fewer now and he no longer woke confused about where he was, worrying that he had fallen asleep on duty. Bel had helped, he realised. He did not have to talk about it to her, but whenever the subject had come up, her empathy soothed him.

Ashe rolled stiff shoulders to ease them, finding the very thought of Bel relaxed him, even if it provoked an uncomfortable physical reaction. He was going to miss her in so many ways. The curricle rounded a stand of ancient beech trees and there was the house, low, rambling and—thanks to Mr Copper's original design and Ashe's ancestors' numerous additions—without any outstanding architectural merit whatsoever. But he loved it, even if he found it hard to stay there for long.

The front door opened as his wheels crunched to a halt on the gravel and there was a flash of white fabric. For a moment he saw Bel standing there, her arms held out to him. Then the vision shifted and blurred and it was Katy, his youngest sister, running down the steps to meet him, her blonde curls flying, skirts hiked up. 'Ashe! You are home!'

'As you see.' He grinned at her, jumping down from the curricle to return her enthusiastic hug. That image of Bel was disconcerting, but he did not want to explore why his mind was playing such tricks on him.

The sound of footsteps behind him made him turn, his arm still round Katy's shoulders, everything else forgotten as his mother, Frederica and Anna came to join the reunion. 'You know I'm all right,' he protested, as they patted and stroked him, trying to make himself heard over the babble of excited voices. 'You got all my letters, I know you did, for you answered them all.'

'Yes, dearest.' Lady Dereham smiled happily. 'You are such a good correspondent; we heard that you were safe almost as soon as the newspapers were reporting the outcome of the battle, so our minds were set at rest much earlier than many families, I am sure. And so many thoughtful letters telling us where you were and when you would be home.'

'Why didn't you come at once?' Katy demanded as they walked up the steps, his two elder sisters still inclined to stroke his sleeves as he walked, as though to reassure themselves he really was there in the flesh.

'Because Ashe had business to attend to, you know

he explained that,' Frederica reproved her. 'And he probably needed a rest before you start bombarding him with questions. Look at poor Philip Carr over at Longmere Hall—the wretched man has had to escape back to town under the pretext of consulting a physician, just because his family would not stop talking at him.'

'Carr's hurt?' Ashe stopped on the top step. *Not another one, not another friend maimed.* 'I had not heard.'

'Only a flesh wound in his thigh, apparently.' Lady Dereham urged him into the hallway. 'He should have stayed in London on his way through, but his mama descended and bore him off and then wondered why he was so taciturn. It has healed cleanly, although he is still limping very badly.'

'My lord, may I say on behalf of the entire staff how happy we are at your safe return?' It was Wrighton, the butler, allowing himself a rare smile as he took Ashe's hat and gloves. 'The household feels the honour of serving a Waterloo hero most keenly, my lord.'

Ashe bit back the retort that he was no damned hero, he was just fortunate to be alive to be fawned over, unlike many men far more worthy of that title. There was no way to say it without upsetting people. He would simply have to adopt an air of manly reticence and hope they would take the hint and stop talking about the damned battle.

'Thank you, Wrighton. I am delighted to be back.'

The arrival of Race and the carriage with his baggage effectively distracted Wrighton and his footmen and allowed Ashe to escape into the drawing room. Behind him he heard his mother ordering *tea and Cook's special lemon drop scones his lordship likes so much.* 'I will be pounds overweight,' he grumbled affectionately as his sisters pressed him down into his usual chair, fussing as though he, and not the unfortunate Mr Carr, was wounded.

'We want to make a fuss of you.' Anna, the elder and most level-headed of his sisters, smiled affectionately as she sat down. 'You must allow us that indulgence, you know. In return, we promise not to plague you with questions about the army.'

'Very well, I consent to being spoiled.' It seemed strange to be spending so much time with women. First the attention he and the other returning officers received from society ladies, then the time with Bel and now he was the focus of four women's world. 'You will have to civilise me again, I expect—I have been in rough male company for too long.'

They sat around him in an attentive semi-circle and he made himself concentrate, think what would please them to talk about. But first he wanted to find out about them. 'Tell me what you have all been up to.'

'I have a new governess.' Katy, predictably, was first to speak. At twelve years old—going on twenty, as her older sisters were known to remark in exasperation—she had no reticence and complete self-confidence. Worryingly she also looked like being the prettiest of the three with hair as blonde and eyes as blue as her brother's. Ashe shuddered at the thought of policing her come-out. 'Her name is Miss Lucas and she is very nice.' That presumably meant she let Katy do what she wanted. 'And I need a new pony, I have quite outgrown dear Bunting, so Mama is driving him in the dog cart.'

'I have been taking dancing lessons with the Rector's daughters.' That was Frederica, seventeen, with a face that everyone described as *sweet* and mouse-brown hair.

'And helping Mr Barrington with the estate books. It is very interesting and he says my arithmetic is exemplary.'

Barrington was the new estate manager, appointed by Ashe on his last furlough. Young, keen, well favoured and hard-working, he had seemed just the man to leave in charge of the estate. He was also the younger son of a respectable gentry family. Now Ashe caught a glimpse of a frown between his mother's brows and glanced sharply at Frederica. *Too young and good looking to have introduced into a household of susceptible young ladies?*

'And I am coming out next Season,' Anna pronounced. 'But you knew that, of course.' She was calm, elegant and usually described as handsome, with honey-blonde hair and blue eyes. She smiled at her mother conspiratorially. 'And I expect I am going to be a great expense to you, Ashe dearest, for Mama and I have very long shopping lists.'

'I suppose that means we need to set the town house in order,' he said, teasing her by looking solemn when all along he had known it was going to be needed. 'Did I tell you I sold the Half Moon Street property?' It was like touching a sore tooth with his tongue; he wanted them to ask who had bought it so he could have the pleasure of talking about Bel.

'Yes dear, you did. Are your chambers comfortable at the Albany?' Mama was giving him no opportunity to indulge.

'Perfectly, thank you. When will you need the town house ready?'

'There is no need for you to do anything, dear.' Lady Dereham lifted the teapot and began to pour. 'We will come up in January and start ordering gowns and planning parties then. I will bring most of the staff from here, if you would not dislike that.'

'Whatever suits.' Ashe accepted a cup of tea. He had no intention of rusticating in the country any longer than he had to, so he had no need for the servants. 'But the place is sadly in need of a new touch; I think we should not leave it until you come up after Christmas. I will write to Grimball and have him make a complete survey and do any repairs, then if you come up to town later this month before you go down to Brighton you can decide what redecoration you would like and he can have that done over the winter.'

'Redecoration? Are you sure? Is that not rather extravagant?'

'With three sisters to come out?' Ashe smiled. 'I am sure it will be an investment.'

He was rewarded by a trio of grateful smiles. Even Anna clapped her hands in delight.

'It is the first week of August now,' Frederica calculated. 'Only two or three weeks and we will be in London!' Watching her, Ashe saw the pleasure falter and she became sombre. Damnation, she was thinking she would be parted from Barrington. Just how far had this gone?

'Think of the ballroom done out in blue silk to match my eyes.' Katy sighed. Her sisters rolled theirs in unison. 'And my bedroom needs new curtains.'

'Shh!' Frederica ordered. 'Stop plaguing Ashe with such nonsense. Blue silk will have faded long before you get your come out, you precocious child!'

Katy subsided mutinously.

'Only, I did wonder…' Lady Dereham completely ignored her bickering daughters, fiddled with the cake slice, then made rather a business of cutting the almond tart.

'Yes, Mama?' Ashe found he was reaching for a third lemon scone and put his plate down firmly.

'I thought perhaps I should be putting the Dower House to rights.'

'Why now? Are any of the elderly aunts in need of it?' But she was right, it did not do to let a house stand empty and neglected and it must be all of three years since Grandmama had died. 'I suppose we could bring it back into use and invite some of them to stay there.'

'No, not the aunts, I think they are all quite content where they are. It was just that I did wonder—now you are back and out of the army and settled—if next Season you would be looking for a wife?'

'A wife?' Ashe regarded his mother blankly. Throughout his childhood she had exhibited the maternal witchcraft of knowing exactly what was on his conscience. It seemed the knack had not deserted her. 'How did you kn…I mean, what on earth would I want a wife for?'

Even well-behaved Anna giggled at that. 'For all the usual reasons Dereham,' his mother said tartly. Lord, he was in trouble if she was using his title.

What did I almost say? How did you know? Is that what just came out of my mouth without apparently passing through my brain? Ashe closed his eyes. An image of Bel sitting by the fireplace, just where his mother was now, filled his imagination. The apparition lifted the teapot, smiled at him and began to pour. He opened his eyes hastily. *No! I do not want to get married.* Bel *does not want to get married to me, or to anyone else, come to that. I am* not *in love with her. She is my mistress; a man does not marry his mistress.*

'I meant,' he said, getting his tongue and his brain lined up again, 'I meant, what would I need a wife for *now*?' Damn it, he could command a company of soldiers, he could fight the French, he could manage a great estate—when he felt like it. Why did he feel completely helpless and at bay when confronted by the women of his own family with *that* look in their eyes?

'You need an heir, unless you want Cousin Adrian— who has the wits of a gnat—in your shoes,' Lady Dereham retorted. 'I need to be able to concentrate on launching your three sisters into society—and I would welcome some mature feminine assistance with that, let me tell you—and finally it is about time you took an interest in this house and this estate and put your own mark upon it. And a wife will help you do that.' She wagged the cake slice at him. 'You are not getting any younger, Reynard.'

'I am thirty,' Ashe said, stung.

'Exactly my point.'

The words came out again, apparently bypassing the conscious part of his brain, apparently from some well of certainty deep inside his mind. 'I will marry when I fall in love, and not before.'

'In love?' Lady Dereham regarded her son with well-bred horror. 'In *love*? That is no criterion for a good marriage, Reynard. Heaven knows who you might fall in love with! Men fall in love with dairymaids, but they do not marry them—not men in your position, at least.'

'I consider it a perfectly reasonable criterion,' Ashe said firmly, deciding that a protest that he had never so much looked at a dairymaid in that, or any other, light was a waste of time. Marrying for love had never occurred to him until a minute ago; up until then he would have agreed with his mother.

Marriage demanded a well-dowered young woman of suitable family, modest habits, intelligence and good health. One assessed which of the available ladies on the Marriage Mart fulfilled these requirements, selected from amongst them the one for whom one felt the greatest liking and respect, and proposed. Short of a Royal princess, there were few females who would consider the Viscount Dereham anything short of a brilliant catch, and he knew it.

'And what will you say if your sisters come to you with some unsuitable man in tow and demand to marry for love, might I ask?' his outraged parent demanded.

'I will trust their judgement.' Ashe was conscious of three wide-eyed, open-mouthed faces staring at him.

'Oh,' breathed Frederica softly. 'Oh, Ashe.'

Oh, Ashe, indeed! She is in love with Barrington and I have just walked straight into that!

'As soon as they reach the age of twenty-one,' Ashe added hastily. 'Unless the man they love also meets the usual criteria of acceptability.'

'Oh,' Frederica said again, flatly.

'That's all right,' Katy announced smugly. 'I intend falling in love with a duke. You will have to approve of him, Ashe, won't you?'

'Which duke?' Ashe asked, diverted and rapidly running the available candidates under review. 'I do not think there are any available.'

'I have six years,' his baby sister informed him smugly. 'One is sure to die and have a young heir, or be widowed or something in that time.'

'Why a duke?'

Katy proceeded to count off points on her fingers. 'They are all rich. I would like being called your Grace and I would outrank Lucy Thorage.'

'She might marry one too,' Ashe pointed out, fascinated and alarmed in equal measure.

'I am prettier,' his sister pointed out, incontrovertibly.

'If you do not wish to go to bed now without your dinner, Katherine Henrietta Reynard,' said her mother awfully, 'you will be quiet and behave like a lady.'

'Yes, Mama.' Katy subsided, leaving Ashe the uncomfortable focus of attention again.

'And what are you going to do to find this paragon?' Lady Dereham enquired. 'Wait for her to appear like a princess in a fairy tale?'

A princess on a white bear who will carry me off to Paradise... But that was Bel. I am not going to have that sort of luck twice.

'I shall do my duty escorting you and Anna next Season. Perhaps I will find her there.'

'I sincerely hope so.' His mother regarded him anxiously. 'I worry about you. You do seem different somehow, dear.'

'Poor Ashe has been through a terrible experience.' Anna leapt to his defence. 'Of course he seems a little altered. Several weeks here at Coppergate with us and he will be his old self again.'

Several weeks in the country? No, ten days at most, and then back to London, back to Bel. Back to uncomplicated bliss.

Ashe spent the next day riding around the estate with Barrington, trying to size up the man, not as an estate manager, for he had already done that and was satisfied, but as a husband for his sister. He would do, he thought grudgingly. A far from brilliant match, but a kind, decent, loving husband was more important for sensitive Frederica than some cold and suitable society marriage.

She would be well dowered. An intelligent, hard-working man like Barrington could build on that foundation to give them a good life. There were a few years before he need worry too much—more than enough time to see if this attachment of his sister's lasted and whether it was returned.

'What do you think of the Wilstone estate?' he asked, an idea coming to him as they reined in to inspect the effects of liming on a stubbornly sour field.

'That was a good purchase, my lord,' Barrington said judiciously. 'Needs work, of course, it had been neglected, but in time it could be very productive. There are fine stands of timber and it borders the new canal— I think you could build wharfs there, a timber yard. It would repay the investment with all the building going on in London. But I had thought you were intending to sell it on.'

'No. I think we will keep it.' The idea was taking more concrete shape as the estate manager talked. 'Make it a special project, Barrington; give it, say, three years and see what you can make of it.'

'What about the house?' Barrington looked interested. 'Sell and just keep the land? The last owner neglected it badly, what with all his debts and so forth. But it is quite sound—just shabby.'

'No, don't sell it. Get it into order. I'll give you a free hand—think what you'd like if it was yours, but stay within the income from the lands.' They moved off, satisfied with the state of the field, the expression on the steward's face showing he was already thinking about the prospect of reviving the rundown estate that Ashe had bought as a speculation the year before. Ashe waited a few minutes, then added, as if the idea had just come to him, 'See if my sister would like to help with the house.'

'Miss Frederica?'

'Yes,' Ashe agreed. 'Frederica.'

If things worked out, then he would give Frederica the estate as part of her dowry and if Barrington couldn't manage to found his fortune from there, then he was not the man Ashe thought him.

'Thank you, my lord, I will get right on to it.'

'Reynard,' Ashe corrected, a warm feeling blossoming inside as he contemplated the possible outcome of his matchmaking. All this talk of love—he must be getting soft. 'But don't neglect everything else,' he added severely, wiping the grin off the younger man's face.

'No, of course not, my…Reynard.'

Hopefully that would take care of Frederica. Anna, he had no doubt, would sail serenely into society and find herself an eminently suitable beau without his help, and as for Katy—well, there were at least four years before he had to face that nightmare, and perhaps one could hire Bow Street Runners as chaperons.

Bel could advise him; he would enjoy talking to her about his sisters. She would take an interest. He could imagine her grey eyes lighting up at the thought of all the alarming things women appeared to find so fascinating: shopping, gossip, matchmaking. But he was trying to matchmake now himself—what had come over him?

'…coppicing?'

'Hmm?' Damn, he was daydreaming. His hack was

standing next to Barrington's and the man had apparently been holding forth for some time about the overgrown woodland in front of them.

'Absolutely,' Ashe said firmly. 'I quite agree it is the best thing.'

'Which? Clear felling and replanting or coppicing?'

Damn again, the man must think him quite buffleheaded. 'Coppice,' he decided at random, finding he was staring into the dense thicket and assessing it as cover for marksmen. Or you could put a field gun just there and cover the whole of the little valley, sweep it with grapeshot. He shivered. No. No more fighting, no more violence, no more gripping a sweaty palm around the butt of a pistol and waiting for death. Peace, growing things, love. That must be it, he was feeling dynastic as a result of seeing all that death and destruction.

Chapter Twelve

'**W**here to next?' Ashe stretched, standing in the stirrups, suddenly aware of the warmth of the sun on his back, the scent of flowers and hay, the sheer delight of the English countryside in summer. For the first time in a very long time—other than when he was making love to Bel—he was aware of his body and of feeling pleasure in it and its reaction to everyday things.

'The Home Farm?' Barrington suggested. 'I need to talk to you about reroofing the long barn.'

'Race?' Ashe did not wait for a reply, but turned the gelding's head towards home, conscious of the power gathering itself between his thighs, of the muscled curve of the animal's neck as it strained against the bit. 'Get up!' As the hooves beat a tattoo along the packed chalk of the track, Barrington's dapple grey thundering behind, he found himself wondering if Bel would enjoy this, whether she enjoyed the countryside, whether he could, after all, hold a house party and invite her.

He beat his estate manager into the yard by a length

and reined in, laughing. 'I'm thinking of holding a house party, Barrington. What do you think?'

'Lady Dereham would be delighted, I image,' the other man responded, swinging down out of the saddle and looping his reins through a ring on the wall.

Yes, she would and there was the rub. It was madness to contemplate bringing Bel here. He could not hope to hide their relationship from close scrutiny by his family, especially as his mother would probably consider her a most eligible candidate for his hand. And besides, they were due to go down to Brighton soon. It would cause endless speculation if he reversed those plans.

Sobered, he put his hands in the small of his back and craned to study the sagging ridgeline of the barn roof. 'Before Christmas, perhaps. This roof, now, is in a poor state,' he commented. 'It'll either have to be done now, quickly, before we want to bring the harvest in or it'll have to wait the winter out.'

It would surprise Bel if she could see him now, standing in a farmyard and worrying about barn roofs and the harvest. What was she doing? he wondered.

Bel was, for once, not thinking about Ashe. She stood in the middle of Madame Laurent's elegant dress shop and sighed in exasperation. 'But don't you *want* a new gown Elinor?'

'I do not *need* one.' Elinor set her mouth stubbornly. 'We came to shop for you, not for me. What use do I have for a full dress outfit? I never get invited to that sort of occasion.'

'Then buy a half-dress ensemble and work up to it! Something that is not fawn or beige or taupe for a change.'

'They are practical colours,' Elinor said calmly.

'Not for evening wear.'

'I do not need evening wear.'

They were going around in circles. Madame Laurent had tactfully withdrawn her assistants to the back of the shop when it was obvious that a fullscale debate was about to ensue between one of her most favoured new clients and her drab companion.

'How are you ever going to meet men if you do not attend evening functions?' Bel asked in a whisper, driven to a frankness she had intended to avoid.

'I meet men at lectures and during the day on business. I meet quite enough of them for my purposes—which do not include marriage!'

'Don't you want to get married?' Bel exclaimed, keeping her voice down with difficulty.

'No. I do not. And you don't either, you say, so why are you trying to persuade me?'

'Because I do not think you are happy at your mother's beck and call and, just because my marriage left me disinclined to repeat the experiment, there is no reason why you should not find a husband you could like.'

What was the matter with her? She wanted to matchmake, to set to couples—yet Elinor was quite correct, she most certainly did not want to remarry herself. But, of course, she had the best of both worlds: the freedom of a widow and the attentions of a lover.

'I am sorry,' she said pacifically. 'I am getting carried away. Perhaps a husband is a step too far. But I am so fond of you and I hate to see you wasting your looks so. Why not wear colours that suit you? Clear greens, ambers, strong, rich browns. Red, even.' It seemed outrageous that her cousin with her striking colouring should look so drab. 'Madame?'

'Your ladyship?' The modiste hurried forward from the rear of the shop.

'What do you have that would set off my cousin's colouring and that would be suitable for a nice, practical walking dress?'

'I have the very thing my lady, newly come in. Paulette, the ruby twill and the emerald broadcloth.'

Elinor rolled her eyes. 'I have better things to do with my pin money.'

'To please me?' Bel tried again. *And Mr Layne, perhaps.* She was not going to give up hope. He was not boring, his temper appeared lively yet equitable and he was intelligent and hardworking. Perfect.

So perfect, in fact, that Bel was conscious that, if it were not for Ashe, she might feel a fluttering of her own pulse at any attention from Patrick Layne. As it was, she could indulge in a little harmless, and probably futile, matchmaking and enjoy his company, quite unruffled.

Bel managed to persuade Elinor into a walking dress and a carriage dress and even a new pelisse to go with either. Both were rigorously plain, but a least none of the garments were dun-coloured.

'Where to now?' Elinor asked patiently, evidently resigning herself to a further round of shopping.

'Hookham's Library.' Bel's driver raised his whip in acknowledgment and the ladies settling back on the cream squabs. 'I hope that is all right with you?' Elinor nodded, no doubt relieved to be back on safe and familiar ground again. 'I would like some new novels, but I mainly want to find some directories which will tell me about charitable institutions.'

'You wish to contribute?'

'Well, yes, if you mean money. But I want to do

more than that, I want to do something practical to help. I feel I live such a frivolous life now I have no responsibilities to the estate. The dilemma is, I cannot choose what type of good cause I wish to support, let alone which one. You would think it would be easy, but there are so many, all no doubt deserving in their way.'

They were still comparing the merits of various types of charity as the barouche swung into Bond Street and began to draw up outside the circulating library. The crowd on the pavement seemed strangely animated, then Bel saw that the porters who opened doors and ushered in customers were attempting to drive away a pair of men in stained uniforms. Both were on crutches, one with the lower part of his right-hand trouser leg pinned up, the other dragging a useless limb.

'On your way,' the head porter was ordering. 'This is a respectable establishment. We don't want the likes of you begging here.'

'Outrageous!' Bel jumped from the carriage without waiting for the steps to be put down and marched up to the group before the doors.

'Just what I said myself, ma'am.' The porter turned a harassed face to her, grateful for the apparent support. 'You go inside, ma'am, quick as you can, we'll soon move them on, never you fear.'

'No—*you* are outrageous, you heartless, ignorant man,' Bel snapped. 'What do you mean, *the likes of you*? These men have been wounded in the service of their country; how dare you insult and abuse them!'

The burly man gaped at her, his glossy tall hat askew from the scuffle. 'Ma'am, this is *Bond Street*.'

'Exactly so. And the reason we are not speaking

French in it or on our way to the guillotine is because of men like these, you ignorant bully.'

'You should be ashamed of yourself,' Elinor chimed in from beside Bel, brandishing her parasol belligerently.

Bel turned her elegant shoulder on the spluttering head porter and smiled at the two soldiers. 'Here, please take this.' She took a folded five-pound note from her purse and handed it to the one with the amputated leg. 'Where do you sleep?'

The man with the dragging leg made a choking sound and she realised he had a badly healed wound on his neck; it must have affected his throat or mouth. 'No, do not try to talk. Elinor, what money have you? They must go and find a doctor at once.'

Her cousin was already pressing a note into the first man's hand. He found his voice. 'God bless you ladies.'

'Where do you sleep?' she repeated her question and the man shrugged.

'Where we can, ma'am. Down in Seven Dials mostly, there's dossing kens to be had there for coppers.'

Goodness knows what a dossing ken was, but if this accommodation was in Seven Dials, one of the most notorious slums in London, then it was the worst possible place for two men in their condition.

'Get into the carriage.' Bel made up her mind suddenly.

'Bel!' Elinor gasped.

'Oh, yes, I am sorry, I should have thought. You had better take the carriage and my footman as escort, Aunt Louisa would not approve. I will take them in a hackney.'

'Never mind Mama! What are you going to do with them?'

'Look after them, of course.' Bel turned back to the

men who were staring at her as they might a carnival freak. 'I have room in the loft over my stables. It is dry and clean and you can bathe, eat and my doctor will tend to you. Will you come with me?'

'Bel, you cannot! You have no idea of their character…'

'I have James here.' She gestured towards the alarmed-looking footman who was trying to interject with protests about what Mr Hedges would say.

'He'll have my guts for garters, my lady…'

Both women ignored him. 'You won't have a footman if you send him with me in the carriage,' Elinor said practically. 'Oh, very well, I will come with you. I agree, something must be done, we cannot leave them here at the mercy of such bigots as this.' With a glare at the flustered doorman, Elinor climbed back into the barouche and gestured to the soldiers to join her.

'Come on,' Bel urged them. 'If you can face the French, you can cope with two English ladies.'

'Yes, ma'am.' She received a smart salute and a grin from the one with a voice and a lopsided smile from his companion.

'Well, give these men a hand up, James,' Bel ordered.

Her vocal soldier informed Bel that they were Jem Brown and Charlie Lewin of the 14th Battalion. 'The Buckinghamshires ma'am,' Brown explained. Lewin had been hit in the neck at Quatre Bras, the day before Waterloo, but the wound had not seemed serious at first, until he had been wounded at Waterloo. 'Lying out for twenty-four hours in the mud with your leg shattered doesn't do much for your wounds, though, ma'am,' his friend explained. 'I had it easier; a ball carried mine off nice and neat.'

Bel swallowed hard, wondering what Aunt Louisa

was going to say if she returned Elinor in a fainting condition, but her cousin was made of sterner stuff than
that. 'A doctor is the priority, then,' she said firmly.
'And to send out for supplies of bandages, gauze and
salves.'

They drove round to the mews and Bel sent James
running for Hedges and the other footman while her
coachman and groom helped the men down. She
expected opposition from the butler. Hedges marched
into the yard, his face grim, then stood assessing the two
men through narrowed eyes. They met his scrutiny with
more calm than Bel would have predicted. Hedges
grunted. 'I reckon they'll do, my lady. Come on, lads,
help them up to the hay loft.'

He watched them struggling up the stairs and turned
to Bel. 'I had a nephew, wounded badly at Salamanca.
Died later on, after he'd come home, but at least it was
in his mother's arms, warm and comfortable and with
those he loved all around. If he'd had no family to go
to, he'd have ended up like those two, and it don't bear
thinking about.' His mouth worked for a moment as
though something else was going to burst out, then he
was composed again, his face expressionless.

Bel stood back while Hedges organised the staff,
sent for the doctor and had the footmen running for hot
water and tubs. 'First thing, get you clean,' she heard
him ordering from the loft. 'Look at the state of you!
I'm not having you on her ladyship's premises in that
state, even if it is only the hay loft. Then you'll be fit to
see the doctor. And then you can eat.'

When the butler came down to the yard again his face
was grim. 'National disgrace it is, the way the army
treats its men. They do it better in the navy, that's for

sure.' He looked up at the long loft, then back to Bel. 'How many more of them have you got, ladies?'

'Just the two,' Elinor said faintly as Mrs Hedges appeared, the kitchen maid at her heels.

'How many more can we take?' Bel asked.

'Up there, my lady? Half a dozen or so.'

'Well, Elinor,' Bel said with a rueful smile, 'It seems I did not have to look far—my charity has found me.'

Ashe remained in Hertfordshire for ten days, surprised at how content he found himself, getting to know the workings of the estate in far greater detail than he had ever done while his father was alive, or while old Simmons, the previous estate manager, had been in charge.

John Barrington was a stimulating companion to work with, his family stopped their overt fussing after a day or two and the sun shone. If it were not for missing Bel, he could have rusticated happily until the start of the hunting season.

But miss her he did, and not, as he had expected, just in his bed. There was that, of course, and on several occasions he had tossed and turned, failing to sleep until he had given up, gone out and swum in the lake in the moonlight. That was some help, until his over-active imagination produced the picture of Bel in there with him, her skin pearly in the silver light, slipping like a fish through the cool water as he dived after her, his hands skimming over her sleek curves.

Ashe missed talking to her. That was the shock. He had not realised just how much time they had spent talking, exchanging opinions and confidences without really being aware of it. He knew she disliked striped fabrics, ormolu and the fad for the Egyptian style and was entirely in agreement with her. He knew she preferred opera to drama and chamber music to orchestral and that there they disagreed. He knew she would like a dog, but not a cat, and that she would rather ride than drive and he had no preferences as far as equestrian exercise was concerned but admitted to a weakness for cats about the house.

Bel declared herself a Whig not a Tory, but expressed distrust of most politicians and was very clear that she preferred short sermons on Sunday, which meant that she would be at odds with several of their neighbours and bored by the Rector. And at that point he realised he was again imagining her at Coppergate, gave himself a brisk mental talking-to and went to discuss pigsty design with the Home Farm stockman.

But despite his attempts at self-control, Ashe was conscious of his heart beating faster as he sifted through the pile of letters, bills and notes that Race retrieved from the Albany porter's lodge when they arrived back in London. He had written three days ago to tell them to forward on nothing more to Hertfordshire, so there was a considerable stack to flick through.

Yet there was no cryptic little note signed B, to greet him, hinting at a time for their reunion, despite his having sent a letter, ostensibly enquiring if she had any further problems with the house, as he would be able to call any day after this date. Disappointed, Ashe poured himself a glass of Madeira and began to work systematically through the pile, tossing the bills aside to deal with later. He had had almost two weeks of paying careful attention to accounts; he was in no rush to immerse himself in them here yet a while.

Invitations, advertisements, solicitations from tradesmen, more invitations… He opened one letter, addressed in a clear black hand that looked vaguely familiar, and found it was from Bel. Not a hastily scrawled, secretive note, but bold as brass, a formal invitation to take tea tomorrow at three o'clock.

Ashe folded the invitation and sat, absently tapping it against his lips as he tried to divine its meaning. Was Bel about to give him his *congé*? Or was she becoming much bolder, entertaining him openly in front of her staff? Or…what?

He unfolded the paper and scrutinised it again. No, surely not his dismissal; the tone, although completely harmless if anyone else happened to see it, was warm.

There was the familiar tightening in his loins as he thought of her, but overriding even that, the desire just to see her, to hold her, to talk. What had she been doing? What would she think of how he had spent the past days? He would welcome her opinion about the actions he had taken to advance Frederica's romance, his ideas for the town house.

'My lord?'

'Eh?' Race was standing by his side, looking faintly martyred. Presumably he had been speaking for some time. 'Sorry, Race, did you say something?'

'I enquired which garments you would wish me to put out for this evening, my lord.'

'I'm going to White's, I think, so the usual for that. And for tomorrow afternoon, those new kerseymere pantaloons and the dark blue superfine swallowtail coat.'

'Indeed, my lord. Most suitable to the occasion, if I may say so.' Race produced a discreet smirk and took himself off before Ashe could retaliate. It really was almost impossible to hide anything from your valet.

Chapter Thirteen

At three on Tuesday afternoon Ashe walked up the steps to what had once been his own familiar front door, knocked and was admitted by Hedges. The butler regarded him with more approval than might be expected, given that on the occasion of their last meeting in Half Moon Street he had been hideously hung over and in the wrong bed.

'Good afternoon, my lord. Lady Belinda is in the drawing room.'

Ashe handed his hat and gloves to a footman, the butler opened the door, announced 'Lord Dereham, my lady', ushered him through and closed it behind him with a soft click.

Bel came towards him, her hand held out, her smiling lips parted as though to speak. He did not give her the chance. His coat was off, thrown to one side as he took two urgent strides across the room, then she was tight in his arms, his mouth crushing down on hers, every soft curve pressed against him as he drank in the taste and the scent of her like a parched man.

She writhed in his arms, inflaming him further; her hands were clenched against his chest, beating a tattoo of desperation every bit as urgent as his. Her mouth was open, working under his searching lips as he swept her further into the room, past the knot of chairs around the hearth and towards the sofa. All he had to do was to get there, although the urge simply to drag her to the floor was overwhelming.

One hand slid down to cup the delicious peach-curve of her buttock; she was so tense, quivering with an excitement that matched his own, struggling in his embrace. They were almost there, almost at the sofa. Out of the corner of his eye, Ashe glimpsed the tea tray on a low table, swerved to avoid it, swept the honey-sweet moistness of Bel's mouth with his tongue—and froze.

The tea tray was laden with cups and plates and more cakes than two people could eat in a week. The realisation sunk in as Bel's teeth closed on his tongue in a sharp bite that had him freeing her with a yelp of pain. From behind him a voice like thunder said, 'Unhand her, you libertine!'

Bel staggered back from Ashe's arms, panting from her struggles to free herself. His appalled expression contrasted with the outrage on her aunt's face as Lady James surged to her feet from the depths of the wing armchair, reticule clenched in one mittened hand, intent on saving her niece from masculine assault.

To an onlooker it would have seemed highly amusing, a farce of the first order; all Bel could feel was a sick apprehension. There was absolutely no way this could be explained away, no way that she was not now exposed, before her own aunt, as a loose woman.

'Explain yourself, sir!' Ashe turned slowly to face Aunt Louisa. Her face, as she recognised him, was a picture of shocked disbelief. 'Lord Dereham! What is the meaning of this outrage?'

'Lady James. I can explain—'

'I would like to hear you try, sir!'

Bel groped for the high curved end of the sofa and held on to it. Explain? How could he possibly explain that away? How on earth had it happened? She had felt so safe, so happy, and now, in a few seconds, it was tumbling around her ears. She swayed, dizzy, convinced that every ounce of blood had drained out of her face. The back of Ashe's neck was red, but his voice was steady as he faced the outraged widow.

'The force of my ardour—'

'Hah! Is that what you call it, you libertine?'

'—for Lady Belinda,' he continued steadily, 'deceived me into believing that my feelings were reciprocated, and, in coming here today with the intention of proposing marriage, I—'

'What?' The question was out of Bel's mouth before she could stop herself. Neither of the other two answered her, or even appeared to remember that she was standing there.

'In short, ma'am, the novelty of finding myself, as I thought, alone with Lady Belinda so inflamed my passions that I threw caution to the winds and seized her, wishing to press my suit with more zeal than, I know, is proper.'

'Proper, indeed! You were about to ravish the poor child upon the sofa, sir. That is not zeal, that is not ardour, that is the action of a ravening beast! You are half-dressed—'

'Will someone please listen to me?' Despairing of

either of them attending to her, Bel poked Ashe in the ribs so that he half-turned towards her. His neckcloth was askew, his shirt half-untucked and his coat gone.

'Lord Dereham,' she said, with as much steadiness as she could command, shock at his words overriding even her shamed confusion, 'I do not believe that I have, on the few occasions we have met, given you any indication that your suit would be acceptable to me.'

'I agree, ma'am,' Ashe responded with equal control. 'Nothing you have said to me could be construed as encouragement for me, or any other man, to make you an offer of marriage.'

'Then why—?'

'You must forgive the ardour of a man seized with feelings too strong to be denied. I had hoped to persuade you.' Ashe had shifted so that Aunt Louisa could not see his face. His intense expression urged her to agree. His lips moved. Bel strained to read them. *Say yes, for goodness' sake, Bel.*

Yes? Marry him? Bel was aware that her mouth was opening and shutting like a carp in a pond and that nothing was coming out.

'Well, you have achieved your aim, young man,' Aunt Louisa said wrathfully. 'Because you are most certainly going to have to marry my niece after this exhibition of unbridled lust.'

'No!' The word burst out of her tight throat. 'No, I am not going to marry him.' With denial came a kind of awful calm.

'Of course you must, you foolish gel! Your reputation is at stake.'

'You must. Bel…Lady Belinda… Think of the scandal.'

'Considering that my aunt is the sole witness of this débâcle, and knowing that she has only my interests at heart, I fail to see where the scandal is going to come from, my lord,' Bel said frostily. Over his shoulder her aunt moved and Bel caught a glimpse of herself in the mirror. Her mouth was swollen with Ashe's kisses, her hair was half-down and the pretty fichu she had arranged at her throat was a wreck. 'Oh, my God! Look at me.'

'Lady Belinda.' Ashe raised his voice over her gasp of horror and Aunt Louisa's furious mutterings. 'Please listen to me…'

Bel slapped his face.

She did it without thinking, her hand flashing out in a reflex that dismayed her almost as much as it must have shocked him. 'How dare you?' she whispered. 'How dare you talk about marriage? How dare you try to force me into something I am resolved never to do?'

There was a silence as they stared into each other's faces. Bel could feel the heat and sting of tears and fought them back. Ashe's eyes were dark with what she could only assume was thwarted anger at her refusal to bow to the conventions and satisfy what his masculine code of honour told him he must do. And the marks of her fingers branded his cheek, to her shame.

From the hallway there was the murmur of voices, the sound of the front door closing. The drawing room door began to open. The three of them, united suddenly, stared at each other. Then Bel spun round on her heel and ran for the door at the other end, the one that opened on to the service passage. As she whisked through it she heard Hedges announcing,

'Lady Wallace, Lady Maude Templeton, Miss Ravenhurst, the Reverend Makepeace, my lady.'

How Ashe and Aunt Louisa were going to explain his presence in her drawing room in his shirtsleeves she had no idea, and, she told herself furiously as she wrenched open the back door that led into her tiny garden, she did not care either.

It was not so much a garden, more of a court, the width of the house and a few yards deep, paved and with tubs of shrubs and flowering plants set about it. But, despite its modest size, in the afternoon it caught the sun and was a pleasant place to sit. Bel remembered too late as she ran down the six steps into it that she had urged her loft-full of soldiers to take the air there whenever they chose: today it seemed they had taken advantage of the offer.

She stood and regarded them, five of the eight who now occupied the loft, brought in over several days by Brown whom she had sent out in a hackney to scour the streets. He had recovered quickly with good food and medical attention, but his friend Lewin was still very poorly and confined to his bed.

They got to their feet with varying degrees of ease and stared at her mutely. Then Brown took a step forward. 'What's the matter, ma'am?' His big fists clenched. 'Who's touched you? You tell me, I'll sort them out.' The group at his back growled agreement.

Bel pushed pins back into her hair with hands that shook. 'No one. I…I had a stupid argument with a friend. I am upset… I am sorry, I forgot you might be here.'

'We'll go, ma'am, let you have your garden back for a quiet sit, don't you fret.' The others began to shift towards the gate, uneasy, she realised, that she was less than poised, less than completely in control. Probably, she thought with a flash of desperate humour, they were afraid she was going to weep.

'No, please, don't go. Stay and I will sit out here too. Tell me how everyone is doing.' Bel forced a smile and saw them begin to relax.

'Well, ma'am, Lewin's sitting up and seems to be getting his appetite back, leastways, for Mrs Hedges's soup. And Jock here…' he tipped his head towards the taciturn Scot with an eye patch who seemed to be resigned to never being addressed by his real name '…his foot's a lot better. And I found two more lads this morning, the doctor's looking at them now.' He talked on, marshalling and presenting his facts efficiently. Bel found herself wondering why he had not become a sergeant, he seemed to have the requisite qualities. She must ask Ashe about how that worked. If they ever spoke to each other again.

Ashe shot one glance down the length of the room to where his coat lay crumpled on a chair where he had thrown it. The door was already opening—he could never make it in time, and besides, the marks of Bel's hand on his face must be crimson.

This entire ghastly episode was like a farce, he thought, despairing for a second before military training kicked in. *Think, improvise, survive.* If this was a farce, then salvation might lay in making it even more of one.

'Scream,' he ordered brusquely, lifting Lady James bodily and standing her on top of a side chair. 'And stay there.' She gave a muffled shriek and waved her arms for balance. As the sound of the entering guests' chatting reached him, Ashe dived under the *chaise*, the poker snatched from the hearth in his hand.

The door closed, the animated conversation petered to a halt. Obviously the new arrivals had taken in the scene. 'Damnation!' he exclaimed, wriggling right back out again and getting to his feet in front of two young ladies, one formidable matron and a rector. 'I do beg your pardon, please excuse my language.'

'Lord Dereham!' Lady James glared down at him from her precarious perch on the chair. 'This is an outrage!'

'I am sorry, ma'am, but it escaped into a hole in the skirting—too fast for me. There was no need to slap me, Lady James,' he added reproachfully. 'I only lifted you up in case it tried to run up your skirts.

'A very large rat.' The bemused guests gaped at him as he set the poker back in the hearth and offered a hand to Lady James, who accepted it with a glare and allowed him to help her down.

'You are a very ingenious young man, are you not?' she asked grimly, settling back in the chair with an awful dignity.

'Taking off my coat in an attempt to throw it over the creature?' Ashe snatched gratefully at an explanation for his missing clothing. 'Ingenious, perhaps, but it was a poorly executed manoeuvre, I am afraid; I missed it by feet.'

'Your coat, my lord.' Hedges approached with the garment, well shaken out. 'I will send for a rat catcher directly. Shall I bring the tea now, my lady, or should I wait upon the return of Lady Belinda?'

Lady James folded her lips, stared arctically at Ashe and then appeared to realise that she had to give him some help for Bel's sake. 'Please bring it in at once, Hedges.' She turned a thin smile on the guests. 'My niece spilt milk on her skirts, jumping clear of the rodent. She retired in some confusion to change.' She gestured to the seats around the tea table. 'Please, everyone, do sit down, I am sure she will not be long. Lady Wallace, how fortunate you were able to come this afternoon, I had feared you might not be back from Exeter in time…'

'If you will excuse me, I will just go and wash my hands.' Ashe took himself off through the door while the others settled down to greetings and exclamations about Lady James's adventure. 'Where is Lady Belinda?' he demanded of Hedges the moment the door closed.

'In the garden, I believe, my lord.' The butler assessed his appearance with professional detachment. 'If you would care to step into the dining room, I will bring some warm water and a towel. Your lordship may also wish to adjust your neckcloth, which is a trifle disarrayed.'

He reappeared as promised a few minutes later, his face a perfect blank. 'Should I send for a rat catcher immediately, my lord?'

'No, you should not, as you very well know, Hedges.' Punching the smug butler, who was now so expressionless as to make it quite clear he had a very good idea about the truth of the situation, would relieve his feelings but could only make matters worse.

Ashe soaped his hands vigorously, his emotions churning. *I asked her to marry me. Why did she slap me? Didn't she believe I meant it? Of course I have to offer for her now.* He used the towel, then tugged his neckcloth back into some semblance of order. Brummell would have had kittens at the sight of it.

'As you say, my lord. I should perhaps mention that Lady Belinda appeared a trifle distressed when she passed me.'

A small understatement, he imagined. His cheek was

still stinging like the devil. 'She is not the only one,' Ashe retorted grimly.

'My lord—there is something you should know… The garden—'

'Later, Hedges,' Ashe threw back over his shoulder as he strode down the hall. *I have got a marriage proposal to get right first.*

Ashe flung open the door into the tiny garden and stopped dead on the top step. He had expected Bel to be pacing furiously, or to be in tears in one of the arbours. What he had not expected was to find her surrounded by a motley group of men in what appeared to be the ragged remnants of British army uniforms, incongruous amidst the topiary and the tubs of bright blooms.

'What the devil?' Had they broken in, intent on burglary, and found Bel, alone and defenceless? His eyes swept over them, assessing, calculating odds. There were five of them, standing close around her. As he stared they closed in tighter with the air of a pack of dogs guarding a bone. Then he realised that not only did Bel not appear at all alarmed, but they were looking at him with deep suspicion, as though he were the threat to her, not them.

The big man on crutches standing closest to Bel glanced down at her, as though for confirmation, then back up at Ashe. 'Is this the *friend* who upset you, ma'am? Because if it is, we'll sort him out for you.'

'This is Lord Dereham,' she said hastily. 'Major Dereham. I do not need any protection from him, I assure you.'

'Major? Stand up straight, lads!' The group shuffled to attention and he saw all of them were wounded, more or less seriously, and that their uniforms, although tattered, were clean and darned.

'No need for the rank. Not any longer, I'm a civilian now,' Ashe said pleasantly, coming down the steps. He swept the group with his eyes as he did so, keeping his weight on the balls of his feet, still not trusting the situation. 'You are all acquaintances of Lady Belinda?'

'Aye, we are that. And I know you, Major, I saw you at Waterloo, just before the end.' The broad Scottish accent drew Ashe's attention.

'Did you now?'

'I did, and I'm fair dumfoonert to see you standing here now, all in one piece, sir, and that's the truth. Seeing what you were doing at the time. Aye, bludy brave, it was.'

He did not want to get into reminiscences of that last, all out, charge, certainly not now. 'I have been more fortunate than you and your friends, by the look of it. And you are here because—?' His eyes locked with the big man who still had his shoulder turned in a way that shielded Bel from Ashe.

'They live here, all of them,' Bel said firmly, stepping out from amongst the men. Most people would not notice anything wrong now, but Ashe could see the tension in her, the rigidity of her shoulders, the bruised look in her eyes. He had improvised as best he could, but she had not escaped that scene unscathed. What was her old dragon of an aunt going to do now? He realised Bel was still explaining about the soldiers and pulled his attention back to listen. '…in the mews. There are eight of them at the moment.'

'So that is why you invited me here?' It was beginning to make sense. Bel was collecting wounded veterans from somewhere and wanted advice on what to do with them.

'Exactly,' she said briskly, turning back to the small group. 'I must go back inside; let Mrs Hedges know if you need anything. I will come down this evening.'

They were treating her with respect, Ashe saw, scanning their faces covertly as they watched her make her way to the steps. Wherever they had come from, and whatever their stories, they did not appear to be intent on taking advantage of her. With a nod Ashe followed Bel, closing the door to leave them alone in the empty hallway.

'Bel—'

'How *could* you, Ashe?' she demanded, her voice shaking with barely suppressed anger.

'I did not know anyone else was there,' he began, but she shook her head impatiently, dismissing the explanation.

'No, not that, I realise you thought we were alone. But how could you ask me to marry you? I thought I could trust you.'

'Damn it, Belinda—' Ashe kept his voice down from a roar with an effort that hurt his throat '—of course you can trust me! And trust me to do the right thing, I hope—'

'Poppycock,' she said baldly, 'You are just like all the rest of them.'

Bemused and affronted, Ashe stepped in front of Bel as she stalked down the passage towards the front hall. 'Bel, my honour demands that I marry you.'

'So that is all right, is it? I marry you, honour satisfied?'

'Yes.'

'No. No, no, a thousand times *no*. It takes two to marry, my lord, and if I ever should again—which I very much doubt—it will not be because it is necessary to save some man's honour.'

'I see. So I am just *some man* to you. Do I have that correctly?'

For a moment Ashe though she was going to either slap him again or storm off. Bel stopped in front of the dining-room door and looked at him from under levelled brows. 'No, you are not, and you very well know it. You are the man I am having an affair with and now I have no idea what to do about you.'

Chapter Fourteen

They could not stand there in the hall glaring at each other, Bel realised. There were more practical and immediate things to think about than her sense of betrayal.

'What happened after I left?' she demanded, pushing Ashe into the dining room in front of her. 'How did you explain being half-dressed?' Was she ruined? Bel closed the door and leaned back against it. What had the other guests seen—and what on earth had Aunt Louisa said?

Ashe gave her a long look, then summarised as concisely as an officer delivering a report. 'I pretended a large rat had run in, causing you to spill the milk over your gown and flee. I lifted your aunt on to a chair to lend credence to that story and explained that this had caused her to slap my face. I said I had then ripped off my coat to try to throw over the creature. I missed, so I said, and had dived after it under the *chaise* with the poker just as the other guests were announced.'

'You are very facile with your explanations,' Bel said tightly, feeling the shock begin to ebb and the anger to build in its place. Inventions came so easily to Ashe, it seemed. He would say whatever he had to, make any claim in order to smooth the way. She knew she should be grateful for his ingenuity, but the emotion proved elusive.

'It seemed to cover all the angles of the situation; there was not much time before they came in to think of anything else.'

'And your explanation to my aunt while I was there? Did that, too, cover all the angles?'

'Apparently not.' Ashe lifted his hand to his bruised cheek and smiled ruefully.

'*Indeed* not,' she snapped. 'I cannot talk to you now. I must go back and you can follow me in a few minutes. I need have no anxieties that you will not be able to behave as though we are the merest acquaintances, I trust?'

'No, I believe I can manage that.' Ashe sounded cool now, his eyes hard.

Damn him! Bel thought as she whisked out of the door and into the drawing room. *He puts me in this impossible position and then is angry when I am not grateful to him for condescending to offer marriage…*

'Good afternoon! I am so sorry I was not here when you arrived, what a ridiculous situation!' Bel fixed a warm social smile on her lips and went to shake hands with Lady Wallace and the Reverend Makepeace. 'Aunt Louisa, I do apologise, leaving you to cope, but I really cannot bear the creatures and I am afraid I panicked… Lady Maude, Cousin Elinor.'

They settled down again, shifting positions to give her room on the *chaise* next to Lady Maude who was, so rumour had it, engaged to Bel and Elinor's cousin Gareth Morant, Earl of Standon. If it was true, the pair were not hastening to announce the fact. Lady Maude was wealthy and intelligent as well as possessing a wide range of influential acquaintances.

'Where is Lord Dereham?' Bel asked brightly as her aunt passed her a cup of tea.

'Putting himself to rights, having dived under the *chaise* with a poker in pursuit of the rat.' Lady James's expression defied anyone to elaborate on the matter.

'Delicious! I do wish I had been here to see it, don't you, Miss Ravenhurst?' Lady Maude, who had a reputation for being both fast and unconventional, seemed immune to the atmosphere or to hints. Or perhaps she delighted in gossip. Bel did not know her well enough to judge. 'Lord Dereham gallantly attacking the creature in a state of undress! Really, when he emerged from beneath the sofa in his shirtsleeves, clutching that poker—I declare I was quite overwhelmed.'

'Most diverting, indeed,' Elinor agreed repressively, glancing from her mother's stony face to Bel's carefully smiling countenance. 'But I do hope his lordship is not detained too long; I am most interested to find out what he recommends for our soldiers.'

'Mr Makepeace also has experience in this field,' Lady Wallace intervened, with a stately inclination of her head towards the middle-aged cleric who was consuming buttered toast in silence. 'Which is why I suggested he should join our little group.'

'Indeed, ma'am.' He put down his plate and regarded them dubiously. 'I have, as you say, experience in this field, and I will do my best to assist, but I must confess that ex-soldiers are not the most amenable recipients of charity and good works. Most are, to put it kindly, ignorant and wilfully independent, however bad their case is.'

'Independence is to be applauded, surely?' Bel inter-

jected. 'And *charity* is not at all what I had in mind.
These men—most of them, at least—ought to be able
to earn their own living, once they have had the chance
to recover from their injuries. I want to give them
medical assistance and a safe, decent place to live while
they look around them for work. That is not charity,
simply a helping hand. Who, however respectable, can
hope to find employment when ill, filthy and dressed in
rags?'

'Bravo, Lady Felsham. Who indeed?' Ashe had
come into the room without her noticing. 'I would
suggest that what is needed is a lodging house of sorts.
One where we can control who resides there and
provide medical assistance and food and clothing. Then
we can assess who is fit for what occupation.'

'That sounds ideal.' Bel smiled with real gratitude,
then felt her expression turn stiff as she caught Ashe's
eye. 'Where would you suggest?'

'I own a warehouse at the back of Oxford Street,'
Ashe offered. 'It will need cleaning, fitting out and so
on—but the location is central. I am more than willing
to donate that to the cause.'

'An excellent suggestion, Lord Dereham.' Lady
Wallace beamed at him. 'I will undertake to supply bed
linen and mattresses.'

'And I know of a manufacturer of beds for work-
houses,' the reverend offered, apparently unoffended
by Bel's rejection of his earlier opinions.

'I will pay for the cleaning and decorating,' she
added, trying not to think about Ashe sitting so near. It
was the practicalities of assisting the soldiers that were
important, she told herself firmly. Her personal life
must wait. 'And fitting out a kitchen. But we are going

to need more assistance with furnishings, food, clothes—we cannot do it all ourselves if this is to grow and help more than a handful of men.'

'If we draw up a list of possible-supporters, I will write to them.' Elinor reached for the notebook she had put beside her plate. 'I can draft a letter and see if it meets with your approval.'

'I think we should hold a subscription dance.' Lady Maude, who had been sitting silently listening, suddenly joined in. 'Papa has put our ballroom in order for next Season, I am sure he will not mind. I will organise it; I am very good at organising balls.' She smiled with all the confidence of a young lady whose father doted upon her, then turned her long-lashed green eyes on Ashe. 'You would support a ball, would you not, Lord Dereham?'

'Only if you will dance with me, Lady Maude,' Ashe rejoined smoothly, earning himself a dimpling smile from Maude and a cool stare from Bel.

They spent a further hour exchanging ideas while Elinor competently made notes, which she promised to copy out and send to each of them, and Bel fought to maintain her composure under her aunt's severe scrutiny and Ashe's carefully maintained distance. She wanted to shout and throw things—a desire she had never experienced in her life before; she wanted Ashe to go away and never come near her again and she wanted to throw herself into his arms and beg him to make love to her.

At least when Ashe had asked her to marry him, he had never mentioned the one word that he might have expected would persuade her to reconsider marriage: love. But of course he did not feel that, and had been too honest to pretend it, even though that would have been the icing on the cake of his careful fabrication to deceive Aunt Louisa.

Bel stared into the tea leaves in the bottom of her cup and wished she had the power to read them. Even if it were, impossibly, true that Ashe felt like that about her, she did not want the burden of being loved and she could not return such an emotion, ever.

Her guests left at last, all except Ashe, who hung back in the hallway, talking to Hedges and discussing going down to the mews to meet the men, and Aunt Louisa and Elinor.

'Belinda, a word with you, if you please.' Lady James closed her eyeglass with a snap and replaced it in her reticule. 'Elinor, kindly wait for me in the carriage. And shut the door behind you on your way out.'

'Yes, Mama.' Her cousin raised one quizzical eyebrow at Bel, as if to say, *Why are you in disgrace?*, and obediently went out.

'Well, Belinda? What, exactly, is your relationship with that man?' Lady James seated herself firmly in Bel's favourite armchair. 'The truth this time, if you please, not Reynard's work of fiction.'

'There is nothing I wish to discuss, Aunt.' Bel made herself sink down gracefully into the chair opposite. 'You heard me reject Lord Dereham's proposal—there is nothing to add to what I said then.'

'Reject it! Hah! Why should you reject it, you totty-headed girl? That man's the best catch you're ever likely to make. Title, money, connections, fine war record and a fine pair of shoulders to him.'

'I have no wish to remarry, Aunt. If Lord Dereham asks me again, I shall continue to refuse.'

Lady James stared at her beadily. 'Are you lovers?'

Bel knew she was blushing. But then, any respectable lady would blush at being accused of having a lover. 'As I said, I do not intend discussing such things, Aunt.'

'Hmm.' Her formidable relative eyed her with something like respect. 'Well, can't say I blame you if you are; he's a handsome fellow and he'll do you a damn sight more good between the sheets than that dull ninnyhammer you married. But that's a risky path, taking a lover; better to be wed if you want a man in your bed.' She ignored her niece's dropped jaw and swept on. 'Does he love you?'

'Certainly not. And I do not want to be loved and I am not in love with him.' *I was simply swept up into some ridiculous fairy tale where I could defy convention, take a handsome lover and get away with it unscathed. Well, I know better now.* The fluffy pink clouds of her happiness were tattered wisps now, blowing in the wind.

'Then be careful how you go on with him, my girl. If you lose your reputation, it won't matter whether you've been in his bed or not, you'll be treated as though you have.'

'Yes, Aunt Louisa.'

It was excellent advice, and she knew it. This was the end of her blissful fantasy and she had to make sure Ashe understood that.

'Where is Lord Dereham?' she asked Hedges after he showed Lady James out.

'Down with the men looking at the loft, my lady.'

'Please ask him if he will join me in the garden after he has finished.' Bel found herself a seat under the arbour well away from the house windows and waited.

She had thought that some moments of quiet reflection would allow her to get her emotions under control and to be able to speak to Ashe with composure. She had not expected that by the time he reappeared, some twenty minutes later, she would be even less poised.

'*Belle.*' He stood looking down at her, his smile rueful. 'We have had an exciting afternoon, have we not?'

'That is not how I would characterise it,' she retorted. 'How *could* you?'

'I told you, I thought the room was empty. I had not seen you for days—I missed you.' Ashe put one hand against the frame of the arbour and looked down at her. 'May I sit?'

'No, you may not. And I do not mean you kissing me. You know I mean you proposing.'

'What else could I possibly do? I had compromised you in front of one of your relatives.'

'You were quick thinking, I will say that for you! But once I had refused, once Aunt had heard your story about being overcome by passion—not that she believes a word of it—why on earth did you persist? You know my feelings about marriage.'

Ashe stared at her. 'You must see I had no alternative, under the circumstances. I have compromised you; the honourable action is quite clear, even if you do not agree with it.' His blue eyes were narrowed as he frowned at her, puzzled, she supposed, that her vehemence persisted after the first shock was over. He looked harder, older, more dangerous than the teasing, flirtatious man she was used to. She had seen it with the soldiers; now he was looking at her in the same way, assessing a problem. She was the problem.

'But you do not mean it—do you? You do not wish

to marry me. It is not as though you love me, is it?' It felt so dangerous, uttering that word, but the question just slipped from her.

Bel expected either an avowal—which she would not believe—or a denial, which she would. 'I do not know,' he said slowly, startling her. 'I had not thought about it before, but now you ask…I must admit to feeling quite sanguine about the thought of marriage to you.'

Ignoring her refusal to let him sit, he dropped into the seat next to her, trapping her between the woven greenery of the side of the arbour and the length of his body. He picked up her left hand and began to play with her fingers, his concentration focused on them. 'I missed you, Bel.'

'I missed you too.' It was foolish to try to deny it. Her heart was thudding uncomfortably and she felt a trifle sick. The repetitive brush of his fingers made it hard to concentrate. 'But that does not mean I love you.'

'Why should me wondering about it make you so angry?' Ashe asked, abruptly dropping her hand and looking into her eyes.

That had been what she had been trying to work out, and becoming so muddled about. 'It sounds like emotional blackmail,' she said at last.

'I see.'

'And I had told you I would never marry again. You knew that when I asked you to be my lover that I did not intend it to be anything more.'

'I know.' He caught her hand again, turned it over in his big one and began to rub his thumb against the tender skin of her palm. 'I believe you.'

'You made me feel as though I was responsible for putting you in a position where you were honour-bound to offer for me. You made me feel as though I had been trying to trap you. I was an idiot to even mention love just now. I am not in love with you—I did not ask because I wanted to hear you say *yes*.'

'Ah.' The pressure of his thumb grew more, making her fingers curl around it reflexively.

'I do wish you would say something—not just *Ah* and *I see* and *I know*.' Bel knew she was sounding irritable, knew that what she really wanted was a magnificent row to clear the air. And then for Ashe to take her in his arms and tell her it was all perfectly fine and they could go on being lovers, without any strings attached, as though nothing had happened.

'Very well.' Ashe released her hand and stood up. 'While I was away I kept thinking about you, imagining you in my home, wondering what you would think about things, what you would say about the everyday problems and decisions. I found I was visualising you as my wife. Is that love? I do not know, I have never been in love. I am trying to be truthful with you.'

'Oh.'

'And I did not want to think about marriage, if you want the complete, unvarnished truth. It was most uncomfortable.'

Oh. That is truthful indeed. No attempts at flattery or evasion there!

'I want my independence, my freedom, just as you want yours.'

'Of course,' Bel agreed brightly. That was exactly how she wanted him to feel. Of course it was.

'But there it was, this thought that kept intruding when my guard was down, this picture of you in my home.' Ashe frowned down at an inoffensive rose, then began to pull off its petals. 'I felt…different and I could not understand it. Then, when I held you in my arms again, when I realised we had been seen, compromised—I felt relief. I did not have to make a choice or a decision and neither did you. We would have to marry.'

How honest. And how thoroughly deflating. Bel knew she was being hypocritical—she had been flattered by the idea that Ashe was in love with her, even as she did not want him to feel like that.

'Well, we don't have to. Aunt Louisa warned me to be discreet, that is all. I was amazed—I had expected her to announce she would write to my brothers.'

'She is a woman of the world.' Ashe shrugged, dismissing her aunt. 'Very well. We will be discreet. No more kissing except behind a closed bedchamber door, I promise.'

'No. No more kissing at all.' Bel stood up, found her legs were shaking and took hold of the arbour frame. 'We must end our *affaire*. Now.'

'You are punishing me for my carelessness, in effect?' Ashe said slowly. 'There is no good reason why we should cease to be lovers, Bel.'

'I am punishing myself.' Bel felt a kind of bitter cold inside her, but she pressed on. 'I was a naïve fool. I thought I could take a lover, live out my fantasy and there would be no risk, no…effect. But there is a risk, and there is an effect. You speak of love and indecision…'

'I speak of real life and real emotions.' He sounded detached. Looking at him, Bel thought she had never seen him look so handsome, so severe. 'Reality is uncertain and messy, my sweet.'

'Yes,' she agreed. That was certainly true.

'We are real people, Bel. There is always the risk that things will change, that what seems safe will fail to be.'

'I will not take that risk; it is not in my nature to be reckless, I see that now. Ashe, I am grateful—'

'No!' His rare temper flared like a coal dropping into oil. One moment he had been detached, faintly ironic and standing a yard away; the next Bel was jerked towards him, mere inches from eyes like ice and the hard, set lines of his face. 'Don't you dare be grateful, Bel Cambourn. Don't you dare be one of those needy women who beg. You made a decision—a scandalous one—and you had the nerve and the courage to follow it through. We came together as equals, you and I. I may have been able to show you something you had not experienced before, but you gave me the privilege of your trust. You owe me nothing, I owe you nothing. Do you understand?'

'Yes, Ashe,' she managed as he let her go and she swayed, off balance. Bel reached out a hand and steadied herself with a touch on his arm. It was like iron with the tension of his temper. 'You will still help with the soldiers?'

'Bel's battalion?' Ashe's smile was wry. 'Yes, of course. Do you think I am going to storm off in a temper and leave them? I have a duty to them, and I thank you for showing me a way to fulfil it.' Relieved, Bel lifted her hand. 'Listen, Bel, we have had a near miss; you are very angry, very shaken. We will not end this *affaire* now, but we will not come together again, alone, for—say—two weeks. That will allow us to calm down. If then you still want to end it, so be it.'

'Yes,' she said shakily. 'Yes, I agree to that. But you

must promise not to speak again about love and marriage—I want neither from you.'

'I promise.' Ashe lifted her hand and kissed her fingertips. 'But tell me one thing though, before we part. You are not refusing me because of any other man?'

'I told you not.' She stared at him, perplexed. 'I swear there is no one else. And I meant what I said—I am not contemplating marriage—not to you, not to anyone.'

Chapter Fifteen

Why had he asked that? Ashe wondered, staring into Bel's wide and puzzled eyes. Was it that it was easier to accept her refusal of his proposal if she loved another man? But he was making no sense. This was Bel: painfully honest, frank, honourable. She would have told him at once if there was someone else, not fallen back on saying she did not want to wed again.

And why should her refusal hurt? It was his pride and his honour, that was all. He had told himself, over and over at Coppergate, that he did not want to marry yet. It was just that she was so very different from any other woman he had ever met and certainly from any other lover. Her innocence made him feel protective, and that was what he was mistaking for love.

'Love is not something one is ever in doubt about, is it?' he asked lightly.

'I imagine not.' She seemed to be trying to match his tone. 'From everything one reads, it comes like a *coup de foudre*. One can hardly mistake it, surely?'

'No, surely not,' Ashe agreed, curiously relieved. It

was this strange back-to-front relationship that confused him. Normally one would meet a respectable woman like Bel, fall for her, marry her and *then* make love to her. The lovemaking would be the culmination of the emotion. Because she was not a lightskirt, he was unconsciously expecting the love.

Relieved by this rationalization, Ashe smiled at her and saw the answering curl of her lips. But her eyes were still as shadowed as his mood. There was never going to be anyone like Bel, ever again, and this ending—if that is what it would prove to be—had come too soon, too suddenly for him to take it in his stride.

'Are you going to be all right?' he asked.

'Of course.' Her chin went up and her back straightened, the almost imperceptible droop in her shoulders vanishing. 'I expect it will be a trifle awkward when we meet in society, but I am sure I will manage. Do you intend to stay in town long this time?'

'Long enough to see your soldiers established in their new home. My family is coming up later this month to decide what they want done to ready the town house for my eldest sister's come-out next Season, and then I expect I will escort them down to Brighton.'

Ashe fought the urge to sit down and tell Bel all about his sisters, his suspicions about Frederica's feelings for Barrington, his worries about Katy, his hopes for Anna. He must learn to keep his distance from her, emotional as well as physical, while she made up her mind about their relationship.

'You are a good brother,' Bel said lightly, leading the way back to the steps. She held out her hand. 'With your plans for Brighton we would be separated soon for some time in any case. Goodbye, Ashe.'

'Goodbye, Bel.' It was more than a form of words—this could be a very final farewell and they both knew it. The next time they met it would be Lord Dereham and Lady Belinda again, perhaps for ever.

He took both her hands in his, feeling the narrow bones, the long, clever fingers, the warmth, the tremor of her pulse. He held them for a long moment, then bent and touched his lips to hers. They seemed, despite the deliberate lightness of the contact, to cling, seeking her sweetness, the taste of her. He felt more than heard her sharp intake of breath and released her.

'Goodbye, *ma belle*.' Then he made himself stride up the steps and through the doorway without looking back.

It is over. She could not let herself believe that in a week or so they could come together again, that they could be lovers once more. There had been such an innocence about their relationship, such a simplicity that she knew they would never be able to find it again.

Yes. It was over. Bel stood in the garden, staring up at the door for a long moment, then gave herself a little shake. *That's all right, then.* She had come out of her scandalous experiment unscathed. She knew all about physical love now; thanks to Aunt Louisa's astonishing forbearance, she had escaped any consequences of her rashness and she and Ashe had parted as friends.

Her mourning was over, her foolish daydreams and yearnings had been more than satisfactorily fulfilled and she had a purpose in life that was worthwhile and demanding. Really, one could not be happier, Bel told herself, climbing the steps and letting herself into the house. She was exactly what she had set out to be: an independent woman in charge of her own life, her own destiny.

'My lady?' Hedges materialised from the shadows of the front hall. 'Is everything all right?'

'Perfect,' Bel assured him with a smile. 'Things could not be better.'

'As you say, my lady.' Something akin to sympathy showed fleetingly on the well-schooled countenance and Bel felt a stab of pain, the sensation that a curtain had flicked back to reveal something unpleasant behind it. Something she did not want to know was there.

'I do say,' she said firmly. 'How are our soldiers?'

'All doing well. I venture to say we will have no trouble finding more men in need once we have the warehouse that I understand his lordship is providing.'

'Indeed.' Bel turned briskly to the drawing room. 'I can see I have much to do and lists to make, Hedges; I shall get on with it.'

There was a little pile of invitations on top of her appointments book, neglected while she had been preoccupied with Ashe. Bel opened the book and found herself flicking back to the page where she had slipped his card, the one that had come with those first roses. She picked it up, fretting at the thickness of the gilt-edged pasteboard with her fingertips, then suddenly decisive, tore it across, twice, and dropped the pieces into the little basket that served as the waste container under her desk.

She fanned out the invitations, dipped her pen in the standish and began to write. Time to get out into the world again, time to move on.

Lady Belinda Felsham thanks Lady Cardew for her kind... A tear dropped on to the last word, blurring it, soaking into the paper. Bel screwed up the sheet, found her handkerchief and blew her nose with more force than elegance. *Lady Belinda...*

Lady Cardew's musicale was delightful. Bel circulated, exchanging gossip against a background of chamber music. Where she could, she steered the conversation to her soldiers and their needs, ruthlessly jotting down the slightest hint of a promise of help on her ivory tablets.

'Thank you so much, Lord Stonehaven,' she said to the elderly peer, who had just found himself promising a weekly contribution to food and fuel costs. 'I should have known you would be so generous.' She dimpled prettily at him, knowing the effect a little harmless flirtation had upon certain old gentlemen.

He was beaming at her as she turned away, only to find herself face to face with Patrick Layne. 'Mr Layne, good evening. What a long time it seems since we last met. Is Miss Layne here, too?' She had neglected her friends in her preoccupation with Ashe, Bel thought guiltily.

'My sister is interrogating a composer on the subject of setting lyric verse.' Mr Layne grimaced. 'I escaped. And whose fault is it, might I ask, that we have not met lately, Lady Belinda? I swear you have been positively reclusive these past days.'

'I have a new project; let me tell you about it.' Belinda tucked her hand through his proffered arm and allowed herself to be guided through the guests towards the champagne buffet.

Patrick listened patiently as she explained, in more detail than she had to anyone else, all about her soldiers and why she felt so strongly about them. He listened, she realised, with complete focus and intensity, leading her on to explain more and more.

'I believe you,' he said, laughingly dodging one particularly expressive sweep of her arm as she tried to describe the size of the warehouse Ashe had donated. 'It sounds as though you need lumber to make room dividers in all that space. May I contribute that?'

'You may indeed!' Bel beamed in delight. 'How generous of you. Will you join our committee?'

'I would be honoured.' Patrick took two glasses of champagne from the footman and presented one to Bel, raising his own in a mock-toast. 'To your new venture and its hardworking committee.'

She touched her glass to his, laughing up at him. 'How do you know they are hardworking, Mr Layne?'

'Because I fear you will prove to be a hard taskmistress, Lady Belinda,' he teased.

'Nonsense, you are teasing me, Mr Layne. I believe one of my faults is that I am not forceful enough.' *But I was when I wanted Ashe*, she thought. Now, after it was all over, she could not believe she had been so brassy, so daring in asking for what she had wanted. It was as though he had bewitched her, she thought, wondering when the spell was going to wear off.

'I wish you would call me Patrick,' Mr Layne said, reminding her that this was quite another man at her side. He was so nice, just right for Elinor. 'And I believe you would be a positive Joan of Arc in pursuit of what you thought was right, however reticent you may be about your own desires.'

Bel felt her cheeks reddening at the perfectly innocent remark. It heaped coals upon her own awareness of how wanton she had been in pursuit of those desires. Her companion looked at her quizzically, obviously wondering what he had said to make her colour up so.

'Patrick, I—' Bel put her free hand on his arm, lost for words.

'Good evening, Lady Belinda, Mr Layne.' It was Ashe. His eyes flickered briefly to Belinda's hand and she made herself leave it where it was for a moment before removing it and sketching a curtsy. 'You remain in town, Layne?'

'As you see, Reynard. At Lady Belinda's beck and call.'

'Mr Layne is kindly contributing to fitting out the warehouse,' Bel intervened hastily, before Patrick made things any worse. 'I have invited him to join the committee.'

'Then we will doubtless see more of each other.' How Ashe managed to make that sound like a threat while speaking perfectly pleasantly and smiling, Bel had no idea. It appeared to be a masculine talent, for Patrick smiled back just as smoothly.

'I look forward to it.'

Bel supposed she should be flattered that their hackles were up over her—if that was what it was—but, given that Ashe was no longer her lover and Patrick had no reason to claim any rights whatsoever, she could only feel vaguely apprehensive.

'Miss Layne is here this evening also.' Bel snatched at a different subject. 'Lord Dereham admires your sister's writing very much,' she added to Patrick. 'I understand Miss Layne is contemplating some lyric verse.'

'I shall seek her out.' Ashe bowed and strolled away, apparently unconcerned about two pairs of eyes fixed on his back.

'My cousin Miss Ravenhurst is also on the committee,' Bel informed Patrick, wrenching her gaze and her mind away from broad, well-tailored shoulders and the memory of just how they looked with no tailoring at all. 'You met her in the park the other week.'

'So I did. I look forward to meeting her again.' Good, he looked quite pleased at the news; Bel had hoped for a spark of interest and was encouraged. Now all she had to do was to make sure Elinor came to their next meeting wearing one of her new gowns. It was a pity that her cousin's natural charm and intelligence were not enough, but Bel very much feared that even the most perceptive gentleman needed help to see past dun-coloured gowns and hideous bonnets.

'Are you well, Lord Dereham?' Ashe regarded Miss Layne with some surprise. It was a blunt query from a single lady to a gentleman. The poetess merely smiled at him maternally, waiting for an answer, her mittened hands folded neatly at the waist of her very elegant gown.

'Quite well, I thank you.' She merely pursed her lips and regarded him sceptically. 'Why? Do I seem pale to you?'

'You do not look as though you have been sleeping well.' Miss Layne smiled. 'You must forgive me, but when a gentleman has dark shadows under his eyes and spends time discussing lyric poetry with a spinster ten years his senior when the room is filled with a bevy of delightful young ladies, one does wonder if the poor man is ailing.'

Ashe thought fleetingly that Miss Layne would get on well with his mother. 'I have merely been burning the candle at both ends, ma'am, which accounts for the shadows. As for the young ladies—you must believe me when I tell you that I value intelligent conversation and elegant sophistication above giggles and naïve banality.'

'I am flattered, Lord Dereham, but surely there is at least one young lady who can supply both intelligence and elegance.' Miss Layne nodded towards her brother who had paused near the chamber orchestra, his head bent to listen to what Bel was saying.

Ashe reminded himself, for the second time that evening, that he had no right to feel possessive about Bel, that Patrick Layne was an apparently perfectly decent man and she could do a lot worse in either a friend or a lover. None of that stopped him wanting to land Layne a facer.

'Lady Belinda seems more than happy with her present conversation.' He made himself speak lightly. Bel laid a hand on Layne's arm and laughed up at him. The smile froze in place on Ashe's lips.

'Yes, they make a handsome couple,' Miss Layne remarked. 'But I fancy Lady Belinda is rather too complicated for my brother.'

'Complicated? Bel? In what way?' *Oh, God...*

Miss Layne showed no sign of noticing his slip with Bel's name. 'Patrick needs a nice girl who will adore him; he is quite conventional at heart, bless him. Lady Belinda needs a man who wants a partner and who will help her find her wings. She needs a man who can think in more than straight lines.'

'Wings?' Ashe watched as Bel dragged an amused Patrick Layne over to talk to three elderly ladies. He strongly suspected that she had sized up the effect a well-favoured young man would have on them and was even now extracting promises of money with the aid of her new ally.

'She has already found her feet, and I do not think that she is going to be happy with simply being a pedestrian in life now,' Miss Layne said drily. 'Something has changed in her over the past few weeks; I suspect that the real Belinda Cambourn is emerging for the first time since before she married.'

A man who can think in more than straight lines. Ashe pondered the poetess's words as she took out one of her endless supply of notebooks and jotted down an impression. Well, that ruled him out. He seemed incapable of thinking about anything except in a *very* straight line—one that led right back to Bel. He had given them two weeks to reconsider their relationship, but a chill doubt was forming inside him that Bel had already decided that it was irretrievably over.

Knowing that he should not, he read Miss Layne's neat notes upside down as she paused, nibbling the end of her tiny pencil and gazed up at the ceiling. *Wings. Birds? No, hackneyed. Icarus? Falling or soaring?*

He had an unpleasant feeling that for the first time in an *affaire* he had come out of it with scars. He was Icarus, with his wings scorched, and Bel, so far as he could see, was happily soaring off, flaunting her bright plumage in the sunshine.

But why was he scorched? Surely he hadn't fallen in love with her after all? Surely he would know if he had? *Hell.* How his mother would laugh now if she could see him, her unimpressionable son, unable to think about anything but a woman—and a woman who didn't want the eligible Lord Dereham at that. What he needed was a nice, uncomplicated encounter with a thoroughly wicked professional to get this nonsense out of his head, and his loins.

'Reynard!' The voice behind him had him turning, very slowly, on his heel. It could not be. It was.

'Mother. And Anna.' He had a certain reputation for *sang froid* to maintain. His family did not make it easy. 'I am delighted to see you, of course.' *Liar.* 'But what the dev…what on earth are you doing here? I was not expecting you in town for at least another fortnight.'

'I started writing to friends to say we would be here later this month and Leticia Cardew wrote back to say what a pity we would miss her *musicale*, so here we are. I did not want to trouble you about the town house, so I have brought most of the staff up with me.' Lady Dereham smiled fondly at her son. 'And what were you doing, standing there like a pillar of salt, might I ask?'

Thinking about love, sex and marriage. 'Discussing poetry,' Ashe said, regretting the ending of the medieval tradition of sending interfering mothers off to nunneries, something several early Reynards had resorted to in the past. 'May I introduce my mother and my elder sister to you, Miss Layne?' The poetess started, removed her gaze from the painted roundels of flitting cherubs on the ceiling and extended a hand.

The ladies exchanged greetings. 'But I love your work,' Anna exclaimed. 'Might I ask where you found the inspiration for the rustic romance in *Hedgerows and Pasture*?'

'I brought your sister here to begin to get used to chatting to young men in company before the Season starts,' Lady Dereham complained, *sotto voce*, as she drew Ashe to one side. 'Not to fill her head with poetry in the company of middle-aged spinsters!'

'Miss Layne has a handsome younger brother,' Ashe suggested blandly.

'Excellent.' His mother unfurled her fan and plied it

vigorously. 'Now, I shall not need your escort, dear, not for the few weeks we will be in town. I intend only accepting the sort of invitations where I can take Anna, and possibly Frederica, with little fuss. Not full-dress occasions, naturally.'

'None of those in any case, not at this time of year, although there's more company than usual up.' Ashe scanned the crowd to see if he could spot Bel. There she was, talking animatedly to an officer in regimentals. He steered his mother in the opposite direction towards the buffet. 'Frederica, too?'

'Yes,' Lady Dereham said with a touch of steel in her voice. 'I thought it best to remove her from Coppergate and give her thoughts a different direction.'

'From what?'

'From your estate manager! Really, Reynard, I realise that men do not think about these things, but you have positively thrown them together with the predictable result that she fancies herself in love with the man.'

'What is wrong with that?' Ashe asked provocatively, feeling more than a little fellow feeling for his middle sister.

'I want her to make a good marriage.'

'I want her to be happy,' he countered.

'I declare, Reynard,' his mother said with a snap, 'if I did not know better, I would think you were suffering from a broken heart and have some romantic notion of fostering love matches as a result.'

'Not at all,' he was goaded to retort. 'But I am certainly coming round to thinking of Cousin Adrian as my heir with some affection if finding a wife is to be so hedged around with calculation. I will call tomorrow morning, Mama, and see in what way I can assist you. Now, I regret I have a commitment elsewhere.'

He strode off through the crowd to find his hostess and make his graceful excuses. And then, he thought grimly, he would take himself off to the salon of one or other of the Fashionable Impures who would be holding court amidst champagne and candlelight and light-hearted banter and banish all this nonsense about romance from his mind.

Chapter Sixteen

She had never been aware of her body before, Bel realised as she strolled along the winding paths in the shade of the elms in Green Park. Not truly aware. She had thought about it when she was not feeling well, or when shoes pinched or she had eaten too much. But most of the time it was just there. Now it had become a constant part of her consciousness. She was far more sensitive to heat and to cold, to the touch of the different fabrics she wore, to the warmth of sun on her skin or the breeze against her cheek.

There was the compulsion to take off her gloves and stroke the textured bark on the trees as she wandered past, to pet a cat for the sinuous silk of its fur, to brush her hair for long minutes past the regulation one hundred strokes at bedtime.

And the smell of things, even smells that were not so pleasant—surely she had not been so sensitive to those either? After almost ten days she had learned not to mope, thinking of Ashe. She had taught herself not to save up titbits of news or silly ideas to share with him.

She could almost get through a whole day—if she did not see him—and not feel as though there was a hollow inside her, waiting to be filled with his company.

But she could not stop dreaming about him—hot, fevered dreams and languid tender ones—and waking in the morning restless and yearning. And even when willpower, breakfast and the business of the day got those feelings under control, there was still this enhanced sensual awareness, Ashe's legacy to her.

And it was a legacy, she was beginning to accept that. She had said nothing to him, but she was certain she was not going to resume their relationship. It was as though the flash of courage that had fuelled her proposition to him had flickered out. Or was it simply that common sense and her sense of propriety had reasserted itself? She should have felt relief at the decision, but all she could feel was a nagging sense of loss.

Bel walked slowly, studying the way the grass grew thick and soft in the shade, seeing each blade, smelling the freshness of it, even as the heat of the day built. She was not looking where she was going, but then neither was the child who was walking backwards down the same path, vehemently disputing something with her older companions who were walking more slowly several yards behind. They came together with a painful thump and the child landed up on the ground.

'Are you all right?' Concerned, Bel bent down and offered her hand. Ocean-blue eyes stared back at her from under a tumble of long blonde hair, then the child's mouth curved up into an irresistible, all-too-familiar smile that took Bel's breath. She was a miniature, feminine version of Ashe. His daughter? Even as the girl put her hands into Bel's and scrambled to her feet, she realised that this child was perhaps twelve, a little too old—unless Lord Dereham had begun on a career of precocious sin at an alarmingly early age. She must be his sister.

'Thank you, ma'am. I do beg your pardon.' The child bobbed a respectful curtsy. 'I was not looking where I was going; I hope I did not hurt you.' She ignored the two young women hurrying towards them and added, 'I am Katherine Reynard, ma'am.'

'Katy!' The taller of the two young women reached them, her slightly younger and shorter companion at her heels. 'Ma'am, I can only apologise for my harum-scarum sister! I trust you are not hurt, or your gown damaged?' Despite the anxiety on the smooth oval of her face, Bel could see that this sister too was an uncommonly handsome girl.

'Not at all, although I believe Miss Katherine might find she has a bruise or two. Neither of us was paying attention to where we were walking, I am afraid.' The third girl arrived and smiled shyly. Not a beauty, this one, with her mousey hair and her rather indeterminate nose. But her expression was sweet and the anxious affection with which she was running her hands over her younger sister to check for injury, touching. 'I am Lady Belinda Felsham,' she added, holding out her hand to the older girl.

Ashe had not spoken much about his family, and she had not probed, feeling reticent in case he thought she was overly curious about his domestic situation. She recalled him saying he had three sisters, but that was all.

'I am Anna Reynard, this is my sister Frederica and you have already met Katy.' Miss Reynard directed a rueful smile at her sister, who was submitting to having her bonnet straightened and her skirts brushed. 'We have been in London a full week and still we are giving the impression of being complete country bumpkins.'

'I believe you must be relatives of Lord Dereham,' Bel said, turning her steps to stroll with them, Katy's hand trapped firmly in Frederica's.

'You know our brother?'

'We have been engaged on the same committee for some charitable work,' Bel explained. It was dangerously pleasant to speak about Ashe. 'I have started a scheme to give medical aid and temporary shelter to soldiers who have returned from the continent wounded and without families to go to.'

'Oh, yes, I can see that Ashe would be concerned to help with that,' Anna said, her face serious. 'What happens to them when they leave your care?'

'One or two who had a skill and were only lightly wounded have gone back to trades already, but I am not sure what we are going to do with many of them.' That was the biggest worry. Bel had no intention of making work, or fobbing the men off with something that did not have any hope of lasting. 'As they recover their strength, I am sure they will start to think of ideas for themselves.'

'Ashe always says that the army is like a family,' Anna mused. 'He found it difficult to adjust, coming home—I am sure men for whom the life was everything are going to find it much harder.'

'Ashe is very different now,' Katy interrupted. 'Mama says she doesn't know what has come over him.'

'Katy!' her sisters chorused. Bel had the impression that this cry of dismay was a frequent occurrence.

'Well, he is,' Katy persisted. 'Look at the way he is

throwing Frederica together with Mr Barrington.' Frederica went scarlet.

'*Katy!*' Anna said sternly. 'Little pitchers with big eyes and ears and even bigger mouths get to sit in the corner at home and not come out with the grown ups. You should not be talking about such things.' She smiled an apology at Bel. 'Perhaps you have younger brothers or sisters, Lady Belinda?'

'No, none.' Bel laughed, then lowered her voice. 'I find your sister refreshingly frank, Miss Reynard.'

'She is certainly that, I fear!'

'Are you in town for long?' Bel enquired. Ashe had said something about readying the town house for them and then escorting them down to Brighton, but she had been so upset at the time she could not be certain.

'We will go down to Brighton with our brother in a week or so, after Mama has decided what she wants done to the house. I am coming out next Season, you see.'

'You are not out yet?' Bel was surprised, then realised that Miss Reynard's calm air made her seem a little older than she was.

'Mama is allowing Frederica and me to attend small parties now,' Anna explained.

'Then you could come to a picnic I am organising to raise money for the soldiers next Tuesday?' Bel found she was anxious to see more of the Reynard sisters. 'Your brother will be there, so I hope your mother would not mind. No doubt Lord Dereham has already arranged for you all to come? And Miss Katherine would enjoy it as well, I am sure—there will be other young people, it is all quite informal. I am asking for pledges to our funds with acceptances.'

Bel raised her parasol against the sunlight as they

stepped out of the shade. 'I believe it will be a very pleasant day—Lady Rushbrook is lending her ornamental gardens near Richmond. There is a lake, floral walks, a bowling green and an archery lawn and the weather seems set fine.'

The sisters agreed with enthusiasm. Anna, predictably organised, had remembered to carry some of their mother's London cards with her, so she was able to exchange one with Bel in form and they parted with mutual expressions of anticipation.

Bel stood looking after the three sisters as they made their way up towards Piccadilly, Katy already skipping ahead now the pressure of keeping company manners was off. How nice they seemed, how close and affectionate. And how much they looked like Ashe, Katy in particular. Bel thought wistfully of a child like her, Ashe's child.

'*Children?*' she said out loud, earning herself a very strange look from a passing governess with two small charges at her side. Children? But she had never thought of them except as a very vague concept. She had certainly never imagined Henry's children, but now, here she was, thinking yearningly of Ashe's! That was a ridiculous indulgence for a woman who had no wish to remarry.

Flustered, Bel turned on her heel and began to walk briskly towards Fortnum's. She had a long list of items to order for the picnic and a bill for unsatisfactory anchovies to dispute.

Ashe, already feeling harassed by the conflict between his agent's advice on the need to treat the woodworm in the ballroom panelling before doing anything else in the room and his mother's insistence that she wanted to see the effect of painting the pale green woodwork cream before she went off to Brighton, was not best pleased to find himself besieged by all three sisters wanting to discuss Lady Felsham's picnic.

'In a moment—Katy, you are going to get paint on your skirts if you stand over there—Mama, I really think we should allow Mr Grimball to try the wood treatment first. Yes, I do know who you mean, Frederica, of course; Lady Belinda's charity is deserving of support, certainly, but I doubt Mama wants—Katy!'

By the time he had rescued the painter from his sister and despatched her upstairs to change her dress, his other sisters had already told their mother about meeting Lady Belinda and the plans for the picnic.

'Why should you assume I would not want to go, Reynard?' she enquired. 'Thank you, Mr Grimball, if you think it best, the wood treatment first and then the cream paint with the mouldings picked out as we discussed.' Lady Dereham led the way back to the small drawing room, the first room to have been put back into order as a sitting room for the ladies. 'Is this the current Lady Felsham or the widow of the late viscount?'

'The widow,' Ashe said shortly, pretending to be engrossed in the colour samples for the hangings.

'I cannot recall her at all. *He* was the most complete bore, famous for it. He once talked to me about drains for twenty minutes at a levée, and of course I could not escape for we were all standing around waiting to be presented.'

'Felsham caught a chill inspecting drains, that is what carried him off.'

'One is tempted to say it was a judgement, poor

man! I am not surprised his widow has turned to good works, it must seem like a riot of pleasure after life with Henry Cambourn.'

'She appears very competent,' Ashe said dispassionately, flattening every iota of emotion out of his voice.

'She is very pretty,' Frederica remarked. 'And her walking dress was so well cut! I mean to look in *La Belle Assemblée*, for I am certain I saw the very same thing in there. It had a pink satin spencer and a pink-and-rose-striped scarf with lace trim. And the skirt was white muslin, Mama, with folded bands at the hem.'

'It sounds delightful. Very tasteful.' Ashe was conscious of his mother's eyes on him. He had obviously overdone the indifference. 'Your praise of the lady seems somewhat lukewarm, my dear. Merely *very competent*?'

'I hardly notice fashion.' Ashe walked to the window to hold up a sample to the light.

'You notice pretty women, though,' Frederica observed pertly. 'I for one am looking forward to this picnic.'

'It was kind of you to invite my family to the picnic.' Ashe accepted a cup of tea from Bel in her drawing room, taking advantage of a moment to speak to her apart from the rest of the committee.

'If I had known they were in London already, I would have sent a card earlier. Although presumably, as a member of the committee yourself, you were already arranging for them to attend.' She was looking particularly lovely that afternoon, he thought, calmly organising tea for the committee as they stood chatting before gathering round the table to finalise arrangements for the picnic.

'Is that one of Mrs Bell's designs?' he asked abruptly. Bel turned from the tea tray, the flounced hem of her afternoon dress whispering against his ankles. It was in the popular Elizabethan style, he decided, with full gathered sleeves of white muslin emerging from a bodice of striped blue silk. Her face was framed by a pretty stand-up collar, its edges pinked into sharp points.

Ashe found himself staring at the shadows it made on her throat and how the sheen of the simple string of pearls echoed the texture of her skin. Only a little while ago he had been able to bend his head and touch his lips to the pulse that beat just there…

'As it happens, it is. How strange—I would not have expected you to be an authority on ladies' fashions.' Bel reached for a teaspoon, then turned to regard him with a cool gaze. 'Or perhaps I am mistaken and you shop there frequently.'

'No.' That was not true. In the time before Bel he would accompany his latest *chère amie* and indulge her with new gowns as a matter of course. He knew where all the leading modistes were and which would serve their frailer sisters and which would not. The thought recalled his uncomfortable evening after he left Lady Cardew's party.

He had taken a hackney cab and gone straight to the first house on his list, had been halfway up the front steps and had stopped. He could not do it. The memory of Bel's shy passion, the scent of her skin, the generous innocence of her response all contrasted so sharply with the sophisticated, perfumed, commercial pleasures that lay through that door that for a moment he felt a disgust that was almost physical.

He had talked himself into a less dramatic and more

reasonable frame of mind soon enough, but even so he had walked the hot, dark streets aimlessly for two hours before returning to his own bed and a long, restless, frustrated night.

'My sisters read *La Belle Assemblée*,' he explained and the suspicion in Bel's face vanished. 'And all the other fashionable journals as well, for that matter. I was treated to a description of your elegant walking dress after you encountered them in the park.'

'They are very charming. I was particularly taken with Miss Katherine.'

Ashe grimaced. 'She terrifies me. Can you imagine what a nightmare it will be for her chaperon when she comes out? And I pity the poor young men. Mind you, she is determined to marry a duke, so most of them will be safe.'

Bel gave a gurgle of laughter that sent a rush of pure lust shivering through him. Every time he believed himself safe, started to think that they really could just be friends and that in time he would become interested in other women again, she said or did something that transfixed him with the desire to sweep her up in his arms and make love to her, there and then.

A glance around the drawing room, the scene of the last time he had yielded to that impulse, had a sobering effect. To bolster it Ashe collected a second cup and carried it across to Lady James, who was already ensconced in her place at the head of the table. The charity might have been her niece's idea, but there was never any doubt who was in the chair at meetings.

'Thank you, Reynard.' She fixed him with a beady eye. 'I hear your mother is in town.'

'Yes, ma'am.'

'I'll see her the day after tomorrow at this picnic nonsense that Bel is organising. Haven't spoken to her in an age. Brought all your sisters up, has she?'

'Yes, ma'am.'

Lady James's thin lips twitched. 'You don't fool me with your meek *yes, ma'am*. Wishing me at the devil, aren't you?'

'Yes, ma'am,' Ashe responded with a perfectly straight face and took himself off to the foot of the table to discuss the progress of the carpentry work with Patrick Layne. Behind him he heard a rich chuckle. She was a battleaxe, but she was a loyal one, supporting Bel and not letting a hint of what she had seen in this very room escape her.

'Do we need another carpenter on the job?' he asked the other man, trying to ignore the memory of those last, heated moments Bel had been in his arms. Working with Layne was helping to damp down the spark of antagonism between them. It also helped, Ashe realised, that it was a while since he had seen Bel and Layne in a social setting. He was not certain how well his tolerance would hold up to seeing her whirling around in Layne's embrace in a waltz.

'No, it will be finished by the end of the week. Some of the men are helping—I have hopes they may get offers from the craftsmen we are using.'

'Order, ladies and gentlemen!' Lady James rang her teaspoon against her cup. 'Take your places, it is time we began our meeting.'

'...so you can see, the finances are in a very healthy state,' the Reverend Makepeace, in his office as treasurer, closed the ledger and sat back. A murmur of pleased comment broke out around the table and Lady James rapped upon it for attention.

'I believe that concludes our business for the day.'

Bel stood up, glad to be able to move around after an hour of sitting opposite Ashe. Most of the time she simply did not know where to look, for every time she glanced across the table his blue eyes were resting on her, his expression unreadable. Then she would look away, gaze about the room until she felt she must look shifty. Finally she compromised by looking firmly at her notebook and jotting things down, quite superfluously, for Elinor was making her usual competent record.

As the others broke up into smaller groups, she found Ashe at her side. 'May I collect you tomorrow in my carriage for the drive to Richmond? My sisters would enjoy travelling with you and my mother would be delighted to meet you.'

'I…' How could he do it? Bel was certain that anyone could tell they had been lovers, just by seeing them together, yet Ashe appeared quite comfortable at the thought of spending an hour with her under the no doubt intent scrutiny of his mother. 'Thank you, but I am going early, with Miss Ravenhurst, to help organise things.'

'Of course, I should have realised. We will see you there, then.'

'Goodbye, Lady Belinda. I will call for you at eight as agreed, shall I?' It was Patrick Layne, hat in hand, about to take his leave.

'Yes, thank you…' Ashe, standing just behind Mr Layne, raised one sardonic eyebrow and walked out. Bel felt the colour come up under her skin as though she had been caught out in a lie. He must have thought she was using her cousin as an excuse. 'It is very kind of you to take *all three* of us,' she said clearly, but Ashe was into the hall and out of earshot.

'Not at all.' Patrick shook hands and departed, leaving Elinor and her mother alone with Bel.

'That young man pursuing you, Belinda?' Lady James enquired.

'Mr Layne? Goodness me, no.' With any luck he was making subtle advances to Elinor, although she could wish he was rather more bold about it. Still, offering a lift to Lady James was proof enough of devotion, she supposed.

Elinor, looking more than usually expressionless, gathered up her notes and stood patiently waiting for her mother. If only she showed some emotion over the man! Still, Bel consoled herself, she had bullied her cousin into buying a very pleasant afternoon gown, had lent her her own best parasol, and if she did not manage to throw Elinor and Mr Layne together in some romantic spot, then she would be disappointed indeed.

And perhaps if she achieved that, Ashe would stop regarding her as though he thought she was chasing Patrick herself. And he had no right to care about that at all, no more than she would have if she found him flirting with a pretty girl.

Chapter Seventeen

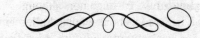

Bel took her disorganised thoughts down to the mews. At least there she could have conversations uncomplicated by emotion, misunderstanding or conventional expectations.

Jem Brown was sitting on the mounting block, his crutch propped up beside him and the *Morning Chronicle* open in his hands. Bel had not realised he could read.

'Good day, my lady.' He tossed away the paper and reached for his crutch.

'No, please, don't stand up.' Bel gestured towards the newspaper. 'Is there anything interesting today? I have not yet had the chance to read it.'

'I wasn't reading the news, ma'am. I was scanning the advertisements.' Brown stuck his hat on the back of his head and gathered up the sheet.

'For work?' One of the grooms emerged from the stables with a wooden chair, dusted it down with his blue-and-white spotted kerchief and set it by the mounting block. 'Thank you, how kind.' Bel settled herself down.

'In a manner of speaking, ma'am. The thing is...' Brown scratched his chin meditatively '...there's a lot of us and what is needed, to my way of thinking, is a way of settling several at once. And there's something in here that's given me an idea like.'

'Go on,' Bel urged.

'See here, ma'am.' He folded the paper and handed it to her. 'Third column on the back page, just below the advertisement for the carriage horses.'

'An inn?' Bel read it and looked up at Brown. The big man endured her scrutiny stolidly. 'Where's St Lawrence?'

'Just inland from Ramsgate, on the Canterbury road. Couldn't be better placed for all the trade to and from the port. And it's a big inn, judging by what it says about the stabling.'

'You want to buy an inn?' Bel queried. 'Do you know anything about running one?'

'If I can run a platoon, I can run an inn,' Brown said. 'I was a sergeant once.' So she had not been wrong, Brown did have the capacity to lead. Bel raised an interrogative eyebrow. 'Swore at a lieutenant, stupid young bu—sprig, and lost my stripes. I can manage it, do the books, keep order. We've got men here who can cook, look after horses, run the cellars. I reckon a place this size—' he tapped the advertisement '—could take twelve of us, one way and another.'

'It would take all the funds and more,' Bel said thoughtfully. It did sound a good idea.

'I know that, ma'am. And I reckon you'll need those funds for more lads in any case. I was wondering if one of your rich friends would lend us the money and we'll pay it back in a few years, regular like.'

'That is an idea, certainly. But I think we ought to look at the place first, don't you, Brown? Get someone to check through the books, see what would need to be done. It may need a lot of money investing.'

'Lewin could do the books, ma'am. He was a book keeper before he joined up.' Bel's astonishment must have showed, because Brown grinned and explained. 'Got himself in a bit of bother with his employer's wife and the army sounded like the healthy option. He doesn't seem so much now, what with his voice and everything getting him down, but he's a bright lad.'

'I'll think about it,' Bel said, getting up from the hard chair. 'And you make a list of all the jobs the men could fill and we'll talk about it after the picnic.'

She walked slowly back up through the garden to the house, mentally reviewing her investments. What would be a reasonable price for an inn and could she afford it? What would Henry have said if he had guessed his wife would ever contemplate buying an inn? Bel laughed out loud, startling the footman on duty in the hall. She could always call it the Felsham Arms.

'This is going to be a complete success.' Elinor leant on the balustrade of the upper terrace two days later and surveyed the closely scythed lawns sweeping down to the lake edge. 'Virtually everyone who accepted seems to have turned up—almost two hundred people!'

'And it feels as though I have shaken every one of them by the hand personally,' Bel said with feeling. The committee members had shared out the meeting and greeting between them and now were circulating, making sure the guests were all enjoying themselves and, with varying degrees of subtlety, working on extracting even more funds.

'Mama is outrageous.' Elinor's tone was dispassionate as she looked for her parent. 'See, she has cornered Uncle Augustus and Aunt Sylvia now.' On the lower terrace below them Lady James was lecturing Augustus Ravenhurst, Bishop of Wessex and his poker-faced wife.

'So she is. I haven't seen Theophilus, have you?' Bel craned to look for the Bishop's only son. With his red hair Theo was usually easy to spot.

'It's an age since I met him—not since I was about ten, I imagine. Mama says he is a scapegrace and a limb of Satan and will not know him.' Elinor twirled the parasol Bel had lent her.

'Poor Theo! He is not as bad as that, and, quite frankly, if Aunt Sylvia was my mama, I would probably turn to wild dissipation in reaction.' When in fact she had managed to behave outrageously with no excuse whatsoever. 'There are Lord Dereham's sisters—that must be their mother, don't you think?'

'Lord Dereham is not with them.' How Elinor managed to insinuate a question into that bland observation, Bel had no idea. If her cousin expected her to express an interest in Ashe's whereabouts, she was not going to oblige her.

'No, he is not. Shall we go down and I will introduce you to them?'

They met the Reynard family at the foot of the terrace steps and between them Anna and Bel performed introductions. Anna began to stroll with Elinor while Frederica lagged behind to look at the progress of a croquet match and Katy skipped along between her mother and Bel.

'I understand my son is an enthusiastic supporter of your charity, Lady Belinda.'

'Yes. He understands the soldiers and they respect him, which is such an asset in the work we are trying to do.'

'I imagine it is. I must admit I was surprised to find him absorbed in charitable work. He has always taken care of our dependents and tenants, of course, but this is rather different. Do tell me, Lady Belinda, how exactly Reynard came to be involved?'

Bel felt herself go hot and cold all over, then told herself it was simply her guilty conscience and Lady Dereham was making conversation, not probing for signs of immorality.

'We met because of my purchasing Lord Dereham's house in Half Moon Street and he told me a little about his military background. When I decided to help the men, he seemed the obvious person to advise us.'

'He discussed his army career with you?' Lady Dereham's fine-drawn brows shot up. 'You have succeeded in gaining his confidence to a greater extent than his sisters and I have, in that case.'

'No doubt he is reticent for fear of distressing you, ma'am,' Bel suggested. 'His experiences must have been harrowing.'

'No doubt.' Bel braced herself for further questions and then relaxed as Ashe's mother enquired, 'Do you stay in London throughout the summer, Lady Belinda?'

'I had intended to,' Bel admitted. 'But now I think I might go down to Margate for a while.'

'Margate? Surely Brighton is more select?'

'So I believe, but at this late stage I am sure I will never secure eligible accommodations in Brighton, and what Margate lacks in royal patronage, I believe it makes up for in the excellence of its sea bathing.' Bel did not think that revealing her intention to inspect an inn with an intention to purchase it would be considered quite the thing. It was not exactly trade, under the circumstances, but it was close enough to be considered shocking, she had no doubt.

Since Brown had shown her the advertisement Bel had made some enquiries of her own and come to the conclusion that Ramsgate might be a little too cosmopolitan and busy, but that a trip to nearby Margate would serve the purpose just as well. Now, talking to Ashe's mother, her resolve hardened; it would be a change of scene and it would remove her completely from all risk of encountering Ashe himself until this foolish yearning for him died down.

She and Elinor parted from the Reynards at the end of the terrace. 'If you will excuse us, we must go and circulate and see if there are any other guests who might be persuaded into taking a more active interest in our cause. If we do not meet again, Lady Dereham, I do trust you have a very pleasant stay in Brighton.'

Bel steered her cousin towards the edge of the lake where Mr Layne was standing beside a vast weeping ash watching the half-dozen or so rowing boats that were dotting the still surface. She had a plan and kept an eye on his broad-brimmed straw hat as they navigated through several brief conversations and two firm promises of help before they reached the water's edge.

'Mr Layne!' He turned and raised his hat. 'Can you row?'

'Why, yes, quite well, I flatter myself. Would you ladies like me to take you out?'

It was even easier than she had expected. 'Yes, please!'

Elinor looked less than entranced at the idea, but permitted herself to be handed down by Patrick and seated while he balanced the small boat. 'I'll untie the rope, shall I?' Bel offered, contriving to both loosen the knot and give the vessel a push as she did so. 'Oh, how clumsy of me! Never mind...' she waved them on as Patrick would have paddled closer '...you go without me; now I see it rock, perhaps I would not like it after all.'

There, now if he has any gumption at all he will contrive to make the best of such privacy, Bel thought smugly, strolling along the narrow strip of bank between the weeping boughs of the tree and the water and watching as Patrick rowed towards the centre of the lake. Elinor had unfurled her parasol and was sitting back, so hopefully that meant she had relaxed somewhat.

Bel paused, finding herself in an unexpectedly quiet and private spot, unable to see the grounds at all and visible only from the boats scattered across the lake. It was pleasant not to have to make conversation for a while and she could puzzle over why the encounter with Lady Dereham had so disconcerted her. For it had, despite the innocuous words they had exchanged. There had been something in the older woman's eyes when she had commented upon Ashe confiding in Bel. And surely there had been something besides polite chitchat in her question about Bel's plans for the summer? Had Lady Dereham wanted her to be in her son's vicinity— or as far away as possible?

She lifted a hand to shade her eyes as she scanned the lake for Patrick and Elinor, but the boats were all too far out now to tell which was which. 'It is very pretty out there,' she commented to a duck that had paddled up, hopeful of a crumb. 'It should be romantic enough for anyone.'

'Nonsense. It might if either of them had the slightest interest in each other.' The voice, so unexpected, made her jump, staring wildly at the duck as though it had spoken. Her foot slipped on the dry grass and she lurched as an arm came from behind her, encircled her waist and lifted her back through the screen of trailing leaves, under the canopy of the tree.

'Ashe!' He set her on her feet, but his arm remained around her waist, holding her close. Bel pressed one hand to her breast, feeling her heart thudding. At his touch every one of the feelings she had been so rigorously suppressing came flooding back. 'You scared the wits out of me—I thought it was the duck talking.'

Ashe, as far as she could see in the deep shade, looked less than delighted to be mistaken for poultry. The old weeping ash enclosed them totally. It was like being inside a giant green parasol with the light filtered through the leaves and only the occasional small gap allowing sunbeams to penetrate. Outside she could hear the loud buzz of conversation, the distant strains of the orchestra on the upper terrace and occasional shrieks of laughter from playing children. Inside they were in a private world of their own.

'I would suggest that you will hear more sense from me than you will from that duck,' Ashe remarked as a plaintive quack from outside marked the creature's disappointment at her disappearance.

'I have no idea what you are talking about,' Bel said stiffly, furious with herself at her reaction to him and her desire to take the short step closer that would bring her right into his arms. The pulse in her neck was racing and quite another, shameful, pulse of arousal quivered into life.

'Your delusion that you can matchmake between Layne and your cousin. She is not remotely interested and he, as is quite apparent to everyone else, is dangling after you.'

'He is not,' Bel retorted furiously. *Patrick? Dangling after me?* 'And that is a horrid expression. *Dangling* indeed!'

Is he? She had acknowledged Patrick Layne's attraction and had dismissed it because she had no desire for anyone but Ashe. But that had been when she and Ashe were lovers. And now? Was Patrick really attracted to her? If he was, why did she not feel happy about it? He was a handsome, kind, intelligent man. *And I am free*, a little voice said inside her head.

'Bel? What is wrong?' Ashe tipped up her chin, turning her face so a shaft of sunlight from above fell across her features. 'There are tears in your eyes.'

'There are no such things.' She swallowed what felt horribly like a sob. 'I have the sun in my eyes, that is all.' *I am free, and I do not want to be.*

'Nonsense.' He gathered her efficiently into the white linen waistcoat he was wearing under his pale tan coat. The broad brim of his fine straw hat bumped against the edge of her bonnet and he took it off, tossing it to one side before tackling the primrose satin ribbons under her chin. 'This is a very pretty piece of frippery, but I believe we can dispense with it.' The bonnet slid down her back to the grass. 'Now, then. Do you want Patrick Layne?'

'No.' Bel put every ounce of sincerity into the

denial. 'Of course I do not. He is a very pleasant man, but that is all.'

'Excellent. Because I still want you Bel. Very much. And it is a trifle disconcerting wondering what deep game you are playing with the poor man.'

'I am not playing any game.' Bel sighed. 'I just want to rescue Elinor from Aunt Louisa and I thought they would suit.'

'Even though you do not think marriage is a good thing?'

'It is not for me, but that is not to say it might be perfectly all right for someone else. And Elinor—'

'Elinor is an intellectual. She needs someone who can match her in that, not a respectable, conventional chap like Layne. Have you got any bachelor intellectuals up your sleeve?'

'None. And you are quite right, I should not matchmake.'

'There's nothing wrong with it in principle—I am in trouble with my mother for matchmaking for Frederica.'

'You are?' Bel gazed up at him, fascinated, her own preoccupations momentarily forgotten. 'With whom?'

'Our estate manager. I think he'll do, and she fancies herself in love with him, but he'll need to prove himself.'

'Goodness, how very kind of you.'

Ashe shrugged. 'I want them all to be happy.'

'And what about you?' Bel murmured.

'I would rather like to be happy too.' Ashe's smile was crooked. 'It is two weeks, Bel—will you come back to me again?'

'Is that why you were following me? To ask that?'

She wanted him, badly, so badly she had no idea whether she could trust her own judgement or not.

'No, this was a coincidence. I came in here for some solitude, to think. A weeping ash—rather apt, don't you think?'

'You are not weeping,' Bel pointed out, the pattering of her pulse making it hard to think clearly.

'No, not yet. I have missed you very much, though.'

'We have met, quite often,' she pointed out, trying to be reasonable and rational. His fingertips, which had been under her chin, slid round to cup the back of her head. Reasonable and rational thought became harder.

'That is not what I mean.'

'You have missed making love?'

'So much that I ache. And I have missed talking to you alone. I have missed your company, *ma belle*.'

'You must not call me that.' She heard the betraying shake in her voice and fought not to move her head against the warm support of his palm.

'No? You have not missed me at all?'

'Of course I have. I have missed talking to you, I have missed making love with you and I have told myself it is right that it has ended and I will miss you less with time. It will become easier.' She saw from his expression that he did not believe it and knew that her own certainty was less than complete. 'Besides,' she added briskly, trying to tell herself that this was not something she should mind, 'you are a man—it is easy for you to find consolation elsewhere, at least for your physical needs.'

'You would think so,' Ashe said. 'But I find that I cannot bring myself to seek that…consolation, however much I need it.'

'Oh.' Bel found she could not meet his eyes, could not look into his face, which he was keeping so carefully neutral without a hint of need or entreaty showing. 'I must choose, then?'

'Yes, because I have chosen, but it needs both of us. I want you for my lover, Bel, you and no one else, but I am not going to persuade you or coerce you or seduce you.'

She had been standing with her hands clasped to her bosom as though that would still the pounding of her heart. Now, seemingly of their own accord, they reached out and flattened themselves against the smooth linen of his summer waistcoat.

Under her palm the thud of his heart seemed uneven, as she had never felt it. Her eyes fixed on the back of her hands as she let them slide up, under the lapels of his coat, up until they encircled his neck and her gaze rose to his mouth. He licked his lips, a sudden, uncharacteristically uncertain gesture and she rose up on tiptoe and pressed her mouth to his, heat to heat, need to need.

'*Aah.*' He sighed against her lips and was still, his arms holding her just as she was for a long, aching moment. Then he pulled her in hard, his mouth claiming hers, claiming her again, his tongue sweeping in to remind her—as if she could have forgotten—of the taste of him, of the passion of him, of what his body and hers meant together.

Yes, she said in her mind as her fingers laced up into his hair, the elegant strength of his skull familiar to her touch. *Yes, this is my man.* Ashe's hands slid down her back, lifting against him, reminding her, as though she needed it, of how his body, roused, felt against hers. He was hard with his need for her, she ached with hers for him. *Tonight, oh, yes, tonight.*

The pressure of his mouth on hers was savage with a need that she responded to shamelessly, unafraid, triumphant that he wanted her like this, above all others.

Mine. My man, my lover, my love…

My love. The thought lanced through her like a lightning strike and she trembled in his arms. *I love him.* It changed everything. It changed her world for ever. It was the end.

Chapter Eighteen

I love you. It was a disaster. Bel freed Ashe's head, put her hands on his shoulders and pushed, dragging her mouth from his.

'Bel? What is wrong?' He sounded as shaken as she felt.

'I cannot. I… This is all wrong. Ashe, I cannot be your lover again.'

'I do not understand.' He stood there in the green shade, inches from her, their arms still around each other, their breath mingling. 'How can you say that? When you kiss me—'

I do not understand either, but I love you and I cannot do this. Not if you do not love me. Not when I want you for ever.

'I cannot explain,' Bel whispered. 'But I cannot be with you any longer. Ashe, I am sorry—'

There were no words. Her tongue dry and clumsy, Bel wrenched herself out of his encircling arms, snatched up her hat and stumbled through the screen of leaves to the lake edge. Out of the strange green shade and into the fresh air she felt as though she had woken from a weird dream.

Reality. She had to pull herself together and be seen. As one of the hostesses, there was no hiding. It was the work of a moment to jam her hat back on her head and tie the ribbons, to smooth down her skirts and to walk briskly along to where the lawn opened out again.

Seconds, and she was back in the midst of the party, smiling and nodding, stopping to scoop up an escaping toddler and return him to his flustered nursemaid. She did not dare look behind her to see if Ashe had come out too or whether he was recovering from her outburst in privacy.

Things were suddenly very clear. Painful, but clear… Bel tried to think, heard her name, stopped. 'Lady St Andrews, good afternoon. Lovely, is it not? We are so lucky to have such fine weather.' An exchange of bows, smiles, on to the next group. 'Mrs Truscott, thank you so much for your kind donation. Yes, such a worthy cause…'

She loved Ashe. No wonder she recoiled now from the thought of simply being his lover. It had been one thing when all she felt for him was liking, attraction and respect. She could share how she felt with him and be honest. An equal. But she could not tell him she loved him, or he would think she expected him to marry her. And snatched nights of lovemaking were no longer enough, not when she yearned for a lifetime together. And not when she could not trust herself not to speak her feelings in the throes of passion.

Bel found herself next to an unoccupied Gothic bench and sank down on it, her fingers twitching her skirts into order without conscious thought. What a blind fool she had been, to imagine that just because her marriage to Henry had been dull, loveless, pointless, that therefore she could never find a man with whom it would be wonderful. And she could hardly tell Ashe now that she had changed her mind, and why—not after protesting so vehemently that she would never marry again.

He had asked her to marry him because he had compromised her and because, she supposed, he was aware that soon he must find himself a wife to carry on his line and share his life. If he had loved her, surely that was the time to tell her? Ashe was no coward, he would not hesitate for fear of a rebuff. Instead, when he had mentioned love, it was to make it more than clear he neither felt it nor understood it.

'Belinda.'

'Aunt Sylvia, Uncle Augustus.' Bel jumped to her feet. 'I am so sorry, I was just resting…'

The Bishop regarded her with stern benevolence, his wife simply sternly. But then she rarely approved of anyone. 'Is your brother back from his honeymoon yet?'

'No, not yet. Sebastian and the Grand Duchess will remain in Maubourg for the summer in any case,' Bel explained. She was sure Lord Augustus did not approve of Sebastian's marriage, but it was difficult for such a pillar of the Establishment to criticise a nephew's connection to a member of the ruling house of an allied state. 'I have not seen Cousin Theo here today. Is he well?'

'Theophilus has departed on the Grand Tour,' his mother said repressively. 'It is to be hoped that a prolonged period of study of the great antiquarian sights will enable him to fix his mind upon a suitable future career.' Her expression implied a grim disbelief that he would do any such thing.

Given that Theo was wild to a fault, it was hard to imagine what that career might be. Certainly not the church! 'His languages are good, are they not?' Bel offered. 'Perhaps the diplomatic service?'

That earned her a frosty stare from her aunt. Oh, well, at least poor Theo was having a holiday; she very much doubted that he was applying himself to serious study.

'Are you remaining in London throughout the summer, Belinda?' The question was not accompanied by an invitation to stay at the Bishop's Palace, much to Bel's relief.

'I am going to Margate, Uncle, for the sea bathing.'

'Not by yourself, I trust?'

'Goodness no, with Cousin Elinor.' Bel crossed her fingers. Elinor was probably not speaking to her after being cast adrift on the lake with Patrick Layne.

After a short lecture on the perils of the unsuitable company to be found at seaside resorts and a warning about the moral inadmissibility of sea bathing on a Sunday, her uncle and aunt moved on, leaving Bel wishing she had a fan with her. What was the time? She glanced up at the clock tower over the stables: only half past two. It would be hours before she could go home and have some peace in which to contemplate a lifetime without the man she loved.

There was Ashe to avoid, Elinor to placate and Patrick Layne to evade also, if what Ashe thought was true. Then there were the endless encounters with the guests and potential donors to endure with a smiling face, alert for every opportunity to secure support.

'There you are!' It was Elinor, alone and none too pleased with her cousin if her thinned lips and aggressively tilted parasol were anything to go by. The hem of her pretty new dress was wet. 'I never want to be that close to a duck again! What on earth did you think—?'

'I am sorry.' Bel spoke before her cousin could manage another word. 'I thought you and Mr Layne might find you would suit if I threw you together. I was wrong.'

The wind taken out of her sails by this frank acknowledgement, Elinor sat down beside her and adjusted her parasol so that it shaded them both. 'Well, I never thought you would give up on the matchmaking just like that. You do realise that Mr Layne's interests lie elsewhere, don't you?'

'You mean with me? Yes, Ashe told me so. I had no idea.'

Elinor's strong dark brows rose. '*Ashe*, is it?'

There was no one close by. Suddenly the strain of keeping it all locked inside was too much. 'Yes. Elinor, I love him.' Said out loud, it was terrifying.

'But that is wonderful.' Elinor beamed at her. 'I do wish you both happy!'

'He does not love me.' It hurt to say it. Bel licked her lips and swallowed, terrified she might cry, here, where everyone could see her. She sucked in her stomach, straightened her back and sat up, deportment-class poised, focusing everything on presenting a tranquil face.

'Oh. But surely—I have seen the way he looks at you.'

'Lord Dereham desires me. It is not at all the same thing, believe me.'

'And?' Elinor prompted, her head cocked on one side like an inquisitive sparrow. Bel could feel the colour flooding her cheeks. 'Bel—you haven't? You and he are not…'

'Yes, we were.' It was highly improper to say any of

this to an unmarried young woman, but Elinor, at twenty-four, was hardly just out of the schoolroom. And Bel knew she could trust her. 'But not any more.'

'Why ever not?' Elinor was shockingly unshocked. She frowned in thought as though Bel's words were some obscure Greek text, then her brow cleared. 'I see. You have realised you love him and to continue as his lover is too painful when what you want is to be wed. He does not love you, but if you tell him how you feel he will be honour bound to offer for you and that would be intolerable.'

'You understand so clearly?' How did Elinor, who was apparently immune to thoughts of love, fathom that? Presumably by applying the same clear-eyed analysis that she used on ancient texts. 'I have been so confused, and then I realised how I felt about him and it was awful.'

'You *are* rather close to it. For someone not emotionally involved it is a simple matter of logic,' Elinor said tactfully. 'What are you going to do now? I can quite see how you would shrink from allowing him to glimpse your feelings.'

'I am going to run away to Margate. Will you come too?' Bel began to explain about the inn at St Lawrence's. 'We could take Brown and Lewin with us, along with a maid for the two of us, and a footman would be handy, I think. We could go down by river on the Margate packet. I am sure the boat journey will be more pleasant than the route by coach, and probably easier for the men than being shut up in a carriage for hours.' She watched Elinor anxiously. 'Would Aunt Louisa mind, do you think?'

'She is going to stay with Aunt and Uncle Augustus

for two weeks with the intention of subjecting Uncle's restoration proposals for the cathedral to the strictest scrutiny; believe me, she will not need me and I will be only too happy to escape the Palace.' Elinor slid her hand into Bel's lax one and gave it a squeeze. 'We will run away together and go dipping in the sea and be so shocking as to inspect inns with Brown and Lewin and take a subscription to the circulating library and read all the newest sensation novels and eat ice cream every day.'

The prospect of such mildly wicked entertainment made Bel smile faintly. 'And forget about men?'

'I do not have one to forget, but for you I doubt it will be that easy, not if you love Lord Dereham,' Elinor said frankly. 'I don't pretend to understand love, but I expect you will mope a little; I won't mind that, you mope as much as you like and I will read.'

'Oh, bless you.' The thought of uncomplicated feminine company was heaven. She made herself sit up straight and release Elinor's hand, doing her best to present a smiling face to the passers-by. 'Miss Layne!' Oh, dear, that was perhaps one female friend she did not want to have to talk to just at the moment. What if Patrick had said something about her to his sister, or she had guessed her brother might be harbouring a liking for Bel?

'What an interesting party this is.' Elinor moved along the seat to make space between herself and Bel and the poetess sat down. She was without a parasol and the tip of her nose was red with the sun, but she had her notebook open in her hand and Bel could see it was full of scribblings. 'I have lost my sunshade somewhere.' She flapped a hand vaguely. 'But I have so many notes. Have you seen Patrick, Lady Belinda?'

'He kindly took me out on the lake,' Elinor interjected, 'but I have not seen him for perhaps half an hour.' She must have decided that it would be a good idea to steer the conversation away from him, for she added chattily, 'Cousin Belinda and I were just making plans for a trip to Margate. We think we will go down on one of the packets; it will be quite an adventure.'

'What an excellent idea.' Miss Layne appeared quite struck by the notion. 'I was only saying to Patrick that I would like to go to the seaside now it is getting so hot, but that I find Brighton rather trying with so many of the Regent's cronies everywhere you go. I shall find him and suggest we follow your example.' She got to her feet and shut her notebook with a snap. 'When will you be going?'

'I…er…it is not yet quite decided,' Bel groped for an answer that did not sound discourteous. 'I have not yet secured accommodations.'

'Do, please, let me know as soon as it is settled. It will be so pleasant to have acquaintances there.' Miss Layne beamed at them and hurried off.

'Oh, dear, I had no idea she would take me up so!' Elinor said in dismay. 'And Mr Layne is certain to accompany her. We can hardly change our plans now.'

'Never mind.' It had been too good to be true, Bel thought. A fantasy of untroubled escape just as her love affair had been a fantasy of uncomplicated pleasure. 'It will give me the opportunity to make clear to Mr Layne that I cannot return his regard, I suppose.'

A perusal of the guidebooks at the library revealed that the Royal Hotel was considered to be the most eligible lodging. *'For neatness, comfort and luxury, the Royal Hotel will not suffer in comparison with any house in the country,'* Elinor read out. Bel, determined to fix her mind upon practical matters, conjured up a smile and hid her yawns behind the packet company's literature. Insomnia was claiming her nights again and she was doggedly ploughing her way through everything Lord Byron had written, trying to distract her mind from a flesh-and-blood man with the highly coloured adventures of the poet's heroes.

Confirmation of a suite being set aside for their convenience came by return, and Brown and Lewin assured Bel that they were more than capable of finding lodgings for themselves in the town once they arrived.

'I have tickets for the packet.' Bel opened a package delivered as she and Elinor sat at breakfast the day after Lady James had departed for her ecclesiastical holiday. She had left her daughter in Half Moon Street with a stack of reading matter, most of which Elinor ruthlessly stowed in a cupboard.

'I am taking nothing but frivolity and guidebooks,' she pronounced. 'When do we sail?'

'Tomorrow morning at seven.' Bel scrutinised the accompanying pamphlet. 'We leave from Ralph's Quay near Billingsgate and we should arrive in Margate at about three or four in the afternoon, depending on the wind.'

'There is a letter from Miss Layne.' Elinor flattened out the sheet. 'She says she had secured rooms at Wright's York Hotel on Marine Parade and leaves this morning. She and Mr Layne look forward to meeting us there…she will review all the subscription rooms to ascertain which is best in advance of our arrival.'

'At least they will not be in the same hotel, so it will be less difficult to avoid Mr Layne. If it were not for the awkwardness of that, I would be glad to have their company.' Bel said, turning over the remains of her post.

Nothing from Ashe, of course. Why should she expect it? She had thrown herself into his arms and then rebuffed him without explanation; the man would have to be a saint to overlook that, and, whatever else Ashe was, he was not a saint. The recollection of just how unsaintly Ashe could be burned through her like a draught of strong wine.

'What is that rueful smile about?' Elinor paused with a piece of bread and jam halfway to her lips. 'Mr Layne? You simply have to continue as before, only this time pretending you do not notice his partiality. Either he will take the hint or he will make a declaration.'

'I do not like to think I could hurt him,' Bel said, suddenly worried. 'It never occurred to me that he might feel like that about me until Ashe pointed it out. You do not think he feels strongly, do you?'

Elinor shrugged in a thoroughly unladylike manner. 'I have no experience of such matters—but you most certainly have not been encouraging him.'

'True.' Comforted, Bel wiped her fingers and gathered up the papers that strewed the breakfast table. 'There is a lot to do, and not much time. Certainly no time to sit around brooding about men. I think we had better make a list and divide things up between us.'

It had not occurred to Bel to spend her guineas on a private stateroom for the space of a few hours' voyage on a fine August day. The deck of the packet boat was spacious and tidy, with benches for those who wished to sit, and between them Brown, Lewin and Peter, the footman Aunt Louisa had left with Elinor, soon had their baggage piled up and securely corded under a tarpaulin.

Elinor, her bonnet inelegantly tied on with a shawl against sea breezes, was guarding a large picnic hamper. Bel strolled up and down the deck with Millie, the maid's eyes wide with the adventure of her first trip outside London, at her side. She surveyed her little party with proprietorial pride, just as Peter turned an unpleasant shade of green and rushed to the side to be comprehensively sick.

'We have not cast off yet!' Bel said with exasperated sympathy. 'Elinor, do you have anything we can dose him with?'

'I've just the thing, ma'am.' Brown produced a flask from under his greatcoat and hauled the unfortunate footman upright. Lewin pressed a blue-spotted handkerchief into Peter's hands. 'Come along, cully, we'll soon put the roses back in your cheeks,' Brown promised. 'Here you go, down the pointed end where the breeze is good and fresh.'

Bel watched the three of them passing the flask around. 'They'll have him as drunk as a lord by the time we get there,' she prophesied, then grinned, suddenly carefree at the thought of their unconventional day's holiday. 'What would your mama say if she could see us now?' she said to Elinor who was watching, wide-eyed, as a cit in a startlingly striped waistcoat pushed his wife, vast in pink bombazine, up the gangplank. Her shrieks of terror competed with the circling gulls.

'She would say that we had taken leave of our senses,' her cousin replied with a grin, jamming her hat down with one hand. 'Fun, isn't it?'

'Yes.' Bel smiled back. *I wonder what Ashe is doing.*

Chapter Nineteen

'I regret to say that Lady Belinda is not at home, my lord,' Hedges said.

'Then please give her my card and tell her I called. When do you expect that she will be returned?' Ashe reached into his breast pocket for his card case. There was something particularly expressionless about Bel's butler this morning. Almost disapproving, which was ridiculous. It was not Hedges's place to disapprove of him—unless whatever it was that had led to Bel's strange mood four days ago was infecting him also.

It had been hard to wait, to brood on what had happened in that dreamlike green space. In a moment Bel had turned from a passionate wanton in his arms to a stranger, rejecting him, spurning the kisses she had incited only seconds before. Ashe had paced the floor of his bedchamber, had sat silent and uncommunicative in his clubs, had thrown away good hands because he was not concentrating on play, and still he did not know what had happened.

It had hardly been something he had said—his mouth

had been on hers from the moment she had melted into his arms. So it had to be something in her head, something that had changed for Bel. And now her butler, who had always seemed to regard him with as much approval as such an individual ever showed, was fixing him with a chilly stare.

'Her ladyship is out of town, my lord.'

'Indeed? Where has she gone?'

'I could not say, my lord.'

Of course he could, Ashe thought, regarding the man through narrowed eyes. He could, but he would not. And that could only be because Bel had instructed the butler not to tell him. Hence Hedges's air of disapproval; it would be enough to be told her ladyship did not want her whereabouts communicated to Lord Dereham for that to be taken as an indication that he had upset her.

His fingers closed around the coins in his pocket, then relaxed. Hedges was not the sort of upper servant who would accept a guinea or two to flout his mistress's instructions.

'Yes, I am sure that is the case.' Ashe allowed the edge of his temper to show. 'Are you forwarding her correspondence to her ladyship?'

'I have specific instructions as to which items to forward, my lord.' He realised suddenly that Hedges was enjoying this as little as he was.

'Her ladyship is well, I trust?'

There was an hesitation, the merest flicker of the studiedly blank expression. 'Her ladyship enjoys her usual good health. If there is nothing else, my lord?'

'No, thank you, Hedges.' Ashe turned and walked slowly down the steps as the door closed behind him.

Her customary good health, but not, he would guess, *her customary good spirits*. And what was the matter with him? Moping because, for once, a mistress had taken the initiative and ended a relationship?

Yes, that for sure. He could identify the coiling strands of wounded pride and frustrated passion knotting in his stomach. But there was something else. He wanted Bel, all of Bel, not just her body. His feet carried him around the curve of Half Moon Street and into the turmoil of Piccadilly. Ashe stared at it as though seeing it through glass a foot thick. What was he doing here? This was unreal, irrelevant, unimportant. He shook his head, trying to clear it, then set off up the slope towards the Albany. What he wanted—no, needed—to do must wait until nightfall.

Distantly a clock struck two. Under his hand the key turned in the lock and the garden door swung open on to darkness. Ashe eased off his shoes and padded along the corridor, into the hall and up the stairs to Bel's bed-chamber. Around him the house breathed in its sleep, timber softly creaking, clocks ticking, the soundless pad of the kitchen cat's hunting footsteps.

It held people, sleeping, but it did not hold Bel. He could feel her absence as a physical thing as he opened the door to what had once been his room, the long-familiar embossing of the door handle reassuring to his hand.

Inside the faint light from the street picked up the great white fur sprawled before the cold hearth, the glint of glass eyes in the head turned snarling towards him.

'Hello, Horace.' Ashe shrugged out of his coat and

folded down cross-legged on to the thick fur. It yielded beneath him and he flattened his palms at his sides, letting his fingers thread into the pelt. The faint smell as he disturbed it was of dusty old fur, of wood ash and of Bel.

Ashe allowed his shoulders to relax and drop, lifted his hands to his knees and let them rest, palm up, cupped. He felt his breathing slow and his mind clear. Long ago, at school, he had learned this from a fellow pupil, the son of a maharajah, sent to the cold, harsh world of an English education. Ashe had befriended the slender, golden-skinned, terrified boy and had marvelled at his poise and his resilience as he adapted to this hostile new world.

And in return for Ashe's cutting tongue and ready fists, both deployed in his defence, his new friend had taught him a secret. He could not remember now what this strange weapon of the mind was called, only that he had used it before battle, when his father had died so suddenly and when Katy had been taken dangerously ill with a fever and the whole family despaired for her life. It left him focused and strong and calm. Now he turned it inwards to try to read his own heart.

The clocks in the house struck and tinkled and chimed the quarters as Ashe sat there, his eyes wide open on to the darkness, his fingers sliding from his knees to mesh in the thick fur. When five clear chimes reached him, each as distinct as a hammer blow, the answer came with them, the words, clear on his lips. 'I love her.'

The relief of understanding his own feelings washed through him, breaking his calm, and Ashe jerked to his feet and began to pace. He had been right when he had said to Bel that surely love was something you recognised when you felt it. The moment he had stopped fighting against it, it claimed him.

Bel had come to fill his mind, his thoughts, his dreams. She had slipped in there without him being conscious of it, driving away his nightmares of battle, replacing them with the sweetness of her, the ache of needing her.

The sheer physicality of this new emotion surprised him. He wanted to shout, to run, to ride at the gallop to wherever Bel was, take her in his arms and shower her with kisses.

But the woman he loved did not want his kisses any more, she was not in love with him and she did not want to marry him.

Ashe found himself by the fur again and sat down abruptly, the burst of energy vanishing as fast as it had seized him. Bel had rejected him and she had fled from him—why, he had no idea. He needed to find her and then, assuming he managed that, he must persuade her to marry him.

Damn it, he thought with a flash of anger, he was eligible enough. Once his mother began to whisper that he was in the market for a wife, every single lady under the age of thirty would be trotted out for his inspection. But he wanted none of them. He wanted the one single lady in society who did not want marriage—or, it seemed, him.

Simply proposing was not going to do the trick, she would just refuse. If he made a declaration of love, she would counter with her accusation of emotional black-mail. So he would have to court her, something he had never had to do before with any woman, and he had to do it without making her feel trapped. Before he had met Bel, Ashe would have accepted quite easily the proposition that he could make a lady fall in love with him if he exerted himself enough. Now that smug masculine confidence deserted him and in its place was a growing chill, the thought of what his life would be like without her now that he knew that he loved her.

'One battle at a time,' he murmured to Horace, pulling the moth-eaten ear nearest to him. 'I've got to find her first.'

The effect of a virtually sleepless night and the pressing request from Lady Dereham to join her and her daughters at the breakfast table in the town house, at an hour which he stigmatised to his valet as the *crack of dawn*, had Ashe stifling his yawns and gazing with unfocused eyes at the back page of *The Times*.

Around him his sisters prattled happily of their plans for the seaside while his mother slit the wafers on her morning's correspondence. 'Excellent!' He glanced up to see she was scanning some missive or another and went back to his sightless contemplation of an advertisement for a new three-volume work on Classical mythology, a subject in which he had no interest whatsoever.

'Reynard!' From the tone, she had obviously already addressed him. Ashe forced his mind back to the present and away from plans to hire Bow Street Runners to check at every tollgate out of London for sightings of Bel's carriage.

'Mama?' He folded the news sheet neatly beside his plate and assumed an expression of filial attentiveness.

'I have here confirmation from the best hotel in Margate that I have secured their most superior apartments for three weeks. I shall write and cancel Brighton immediately.'

'Margate? But, Mama, the shops…' Frederica wailed.

'But the parties at the Castle Inn…' That was Anna.

'I wanted to drive a donkey cart again,' Katy said mulishly.

'I have been worried for some time about the tone of some members of society one finds at Brighton at this time of year,' Lady Dereham pronounced. 'Too many rakes and beaux. And the sea bathing at Margate is much superior, the beach is sand and the bay well sheltered.'

'This is rather sudden, is it not, Mama?' Ashe asked, frowning at her. There was something that did not quite ring true about his mother's explanations.

'I have been thinking about it ever since Lady Belinda Felsham told me she was going there.' She paused and studied Ashe. 'Your mouth is open, dear.'

He shut it with a snap. 'Be…Lady Belinda has gone to Margate?' *It is going to be this simple to find her?*

'Yes, with her cousin and the Laynes, I believe,' his mother said tranquilly. He almost took her tone at its face value, then something in the closeness with which she was watching him caught his attention. This was nothing to do with dubious company at Brighton—Lady Belinda had caught his mother's eye as a suitable bride. He frowned, deliberately, and saw the anxiety in her eyes.

'Do you still wish me to accompany you?' Ashe let a faint tinge of reluctance colour his voice. 'I had made plans to meet a number of friends in Brighton. I suppose I could go there and travel round the coast once or twice to see you.' To have discovered Bel's whereabouts so easily was a miracle, but he had no intention of letting his mother guess he had already lost his heart. This wooing was going to need subtlety, not the intervention of well-meaning relatives.

'I am sorry to disrupt your plans, dear,' Lady Dereham said hastily, 'but I really do feel I would need you more than ever in a strange resort.'

Ashe pursed his lips and regarded the four pairs of eyes fixed on his face. It was cruel to tease them, and, if they could only guess, he was within an inch of leaping to his feet and hugging his mother out of sheer gratitude. 'In that case, of course I will accompany you,' he said, smiling, and trying to ignore the sensation in the pit of his stomach that was warning him that it was only the easy part out of the way. Now he had to woo his reluctant love.

'Do you intend to dip?' Miss Layne viewed the ranks of bathing machines drawn up on the sweep of golden tan sand below the Marine Parade dubiously.

The two parties had exchanged notes the night before and had met by agreement outside one of the numerous establishments advertising steam and vapour baths, warm saltwater baths and attended dipping from the shelter of a bathing machine.

'I *think* so.' Elinor, equally dubious, watched a female bather, clad head to foot in fashionable attire, being helped up the steps into a bathing machine. The horse was harnessed to the shafts and a muscular woman kilted up her skirts and hauled herself up on to the seat beside the driver. The vehicle set off down the beach and into the mild surf. Once the water was up to the base of the compartment, the driver slid down, unhitched the horse and rode it back up, ready for the next customer.

'What is she doing now?' Miss Layne enquired, raising her eyeglass in an effort to see better. 'Patrick, you have a telescope.'

'And I am certainly not going to deploy it upon a bathing machine occupied by a female,' he said with a grin. 'What sort of fellow do you take me for? Do you want me escorted off by the beadle?'

'I only want to see what is happening,' his sister protested. 'Oh, look, the woman is letting down the hood.' Sure enough, a great canvas awning was falling down to shield the entrance into the machine and covering an area of sea quite one hundred feet square, by Bel's estimation.

'There is enough space to swim in,' she said thoughtfully. The idea of being forcibly dunked by one of the large dippers was not appealing, but she could swim quite well and the thought of doing so in the sea was very tempting.

'It all looks far too cold and exposed for my liking.' Miss Layne shivered. 'I intend to take one of the warm water baths. What about you, Patrick?'

'Oh, I shall swim,' he said. 'Without the assistance of one of the dippers, I might add. Shall I go and find out what is the best time to come back this afternoon?'

'If you would, dear. I shall go and put my name down for a warm bath.'

'Please, add mine,' Elinor added hastily. 'The more I think about it, the less I fancy all that cold water.'

Bel adjusted her parasol to shield her cheeks from the sun and sat down upon one of the benches that lined the Marine Parade. The scene on the beach below was sufficiently engrossing to while away any amount of time, and beyond the bay there were the comings and goings at the pier to add animation.

Behind her a chattering group of washerwomen strode up the hill, their baskets overflowing with towels from the various bathing establishments and sweating porters in their white smocks struggled with the luggage from the packet boats and hoys newly tied up.

She eyed the ladies timorously walking out to the bathing machines, studying their complex bathing costumes. Her own, an elaborate confection of pink and green fabric, had fluttering green zigzag trim at the hem and neck, which she suspected was supposed to be seaweed. The only relevance it had to bathing, as far as she could make out, was that it was cotton and would therefore dry easily, and fastened at the front, which would make it easy to undress to reveal the utilitarian flannel garment beneath in which she was supposed to take to the waters. Bel had no intention of trying to swim in that. Thanks to the all-covering hoods, invented fifty years before by the enterprising Mr Beale, she could disport herself naked in perfect modesty, just as that worthy Quaker had intended.

And as the men still did, she thought, rather naughtily letting her gaze stray along the beach to where the men's machines were drawn up. Gentlemen were strolling down to those in light cotton trousers and shirts, straw hats tipped negligently over their brows. As she watched, a tall figure came into view, raised his hat in response to a greeting from a fellow bather and the breath caught in her throat. Blond hair glinted in the sunshine and no one else, surely, moved with quite that long-limbed elegance?

'Ashe?' Her fingers clenched around the iron rail

and she gave a little gasp of pain as the rough, rusty surface cut into her thin cotton gloves. He had followed her here? Somehow, despite the fact that she had told her staff to refuse to say where she had gone, he had found her. Bel sat quite still, the joy bubbling within her, as she watched him swing up easily into the bathing machine and disappear inside the wooden cabin.

'Bel? We are ready to go now.' Elinor and the Laynes stood beside her, eager to be off on the next part of their morning's exploration. 'We are going to take out subscriptions at the lending library, don't you remember?'

'Oh. Yes, of course. Only it is so lovely here, I think I will just sit a little and take in the air. You register my name for me, please, Elinor.' Ashe cared for her—there was no other explanation for the fact that he had abandoned his family party and come here. 'It is quite all right,' she said, urging a dubious Elinor to follow the Laynes towards the High Street. 'I will be quite safe—look how many respectable families there are here.'

Ashe's bathing machine began to move, down to the sea. In her mind's eye she could imagine him in the dark space, stripping off his clothes, bracing himself with those long, muscular legs against the sway of the vehicle, stepping out into the light under the canvas and…

'There are, indeed,' Elinor exclaimed with a laugh. 'Look who is walking down the hill towards us—Lady Dereham and all three girls.'

'What?' Bel swung round as Elinor waved and Katy ran to meet her.

'Good morning, Miss Ravenhurst, Lady Belinda! Isn't this exciting? I was disappointed about Brighton, but this will be just as good and Frederica is taking me bathing tomorrow!'

'Yes, very exciting,' Bel agreed, the backwash of disappointment leaving her queasy with reaction. Ashe hadn't come for her after all, he had come with his family. He had no idea she was here. She made herself stand up as Lady Dereham and her two elder daughters reached her and shook hands, finding a bright social smile from somewhere. 'What a surprise, I thought you were fixed upon Brighton this summer.'

'And you are all here together?' Elinor asked, earning her Bel's undying gratitude.

'Yes, indeed. Reynard had gone sea bathing.'

'No doubt he was surprised I had recommended Margate,' Bel remarked idly.

'I did not mention that you had done so.' Lady Dereham watched her daughters petting a small dog another promenader had at the end of a green cord. 'Although I am sure your opinion would have weighed with me if I had needed to use any persuasion.'

So Ashe had no idea that she was there. The last trickle of hope ebbed away. After the way she had reacted at the picnic, she should have had no hope that he would have any interest in her any more and yet some foolish part of her heart held on to the dream that he did care for her, more than as a lover and a friend.

The awning at the seaward end of his bathing machine unfurled itself to the waves. Bel dragged her gaze away and fiddled unnecessarily with her parasol. 'I am afraid we must catch up with our friends the Laynes, but I am sure we will meet again, Lady Dereham.'

'You have gone very pale,' Elinor observed as they walked up the gentle hill towards the circulating library. 'Was it a very great shock to discover Lord Dereham is here?'

'I thought—just for a moment—that he had sought me out and followed me,' Bel confessed. 'Such foolishness, after the way I snubbed his advances. Why should he?' Elinor opened her mouth to respond. 'That was a rhetorical question,' Bel added with a glimmer of a smile as they reached the door of the library and Patrick Layne came to open it for them. 'I know the answer perfectly well.'

Chapter Twenty

Ashe eased his shoulders more comfortably against the stack of casks and watched the entrance to the Royal Hotel with the same stoical patience he had exhibited for the past hour. Surely Bel had to come out some time? Luncheon was long over, the sun was shining, the crowds were promenading. One did not come to a seaside resort to sit inside one's hotel.

Unless, of course, meeting his mother and sisters had made her keep to her room to avoid seeing him. But that was not like Bel, he told himself. She had too much pride to skulk. If she did not want to see him, she was more than capable of sweeping past him with her nose in the air. He just wished he had a rational plan for courting her.

That damned Patrick Layne was here with his feet well and truly under the table, whatever his sister said about his lack of suitability for Bel. His unpredictable love was upset and who knows what she might do, who she might turn to? If he caught that man pressing his attentions on her... Ashe grimaced and relaxed his hands that had balled into fists. If Bel wanted Layne's attentions, then who was he to stand in her way? He was her discarded lover, not her husband and not her betrothed. He had no rights.

The doorman at the Royal hurried into the street, bowing and scraping as Bel, Elinor and their maid came out. Ashe straightened up, keeping in the shadows, his eyes hungry on Bel's face. She was wearing an expression that he knew signified embarrassment and determination. When he dragged his eyes from her face to look at the whole of her, he saw why and could not repress a smile.

It was a puzzle why otherwise rational females should find sea bathing an excuse to wear quite ludicrous garments, but they did and it appeared that his love was not immune from this form of lunacy, even if she had the taste to be highly dubious about the result.

Falling in behind the three women at a discreet distance, Ashe was able to admire the froth of seaweed-green pinked ruffles around the hem of the garment, the lurid green and white peppermint stripes of Bel's canvas half-boots and the plume of feathers that threatened to dislodge the utterly impractical bonnet which crowned her head. Under this rig she was doubtless clad in an all-covering flannel shift to preserve her from the gaze of any lecherous crabs or lobsters that came within range.

Ashe grinned as he walked, his mood lifting as he imagined Bel being ruthlessly dunked by one of the muscular female dippers whose job it was to ensure their shrinking charges received the regulation three total immersions that medical opinion had decided was the best for health. She would emerge from the experience shaken and probably grateful for a nice cup of hot chocolate and an ice provided by a friend. He would be careful to behave in a completely neutral manner, do nothing to alarm her, appear delighted that she was so comprehensively chaperoned. Do everything, in effect, to try to stop her associating him with naked, uninhibited, physical passion.

Bel waved to Elinor and the maid and descended the steps to the beach. The other two women walked on to the entrance to the warm baths together and vanished inside. Ashe hitched one hip on the balustrade and waited until at length Bel reappeared on the beach below in vigorous discussion with a stalwart dipping woman. She appeared to be refusing something, then the woman helped her up the steps into a bathing machine and walked back up the sand. The driver backed a horse into the shafts and the machine set off down the beach.

She was going to go in without a dipper, relying, as he had earlier, on raising the little flag on top of the machine when she wanted the driver to return. Ashe found he was running down the steps without consciously making a plan.

'Sir? Looking to go in again, sir?' It was the proprietor who had rented out the machine he had used that morning.

'Yes,' Ashe nodded. 'Straight away, if you please.'

The door closed, leaving Bel in near darkness. Light filtered through cracks in the wooden walls of the hut on wheels in which she was enclosed and she wondered why no one had thought to put windows in the roof. She reached out her hands and found she could just touch the planks on either side. Beneath her feet what felt like wet carpet squelched. With a lurch the vehicle began to move and Bel sat down hard on the narrow wooden seat that ran front to back. Above her head there was a shelf for her outer clothes and for the pile of towels that were provided as part of the fee of one shilling. She had saved three pence by not taking a dipper's services, although she had tipped the woman for helping her in and explaining the limited facilities.

The machine lurched again and there was a strange slapping noise, which Bel realised was the waves splashing up under the floor. Hastily she took off her bonnet, laid it on the shelf and began to unbutton her gown. At least it was easy to get out of, leaving her in the sack-like grey flannel bathing shift. She eased off her half-boots and stockings and stood up uneasily on the cold and sodden carpet while she stacked everything carefully away.

The machine stopped. There was movement outside, then a rattle and a flap and the driver shouted, 'All set!' Bel waited a moment, then lifted the bar on the door and peeped out, blinking in the brightly lit space. All around was the white canvas hood of the bathing machine, at her feet the green water, swelling up to splash her feet as she hesitated at the top of the steps. Below, the sand shimmered in shafts of sunlight and a shoal of tiny fish flashed across the space and were gone.

From outside she could hear the screech of gulls, the shouts of excited children, the cries of the sailors manning the vessels further out in the bay, but here, in her own little sea world, all was tranquil.

Bel dipped a cautious toe in the water that was chuckling and splashing over the top step. It was cold, but only, she guessed, in contrast to her warm feet. Sunlight reflected on the ridged sand, sparkling off a shell as she gazed down, mesmerised. The skirts of the flannel shift flapped around her calves and, impatient, she pulled it off over her head and tossed it on to the bench.

Walk down the steps or jump? Bel took a deep breath and jumped, plunging under the water, then coming up with a shriek that was half-shock, half childlike delight to be in the sea. She found she could stand on the bottom, her shoulders out of the water. Between her toes the sand sifted delightfully and she wriggled them, scaring the inquisitive little fish as she pushed back the soaking mane of hair from her face.

It felt quite different from the still, greenish waters of the lake where she had learned to swim. This water was vibrant, shimmering, alive with wavelets, and her whole body came to life with the sensual caress. Bel kicked off and swam up to the edge of the canvas, then turning, back across the width, delighting in the buoyancy of the salt water.

She stood, running her hands down her body, shivering with the sensual freedom of being naked in this translucent world. But already the restriction of the enclosure was frustrating her—she wanted to swim free, watch the horizon. Daring, Bel ducked her head under the water and opened her eyes. For a moment it stung and the image blurred, then she could see all round her own bathing machine for yards on all sides. Dare she swim under the awning's edge and pop her head up like a seal in open water?

No, of course not, it was a scandalous thought. Bel dived again and lifted a shell from the sand. Increasingly confident, she swam as far under the water as the awning, then under it, then with a panicky flick of her feet, turned and hastened back into her safe cocoon.

There was another shell. She dived for that, then hung in the water with it clenched in her fist as she tried to make sense of the dark shape she could see coming towards her. That had not been there before—a seal? A shark? Bel surfaced, spluttering and paddled back to the steps in a panicky flurry of foam just as the shape slipped under the edge of the awning and surfaced. Not a fish, not a sea mammal. A man.

'Ashe!' Without thought Bel tumbled down the steps and into his arms. He was naked, sleek with water, his hair otter-dark, his skin cool over the hard heat beneath. Bel wrapped her arms around as much of him as she could and clung. 'Ashe—oh, but I have missed you.'

'How can you complain about missing me, you ran away,' he countered reasonably, lifting her under her arms so that she slid up his chest. 'Put your legs round my waist.' It was an utterly indecent position and one that demonstrated clearly that cold sea water had no effect at all on the evidence of how much he had missed her.

Something—common sense, she supposed—struggled to make itself heard. 'This is so wicked!'

'Pleasantly wicked?'

'Yes,' Bel confessed, blissfully overwhelmed by the shock and the sensation of wet, naked man holding her so close. 'Oh, Ashe, I do—' She almost blurted it out, the way she felt about him. Bel smothered her own words against his mouth, losing herself in the heat and the demand of his possession, rubbing her body shamelessly against his, all her reservations about making love with him again swept away. Vaguely she was aware that she was going to regret this later, but now she did not care.

Ashe lifted her again, wriggled his hips and slid into her in one smooth thrust, making her gasp at the heat of him filling her. 'Lie back and float,' he commanded, letting her go, and she did, her legs holding her tight to him, the bobbing movement of the swell sending *frisson* after *frisson* of pleasure shooting through her as their joined bodies rocked. Bel closed her eyes as he began to run his hands over her breasts, teasing the nipples under the water so they peaked as hard as tiny beach pebbles between his tormenting fingertips. It felt as though they were making love in the clouds, almost weightless, flying.

All the sensations were subtly different, she could not relate anything her body was feeling to what she had experienced before. Adrift, yet anchored, ecstatic yet fearful, Bel opened her eyes to find his on her face, wide and blue, darker than the sea, deeper than the sea, drowning her. 'Ashe!'

I love you! He wanted to shout it; instead, he took Bel by the shoulders and hauled her back desperately against him, murmuring the words over and over into her mouth as she opened for him, letting him feast on the salty tang of her lips as he lost himself in her. His hands were cupped around her hips, holding her as he braced his feet on the firm sand and began to thrust. He was not going to be able to hold on for long, he needed her too much. The thought came like a lightning flash behind his closed lids: *Don't withdraw, get her with child, she will have to marry you then.* He fought it, knowing it was wrong, wanting nothing more in the world than Bel, blossoming with their child.

Bel was clinging to him as if for life itself, her mouth free of his now, her lips roaming frantically over his neck, his shoulder, wherever she could reach, her breath gasping as he plunged into her, deeper than he had ever been. He felt the pleasure take her, throw her over the edge beyond reason as her head fell back on a sobbing cry and with an effort he did not know he was capable of, Ashe lifted her away from him, holding her tight as he shook with the force of his own release.

'Oh,' she murmured softly against his neck as he forced his shaking legs to walk to the steps, climb them and sit down at the top, holding her.

He felt like a sea god, like Neptune on his throne with a nymph in his arms, capable of anything, lord of all he surveyed. 'Oh,' Bel said again. 'That was so…so…' Ashe rested his cheek on her hair as he thought of some of the adjectives. *Wonderful, blissful, astonishing, perfect.* Whatever had been wrong at the picnic was now all right again.

'I was never going to do that again,' she said ruefully, her breath fanning warm on his wet chest, shattering his new-found security.

'Why not?' He knew he sounded harsh, did not care.

'It is wrong,' she said sadly, slipping out of his grasp and down into the water, hanging there, her hair fanning out around her, her eyes solemn on his face. His own mermaid.

'Why? Why now is it wrong and before it was not? Explain to me. What has changed, Bel?'

'I have changed.' A shoal of fish darted across the space behind her, a flash of silver that drew his eyes from her for a moment. When he looked back, she was rubbing her hand across her eyes.

'Bel? Are you crying?' Ashe pushed off the steps and stood beside her. What cause had she to weep? It was his heart that she was breaking. He lifted his hand and brushed the back of it across her cheek, the feeling of tenderness for her struggling with the urge to shake her until she explained, told him she loved him.

'No, just salt in my eyes.' She turned her cheek against his hand for a moment. She was a very poor liar, Ashe thought. 'I must go and get dressed. We should not be here like this.'

'In my arms just now you were like molten silver. It hurts you to turn me away—you want to cry. Just now I felt what you felt and it was not wrong, Bel.' She glanced up, the reflection of his desperation stamped on her face.

'It is wrong in my heart,' she said and reached up to him, pulling his head down to hers, finding his mouth with desperate lips. She kissed and clung as he fought to be gentle, not to ravage her mouth with the love and frustration and incomprehension that was filling him. She pulled back, her mouth a whisper from his and murmured something, so softly that all he could sense was the movement of her lips. What had she said? *This is breaking my heart?*

'Go now.' She stepped back, her cold hands pushing against his chest. She was shivering now, from chill or emotion he had no idea, but he could not let her stand here like this while he struggled to understand.

'Yes, I will go.' Ashe made himself smile, saw the answering curve of her lips as she tried to send him reassurance. Which of them was reassuring the other, and what about? he wondered bitterly, with one long last look at her before he dived under the edge of the awning and kicked hard in the direction of his own bathing machine.

He surfaced, tossing his hair back from his face and climbed into the cabin of the machine, reaching for a towel and rubbing with painful vigour over his salty wet skin, haunted by the thought of Bel drying herself alone, just a few yards away.

Ashe had no difficulty cataloguing the emotions that were warring within him. Hurt masculine pride, frustrated love, baffled incomprehension were uppermost. He dismissed the first, despising himself for it, absorbed the aching hurt of the second and wrestled with the third as he dragged his thin cotton trousers on over still-damp skin.

If he had done something to hurt her, she would have told him so, she would certainly not have gone into his arms with that uncomplicated passion he had just experienced. If there was another man, she would have told him that too—and she certainly would not have allowed him to so much as kiss her cheek. And she was unhappy, so unhappy. Yet that was the one thing she would not explain.

Ashe tied his neckcloth in a slipshod knot and dragged on his coat, then reached out and pulled on the cord that would raise the flag to summon the horse and driver. Something was stirring inside him; then he realised what it was—hope. If Bel was unhappy, it was because she did not want to renounce him. Something was making her do it, not her own inclinations. All he had to do was to find out what—or who—was behind this and then his way would be clear.

Ashe stood in the doorway as the sound of the horse splashing through the water reached him and the driver began to haul up the awning. He shut the door and perched on the outside bench as the animal was backed into the shafts. The flag was up on Bel's bathing machine too. *I am going to marry you, Belinda Cambourn*, he vowed silently, as the machine lurched back to shore. *Court you, win you, wed you.*

Chapter Twenty-One

$\mathcal{S}$he had three choices, Bel told herself as she sat giving a good imitation of a woman deeply engrossed in Ackermann's *Repository of Arts, Literature and Fashions &c*. Distracted for a moment, she wondered what the *&c* covered, then flattened the journal open at the section of 'General Observations on Fashions and Dress'. A lady might be excused for sitting in Garner's reading rooms staring at that for quite some time.

Three choices. She could flee back to London, either dragging poor Elinor with her or leaving her with Miss Layne. On the face of it, that was the easy thing to do, for it would remove her completely from Ashe and she had proved only yesterday that she was completely incapable of behaving with any restraint or sense the moment he touched her.

On the other hand, it was cowardly to run away and most unfair on her cousin and on Brown and Lewin, who were expecting her to go and look at their inn that afternoon. And how would she ever learn to live without Ashe if she could not confront this?

Or she could stay here in Margate and do everything possible to avoid seeing him. Which would involve dodging round like a criminal and giving offence to Lady Dereham and her daughters.

Or she could steel herself to meeting him socially, act as though there was nothing but acquaintance and their mutual interest in the wounded soldiers between them. Which would be so hard when she feared that her love must show in her eyes every time she looked at him, and her hand was trembling even now, just thinking about him. She must compose herself, think of light subjects for conversation, prepare her defences thoroughly.

'Good morning, Lady Belinda.' The journal fell from her hands to the floor and Miss Katy Reynard hastened to pick it up and smooth the crumpled pages. 'I do beg your pardon, I made you jump. There, I do not think the fashion plates are damaged.'

'Thank you.' Bel accepted it back and fixed the smile on her lips before she looked beyond the girl. The entire Reynard family was there. So much for preparation. She rose to shake hands with Lady Dereham and the two elder sisters. 'Good morning, you find me very reprehensibly immersed in the latest fashions.'

'That I confess is our intention also,' Lady Dereham admitted. 'At least, to provide ourselves with some light reading of various sorts. We are taking a foot tour of the town to view all its amenities and for Reynard to call at the bank.'

Bel made herself look beyond the ladies to where Ashe was standing, a folded newspaper in one hand, his hat in the other. He bowed gravely and she inclined her head. *There, that was easy. I did not faint, nor fly into his arms and no one has remarked upon any peculiarity in our manner.* Then she met his eyes and read neither desire nor anger, but something new, intense and strange. The pulse in her throat fluttered and she looked away hastily.

'Have you seen the sea view from here? It is very fine.' Frederica, who was perusing a copy of the *New Margate Guide*, unwittingly came to her rescue, pointing from the window. 'There are the towers of Reculver church, see? There is such a romantic story here about how they came to be built.' She began to read as her brother came to stand next to Bel.

'Lady Belinda. We are taking a carriage for a drive along the coast to Broadstairs this afternoon. Would you care to join us?'

'How kind of you to ask. But I have an engagement this afternoon—perhaps some other time?' Bel looked down and saw the journal was crumpled in her grip. Now she would have to buy it. 'Oh, dear, look at that,' she said, trying to flatten it again, making a business of it to draw those steady blue eyes away from her face for a few moments of relief.

'Allow me.' Ashe took it and strode off to the counter.

'Lord Dereham!' He was already paying. 'Thank you, but that is very extravagant.'

'Four shillings? Merely the cost of four uses of a bathing machine—without an attendant,' he observed blandly as she twitched the neat parcel from his grip. 'Now tell me, where are you going this afternoon? Is Layne escorting you?'

What was that? A flicker of jealousy? 'No,' Bel responded with composure, deciding to use shock tactics. 'I am meeting Brown and Lewin in a public house.'

'Brown and—' He frowned. 'Two of your soldiers? The big one who growls if anyone comes near you and his friend with the damaged throat?' She nodded. Of course he would remember; a good officer knew the names of all his men. 'What are you up to, Be…Lady Belinda?'

'Brown found details of an inn for sale in St Lawrence, on the London road out of Ramsgate. He thinks it might be suitable for quite a number of the men to run together.'

She had expected that she would have to persuade the others on the committee that this was a good idea, but not, apparently, Ashe. He was nodding. 'A good idea. They know horses, they know how to work as a team, some of them will be able to cook and all of them will know about beer.'

Bel felt her spirits lift at his response and found herself smiling. 'Brown can run it, he was a sergeant.'

'I thought he might have been. What did he do?'

'Swore at a young lieutenant—he would not say any more.'

Ashe grinned. 'I would have liked to have seen that—he strikes me as a man who does not suffer fools gladly. And how much is it? Can we afford it?'

'I intend purchasing it myself, as an investment.' Bel found that she was tensed for his response and her chin was up. 'If it is suitable, of course. Lewin was a book keeper, he is checking the records.'

'You have it all worked out,' Ashe said. His tone was pleasant, but there was an edge under the words. 'You did not see fit to consult the rest of the committee? Or perhaps that is why Layne is here.'

'No, I shall look at it first. I found myself wanting

to leave London and this seemed as good a destination and reason as any,' Bel responded. There must have been something in her voice, for she saw Lady Dereham glance in her direction. 'Miss Layne heard we were coming down and found the idea attractive,' she added with a completely contrived smile.

'I will accompany you,' Ashe said abruptly.

'You are already committed to your family for this afternoon,' Bel pointed out, strolling nearer to the others who were grouped around Frederica, reading aloud from the guidebook about the ruined church at Reculver.

'...*we recollect the pious labours of those ladies who raised these sacred fanes in commemoration of their escape from a watery grave, and as landmarks to the adventurous mariner, whereby he may avoid those dangerous shallows which wrecked their brittle barque*. And it is about to fall into the sea, along with the remains of a Roman fortress,' she added.

'Nothing endures for ever,' her mother observed. 'Reynard?'

'I was going to ask if you would mind very much if we changed our drive to tomorrow, Mama. The weather seems set fair for several days and I find that Lady Belinda has located a suitable source of employment for some of our soldiers and has an appointment to view it this afternoon. I do not feel she should be doing so unescorted.'

'But of course.' Lady Dereham smiled approval. 'I have not the slightest objection and, naturally, Lady Belinda should be escorted.'

'I would not dream of disrupting your plans,' Bel protested, vaguely aware of someone else approaching their group but too concerned with not finding herself tête-à-tête with Ashe for an afternoon to look. 'I will have my cousin's company and two of the soldiers…'

'May I be of service? Good morning.' It was Patrick Layne, smiling, bowing, shaking hands. 'I could not but help overhear—are these our soldiers you speak of, Lady Belinda?'

She did not want him either. Bel bit down on a sharp request that the men simply leave her alone, and explained all over again about the inn. Hopefully it would shock Lady Dereham that Bel should involve herself in such a thing and she would cease to urge Ashe to accompany her.

'What a good idea,' Ashe's mother said warmly, dashing that hope. 'But you must certainly have a gentleman's escort.'

'She has it,' Ashe said. Bel thought she could detect teeth being gritted.

'But you have your delightful family to look after,' Patrick intervened. 'My sister has made it very clear to me that she is spending the entire day immersed in her latest poem, so I am entirely at your disposal, Lady Belinda.'

'As am I,' Ashe said. It was less a grit, more of a snarl this time.

'Perhaps you should both come.' Elinor appeared, somewhat dusty, from the depths of the book stacks. 'Good morning, everyone, do excuse me, but I have just discovered an excellent antiquities section including a book my mother has been anxious to acquire and I was quite absorbed.' She beamed equally upon the men. 'After all, there are two ladies to escort.'

'There, now,' Lady Dereham said peaceably, 'that solves that. I am more than happy for you to take my barouche, Reynard.'

'I have found a pamphlet of walks in the vicinity,' Anna added. 'There is one to a delightful-sounding pleasure gardens just a mile and a half away, called Dandelion of all things! Shall we go there this afternoon, Mama?'

The Reynards made plans and polite conversation with Patrick while Bel bit her lip and restrained herself from taking Elinor by the elbow, marching her off and demanding just what she thought she was doing, saddling her with two antagonistic men. And what was Ashe about? She had expected almost anything other than this degree of attentiveness in full view of his family. It was almost as if he were paying court to her.

Which was ridiculous. Bel studied him from beneath her lashes as he chatted easily with Elinor, drawing her out and making her laugh. He turned his head suddenly and caught her watching him. One eyebrow rose interrogatively and she made herself stare haughtily back—which was a mistake. Ashe smiled and her heart stuttered in her chest, then he was serious again, listening to her cousin. He knew she would not be his lover again, he knew she did not want to marry again. No, she corrected herself, he *thought* he knew she did not want to marry again. Which was, unless she was prepared to risk her pride and her dignity and what remained of her battered heart, how things would remain. For ever.

'If you will excuse me, I must go and do some shopping. Cousin Elinor, would you prefer me to leave Millie with you, or the footman?'

Ashe made himself stand, as though simply waiting for Miss Ravenhurst to turn her attention back to him. He kept his eyes on her face and did not indulge in the luxury of watching Bel as she walked away.

'What exactly are you up to, Miss Ravenhurst?' he enquired softly as Elinor turned back to him. The redhead coloured up, but she maintained her composure.

'Up to, my lord? I am afraid I do not follow you.'

'Why are you encouraging Layne to dangle after your cousin?' He watched the other man warily, but he was helping Katy focus the reading-room telescope on the end of the harbour wall and appeared quite unconscious of being under scrutiny.

'Perhaps I wanted his company myself, my lord,' Elinor suggested outrageously. 'I doubt if my cousin will object if I flirt with him all afternoon.'

'I have observed Lady Belinda's previous efforts to pair you off with Layne, Miss Ravenhurst—you are not going to convince me that you are angling for his attentions.'

'And if you have observed so much, Lord Dereham, you should realise that Belinda is not angling for them either.' She regarded him shrewdly, an uncomfortable echo of her formidable mother in her expression. 'There is no need to be jealous, you know.'

'*Jealous?*' Ashe just managed to articulate the word in a hiss, not a bellow. 'Of course I am not jealous. I simply do not trust the fellow's intentions.'

'I believe them to be completely honourable,' Elinor countered with an earnestness that Ashe suspected was deliberately provocative, 'but it is very kind of you to take such an interest.'

Ashe regarded his tormentor in fulminating silence for a long moment. 'Do I need to tell you, Miss Ravenhurst, that my feelings towards your cousin are not those of kindness?'

'No, Lord Dereham, you do not. I imagine they swing rather wildly between an urge to strangle her and a quite different emotion altogether. Unfortunately, I am not sure if Belinda realises that and, although I am not at all experienced with this sort of thing, you do appear to be making something of a mull of bringing it to her attention.'

Amusement twinkled in her greenish eyes and through his irritation he thought that, animated like this, she was far from the dowdy bluestocking everyone dismissed her as. 'And now you would like to strangle me too, so I will run away.' Her smile was pure provocation. 'If it is convenient, could you call at two?'

She took his curt nod for agreement and took her leave of the Reynards, pausing to confirm the time for the afternoon's expedition with Patrick Layne.

Ashe sat down and snapped open the *Morning Chronicle* as an effective barrier to think behind. How was he going to find some decent privacy to court Bel if his entire family and that damned Layne fellow kept intruding at every turn? He was certainly not going to find it traipsing round every nook and cranny of an inn in company with two ex-soldiers, a bluestocking and a decent fellow whose eye he would very much like to black.

'How interesting,' Elinor observed, as the barouche came to the crossroads in the centre of the village of St Lawrence. 'The church tower is of Saxon origin.' She consulted the guide book again. 'This appears to be quite accurate—so often they confuse late Saxon with early Norman, you know.'

Her cousin had maintained a flow of informative chat

for the entire journey. Bel, who would normally have been bored to death by talk of Saxon towers, ancient seats and the remains of Elizabethan warning beacons, had been grateful for the necessity placed on the two men to respond appropriately to Elinor's flow of antiquarian information. Ashe and Patrick had settled down diagonally opposite each other with polite enquiries and smiles that she would have trusted about as far as she would have trusted those of a brace of crocodiles.

Now, at least, she could see their destination. 'Look, there it is—the Kentish Samson.'

The creaking and faded inn sign showed a huge man rending a thick cable apart with his bare hands. 'Richard Joy,' Elinor informed them helpfully. 'He lived here in the last century and was famed for his strength.'

'Which is more than can be said for the structure named after him.' Ashe eyed it critically as they drew up in the inn yard. Shutters hung off their hinges, stable doors stood open on to dirty, empty stalls and the yard itself did not appear to have been swept for a year.

'It may not be structural,' Patrick countered, standing to help Bel down as the groom folded down the steps. 'Do mind where you put your feet.'

'Half the window frames look rotten,' Ashe observed, handing Elinor out.

'But the roof line is perfectly sound,' Patrick responded, apparently intent on making Ashe sound negative. He took Bel's arm and pointed upwards. 'See? The ridge line is quite straight, which is a good sign, and there are few slipped tiles.' Having secured her arm, he tucked her hand firmly under his forearm and walked towards the back door. Conscious of Ashe's gaze on them, Bel forced a smile and left her hand where it was. She supposed she should feel flattered that Ashe was so hostile, but as he seemed more motivated by antagonism to Patrick than affection for her, she was not much encouraged.

'My lady.' It was, thank goodness, Brown with Lewin hopping on his crutch behind him. The ex-sergeant kept his voice down, waiting for Ashe and Elinor to join them. 'It looks good—needs some work—but the books seem honest and if it was fettled up right I reckon it'd be a little gold mine.'

'You had better show us round then, Sergeant,' Ashe said, earning himself a sharp look from the big man.

'I don't rightly hold any claim to that rank now, Major.'

'Nor I to mine. Very well, Mr Brown, let us go and see if you have found yourself an inn to run,' Ashe returned, assisting Elinor over a puddle.

They spent an hour poking through the place from attics to cellars, dogged by the owner, anxiously twisting his hands into his stained apron. 'It's a good place,' he whined, 'only since my wife died I don't seem to be able to get a grip on it like I used to.'

'Since she ran off with that Sergeant of Marines you mean, Tom Hatchett,' one of the men in the bar shouted unkindly. 'Sooner you sells it and we get a landlord who can keep a sweet barrel of Kentish ale, the happier we'll all be.'

'Let's have a look at the books,' Ashe said, seconded by Elinor, a notebook ready in her hands. They followed the landlord and Brown and Lewin into the inner parlour, leaving Bel with Patrick in the bar.

'Outside, I think,' he said, holding the door for her. 'This isn't a place for a lady, although I think we could get the carriage trade in once it was done up.'

'Yes, I think so too. I really feel quite optimistic about it.' At least something was going well. She could quite see that Brown's claim that a successful inn could employ a dozen men was no exaggeration.

'Reynard is not so confident,' Patrick observed, holding a door open for her. Bel stepped through into what appeared to be a harness room, now more a haven for spiders and rubbish.

'I think he is merely sceptical. He does not want me making a poor investment.' Bel lifted an empty sack to see what lay beneath, then dropped it again with a grimace as thick rolls of dust fell to the floor.

'He seems most protective of you.' Patrick came fully into the room behind her, his body blocking out the light. 'Lady Belinda…Belinda. I must ask you, what is Dereham to you?'

'Nothing—other than a friend and a fellow committee member.' She should enquire haughtily what right he had to ask, she realised as soon as she began to speak. It seemed her guilty conscience about Ashe would be her undoing.

'I am glad to hear you say it, although I doubt that is how he sees himself.' Patrick sounded more serious than she was used to hearing him.

'What right have you…?' Bel began, but he moved closer, holding up a hand to silence her.

'You will forgive me if I observe that you have spent some energy on matchmaking between me and Miss Ravenhurst.'

'Yes. I am sorry, that was foolish of me, I just thought that perhaps you would suit—' She broke off and regarded him ruefully. 'But you would not, would you?'

'No, Belinda, we would not. Miss Ravenhurst is an

admirable young lady, both intelligent and amiable, but I am attracted to quite another woman you see.'

'You are?' *Oh, Lord, he is going to make a declaration.*

'Belinda, have you no idea how I feel about you?' His brown eyes were earnest as he reached out and caught her hand in his. Bel tugged, but he held her firm, pulling her towards him so that her captured hand was pressed to his breast.

'No,' she lied. Ashe had warned her, but she had not taken him seriously, knowing that Patrick was wrong for her; she still could not believe he thought they were suited. 'No, I had no idea. Mr Layne, I truly value you as a friend, but I could never regard you in any other light, believe me…'

'Just try to think of me in that other light.' He secured her other hand. Trapped between his body, which suddenly seemed much larger than she had thought, and the metal saddle racks and wooden boxes, Bel found she had nowhere to go. 'Bel, I cannot offer you a title, but I can offer you my devotion and my—'

'No!' She pushed against his chest. 'Mr Layne… Patrick, I am of course honoured by your regard, but I am certain that we would not suit.'

'Let me show you how suited we could be, Belinda.' And he bent his head to kiss her.

Chapter Twenty-Two

❧

Patrick's attempt at a kiss would have been more successful if Bel had not ducked her head at the last moment, fetching him a nasty blow on the bridge of his nose from the high poke of her straw bonnet.

'Hell!' He staggered back, clutching his face with one hand, the other still clasping her wrist, and came up hard against Ashe, who was striding into the harness room.

'Hell indeed,' he said grimly, taking Layne by the shoulder and turning him, the other hand already clenched into a formidable fist.

'Ashe!' Bel, propelled by the force of Patrick's turn, spun with him, landing against Ashe's chest as the other man released her. 'Ashe, stop it.'

She stood between the two men as they glared at each other. Patrick's hat was off and a darkening weal cut across the bridge of his nose. Ashe was poised on the balls of his feet as though ready to spring.

'Did he hurt you?' he demanded.

'No, of course not. I turned suddenly and caught

him a glancing blow with my bonnet brim. Really, my lord—'

'And your wrist?' Ashe seized her right hand and lifted it. In the gap between her cuff and the edge of her light summer glove the skin was reddened.

'Mr Layne caught at it instinctively to save his balance when I knocked into him,' she improvised. 'And then you jerked him out of there at such speed I was dragged too.' Bel tried to interpose herself between Ashe and Patrick and found herself bundled very firmly to one side.

'There is no need to lie for me, Lady Belinda,' Patrick said with cold dignity. 'My lord, I was making Lady Belinda a declaration when you intruded. I must request you to retire, you are embarrassing her ladyship.'

'Embarrassing her more than you making her a declaration in a filthy hovel? One that she finds so distasteful that she tries to break your nose for you? One that she must be restrained to hear, you bastard?'

'Really, my lord, I must protest. The intemperance of your language before a lady is completely unacceptable. The force of my ardour—'

The echo of Ashe's words when Aunt Louisa had caught them in the drawing room was too much for Bel's overstretched nerves. She gave a gasp of shocked laughter, then clapped her hands to her mouth as Elinor, followed by the two soldiers, the landlord and several interested customers, spilled out into the yard.

'You can take this for your ardour,' Ashe said grimly, punching Patrick square on the jaw. He went down in an ungainly tangle of limbs, but got to his feet gamely, his fists clenched.

'Here, gentlemen, not in front of the ladies!' It was

Brown, nimble now on his crutches, swinging his formidable bulk between the two men.

'You will meet me for this,' Patrick said fiercely.

'Damn it, *you* will meet *me* for the insult to Lady
Belinda.' Ashe glared back at him.

'You cannot meet anyone,' Elinor declared coolly,
in a voice of flattening common sense as she came to
take Bel's arm. 'You have no seconds. It would be
most irregular.'

Ashe turned to look at her, a glimmer of a smile just
touching his mouth as she met his hot blue stare with un-
flappable calm. 'Thank you for that observation, Miss
Ravenhurst. Brown, Lewin, you will have to stand for
us.'

'Aye, well, there's no one else. I've seen these affairs
before,' Brown observed. 'And it's the challenged party
what gets to choose the weapons. You've challenged
each other so we need to sort that out first.' He frowned,
then fished in his pocket and drew out a heavy coach
wheel, tossing the penny coin to Ashe, who caught it
one handed. 'And you lot!' He raised his voice to a
bellow. 'Get out of here and mind your own affairs.'

The spectators shuffled off reluctantly as Ashe
balanced the coin on his bent thumb, said 'Call', and
sent it flying upwards.

'Heads.'

They all bent to observe it as it lay on the filthy
cobbles, King George's fleshy profile uppermost. 'I
choose pistols,' Patrick said. 'If we have any.'

'I have a pair. Tomorrow at six on the cliffs?' Ashe
asked.

'Right.' Patrick nodded.

Bel looked from one man to the other. They did not

seem unduly hostile now, it was incomprehensible. 'Stop it,' she said, finding her voice again. 'This is madness.' She might as well not have spoken.

'Good day, Lady Belinda. I will hire a gig to return to Margate.' Patrick Layne bowed punctiliously and strode out of the yard.

'Right.' Ashe tugged his glove back more firmly over his knuckles. 'Have we finished looking at this place?' Bel and Elinor exchanged incredulous glances. 'It looks good to me. If you do not wish to purchase it, Lady Belinda, I certainly will, if Brown and Lewin feel it matches their needs.'

'Aye, my lord, it does that, I thank you.'

'Very well.' Ashe reached into the breast of his coat and produced his pocket book. There was an exchange of something that crackled. 'Tell him to take it off the market and my man of business will be in touch with him directly.'

'I want to buy it,' Bel said flatly as they got back into the carriage.

'You will surely not wish to be involved in negotiations. Let my man handle it, we can discuss who makes the purchase later.' Ashe settled himself opposite the ladies, as at ease as a man who had just spent an hour strolling round the garden, not one who had been involved in fisticuffs ending in a challenge.

'And you will stop this duel nonsense,' she began.

Ashe raised one brow. 'Certainly not, and I will not discuss it further.'

Bel opened her mouth and received a sharp jab in the ribs from Elinor. Her cousin was doubtless right. Expecting a man to take a sensible view of an affair of honour was like expecting the sun not to rise in the

morning. She held her peace as they travelled in silence
back to the resort, her brain spinning with fruitless ideas
for stopping it.

She dismounted at the hotel with a stiff nod to Ashe
and swept inside and up to their suite, Elinor hastening
behind her.

'How do we stop them?' she demanded the moment the
door was closed. 'Tell Lady Dereham and Miss Layne?'

'They will not be able to do anything.' Elinor
frowned. 'And we will be worrying them, for I doubt
the men will tell them.'

'No doubt they intend just to leave a letter with di-
rections on where to find their respective wills.' Bel felt
savage. 'And if one of them kills the other, then the
survivor will have to flee abroad. They have probably
got Brown reserving a hoy at Ramsgate against just
such a contingency.'

'Well, it is illegal,' Elinor said thoughtfully. 'We
could inform the magistrates. After all, we know where
and we know when.'

'So we do.' Bel jumped up and kissed her. 'That is
brilliant! Should we do it now?'

'No, later this evening,' Elinor decided. She hesitated. 'You do still love him, don't you?'

'Ashe? Oh, yes. So much. I thought he had followed
me here, but of course, he had not. We…met while we
were swimming.' Elinor's mouth formed a perfect O
of shocked surprise. 'I should never have…not
again…and afterwards I told him that. If he had felt
anything for me other than physical desire, surely he
would have said so then?'

'I have absolutely no idea, I am glad to say,' her

cousin retorted with some asperity. 'I knew I was right to resolve upon a single life.'

'I ought to wish I had never embarked upon the affair,' Bel said painfully. 'But I cannot. It is breaking my heart and yet I cannot wish I did not love him.'

Ashe stood on the cliff top, watching a fishing smack making its way towards a small buoy that bobbed scarlet and black against the grey morning sea. The sky was lightly overcast with cloud, the wind still cool up here on the sheep-cropped turf.

A few yards away Layne stood likewise, affecting an interest in the seascape while Brown and Lewin loaded the pistols. At the edge of the road, against a distorted clump of trees, the doctor's closed carriage lurked, far enough away to give some credence to the tale he would tell of just passing by when he heard a shot. If there was a death or a serious injury today the doctor could be incriminated if it were proven he knew about the duel beforehand.

Ashe pushed the flicker of speculation about Layne's intentions, and his skill with a pistol, to the back of his mind. It was better to starve the imagination in situations like this. He touched his thumbs and forefingers together and began to discipline his breathing, wishing for the comfortable white pelt of the bearskin rug beneath him as he strove for balance and focus.

'Right, then.' Brown had reached his side unnoticed. 'Here's your pistol, Major.' He hesitated. 'Lady Belinda's going to be mad as a wet cat if we bring you back with a hole in you.'

'She won't blame you,' Ashe said with a grim smile. 'She knows exactly whose fault this is.' He walked towards Layne, bowed as they met, then turned on his heel to stand back to back with the other man.

'Walk,' called Brown and he began to pace. 'Stop. Turn. Take aim.'

Ashe lifted the pistol, his arm straight, his body turned to offer the smallest target to Layne's bullet. The tiny black mouth of the other pistol leered at him as he took his aim.

'Stop in the name of the law!' The shout had them all turning. Ashe threw up his pistol hand so the weapon was pointing skywards and saw Layne do the same as the gig bounced towards them over the hummocks, two red-faced men in bag-wigs glowering at them.

'How the hell—' Layne began.

'Look behind them,' Ashe said grimly as a second gig, driven by Miss Ravenhurst, swung off the road in the magistrates' wake. Bel spilled out of the vehicle as it came to a halt and ran, stumbling, across to him, her skirts kilted up to scandalous heights. Ashe lowered his hand and fired into the ground, hearing the echoing bark of Layne's safety shot.

'Gentlemen,' he could hear Layne saying fluently, 'we are merely rabbit shooting, you have obviously been sadly misinformed if you feared something else was afoot.'

'Rabbits, my eye, sir! With Dr Lambert's carriage—'

'What carriage?' enquired Layne coolly, gazing around. 'I greatly regret that you have been led on a wild goose chase, your worships.'

'Just get out of our parish next time you want to shoot rabbits,' the stouter magistrate ordered, heaving himself back into the gig. 'Madam,' he said with dignity to Bel who had arrived breathless on the scene, 'I bid you good day.'

'What do you mean, Mr Manningtree—*next time*?' she demanded. 'You have stopped them.' Her bonnet was hanging down her back by its ribbons, her slippers were grass stained and her muslin skirts creased and rumpled from where she had screwed them up as she ran. Ashe wanted to shake her until her teeth rattled.

'Madam, this is a *duel*,' the thinner one explained, glaring at Ashe in such a way that made him sorry for any poacher who came up in front of this bench. 'Once *gentlemen* have resolved on this course, they will not be deterred unless one of them apologises—or is dead. Our sole concern is that they do not continue within our jurisdiction. Good morning to you.'

'Ashe, no!' She turned to him, her mouth trembling. 'This is finished now, surely. Tell me you are not going to persist with this idiocy.'

'Not even if you hound us out of Kent, Bel,' he said. His anger with her was still hot, but he wanted to take her in his arms and kiss her until those lips were trembling with desire and passion and not fear for him. 'You will just have to let us get on with it.'

He expected—feared—her tears. He had not expected anger, but that was what lit up her eyes. She marched up to him, so close that their toes bumped, grabbed him by the biceps and shook him. Ashe rocked back on his heels a little, braced for a slap, but all she said, her voice intent and shaking, was, 'You and your damnable honour. You will break my heart, Ashe Reynard, won't you? But, of course, this is more important. Off you go and kill each other.'

Break my heart? 'Bel?' But she was gone, running across to where her cousin waited, her white face turned to them, her hands on the reins of the hired gig. A slow, incredulous smile spread across his face.

'There is nothing we can do?' Elinor demanded as she steered the sluggish pony back down the hill to the seafront. 'They will just go somewhere else?'

'That is what Ashe says. That is what the magistrates said—all they wanted was to chase them away so they did it in another parish, can you believe! Why could they not have arrested them?'

'Arrest a viscount? With no actual shots fired? I doubt they have the courage.' Elinor sighed. 'All we can do is wait. Shall I have tea sent to our room?'

'We cannot watch for them to return if we wait up there.' Bel went into the public drawing room, which was set out with groups of *chaises* and armchairs. A number of formidable dowagers had staked out a claim to the best viewpoints to observe and criticise the passing throng.

'Here, these seats by the window.'

'That is where Lady Throckington and her companion always sit,' Elinor protested.

'She will just have to sit somewhere else today.' Bel sat in a chair overlooking the Marine Parade and facing the way they had entered the town. 'Here, you face in the opposite direction in case they circle around.' She hitched her chair closer to the glass.

'Bel, you will be visible from outside.' Elinor twitched a curtain across to provide some sort of screen. 'We are not the men in the Bond Street coffee-house windows, you know!'

Ninety minutes and two pots of tea later they were still sitting there. Lady Throckington had arrived, glared, and retired defeated by Bel's flat refusal to be shamed into moving. She sat in the next group of chairs along and fixed the two younger women with a basilisk stare while carrying out a loud and rather one-sided conversation with her companion on the manner and morals of today's generation.

Bel, who had hardly noticed her, was beginning to feel desperate. Surely they should be back by now? Surely such a delay meant that one of them was wounded, at the very least? Her imagination filled with horrid pictures of Ashe white, dead, on the green grass. Of Ashe, Patrick's blood still staining his hands, running for a boat and exile. Of…

'Miss Ravenhurst?'

'What? There is a mistake, it must be a message for me.' Bel swung round to find one of the pageboys holding out a salver with a sealed note upon it.

'No mistake. It is addressed to me.' Elinor picked it up and slit the seal.

'I was to wait for a reply, if you please, ma'am.'

'What is it?' Bel demanded, her heart in her throat.

'Oh, nothing of any moment.' Elinor frowned down at it. 'I wonder what to do for the best.' That appeared to be a rhetorical question, for she stood up. 'I will not be long—will you wait here?'

'Yes, of course—but, Elinor, I need you with me.'

'Of course. Truly, you will not be alone long. Now, where is the nearest writing desk?'

Biting her lips, Bel turned from watching her cousin's retreating back and fixed her eyes on the road. Had she missed them? Surely Brown and Lewin would come and tell her if the worst had happened? The minutes ticked by and still Elinor did not return.

Then there was a movement beside her and she half-turned, her eyes still fixed on the street. 'Where on earth have you been—*Ashe*!'

'May I sit down?' He placed his hat on a chair, propped his cane against it and sat, one leg elegantly crossed over the other, an immaculately groomed figure in pantaloons and Hessian boots, his coat of superfine fitting to a nicety, his linen crisp.

The room swam around her. Ashe was alive. He was here and not dead, not heading out of Ramsgate harbour.

'You stopped and *changed*?' she demanded, relief fuelling her fury. Lady Throckington raised her quizzing glass and Bel dropped her voice to an enraged hiss. 'You knew I would be frantic and you stopped to *change*?' Then thought became easier and she gasped, 'You haven't been wounded?'

'No. And neither has Layne. We both deloped.'

'So neither of you ever had the slightest intention of killing each other?'

'Don't sound so cross about it Bel, I thought that was what you wanted. No, no coffee, thank you.' The waiter bowed and took himself off.

'Of course that is what I wanted—but why have you had to go through this farce? I have been worried to distraction.' Her eyes searched his face anxiously, the way he was sitting. He truly did appear to be unharmed.

'Because it was a matter of honour,' Ashe said quietly, watching her face. 'And that is how matters of honour are settled—or a gentleman has no honour.'

'But you *like* Patrick,' she puzzled. 'You did not truly believe he would hurt me—or you would not have deloped. You did not mean to kill him.'

Her voice had risen again, heads turned as her words

became audible. 'I do disagree with *killing animals* for sport,' Bel said clearly and faces turned away.

'Once I had hit him there was no going back.' Ashe leaned forwards so they could continue their conversation more quietly.

'Then you should have apologised.'

'But I wanted to hit him,' he admitted ruefully. 'And I enjoyed it.'

'Why are you here?' Suddenly she was finding his closeness almost unbearable. She wanted to be in his arms and that was impossible. She wanted to speak openly to him, but that too was impossible. He had frightened her almost out of her wits and for that she wanted to hit him. Hard. Bel contented herself with a frosty stare.

'Because I want to know what you meant by what you said on the cliff top,' Ashe said softly, leaning forward, his clasped hands between his knees, so close that she could feel his breath. 'You said "you will break my heart". What did you mean, Bel?'

'I...' Had she really said that? She had thought the words were only in her mind. 'I meant it would be so terrible to have to tell your family that you had been killed, or had to flee abroad, all because of me.'

'Little liar,' he said amiably, his tone belying the intensity in the dark blue eyes. They were the colour of storm sea again: deep, dangerous, intense. 'You will tell me what you meant. The truth now, Bel.'

'That is what I meant,' she lied, looking around her for Elinor and some rescue. 'Where has Elinor got to?'

'She has gone to the library to meet Miss Layne and then they will have luncheon.'

'But she knows I was frantic! How could she leave me?'

'Because I told her to.' Bel sat stunned by her cousin's desertion. 'She knew we were both all right. I told her in my note that I wished to speak with you alone. At length.' There was no mistaking what he meant by that. Bel could feel the heat building inside her, treacherous, betraying, weakening.

'We have said all there is to say.'

'No we have not. Bel, you will tell me what you meant. Come, let us go up to your suite.'

She gasped. 'No! Of course we cannot, that is scandalous!' The quizzing glasses swung round again. 'The price of French silk,' she extemporised wildly. 'Quite scandalous.'

Ashe appeared unconscious of the fact that they were in a public place. 'Oh, I think we can, Bel. You see, we need to talk and it is going to be the sort of conversation we need to have naked.'

'Na—' Bel slapped her hand over her mouth before she could say it. 'No. I will sit here all day if need be.'

'So be it.' Ashe sighed and sat back, beginning to tug at the fingers of his right glove. 'I have never thought of myself as an exhibitionist, but if that is what you want…'

'You cannot mean to sit there and take off all your clothes,' Bel whispered. 'I refuse to believe it.'

'I will have to stand up to remove my pantaloons,' Ashe said thoughtfully, finishing tugging each finger and pulling off the glove. He tossed it on to the table and began on the other. Slowly. 'And then I will have to stand up to undress you…'

Bel pursed her lips and sat bolt upright in her chair, staring out of the window. He did not mean it. He could not possibly mean it.

The second glove landed on the tea table with a soft

leathery sound. Out of the corner of her eye Bel could see Ashe's long fingers begin to toy with the top button of his coat.

Lady Throckington's quizzing glass was trained on his profile. 'A handsome young man that,' she informed her companion loudly with all the outrageous frankness of women of her age and class. 'Boxes, I have no doubt. Strips well, I should imagine.'

The companion, no doubt inured to an employer who was not above ogling good-looking footmen, did not respond. The tips of Ashe's ears went pink. But the button was undone. He moved on to the next one.

'Well, Bel, that old trout will appreciate the scene, even if you do not.'

'You would not dare.'

Ashe smiled, a slow, sensual smile that made every cell in her body remember how that mouth felt on her skin, how those long, clever fingers could drive her to madness.

'Try me.'

Chapter Twenty-Three

His coat undone, Ashe began on the buttons of his waistcoat. Frantically Bel counted them. Four. *One... two...*

'I am going.' She put her hands on the arms of the chair and started to stand.

'With me?'

'No.'

'If you set foot in that lobby, still refusing to take me to your room, I will pick you up and carry you.' Bel sat down.

Three.

'You do not know which one is mine.'

'Second floor front, first door on the left. The key is in my pocket. Which reminds me, I must take it out against the moment when I have no pockets about my person.'

Four.

'Where did you get it?'

'Cousin Elinor, of course.' Ashe pulled the ends of his neckcloth free. 'I will do this, Bel. I never make threats, only promises.' He started to unwind the long white muslin strip. Lady Throckington's mouth dropped open.

'Very well,' Bel capitulated. Anything rather than a scene in here. Once she was in the lobby, she could run. He could hardly snatch her in the street. 'You must tie it again,' she hissed as he sat back with a grin.

Ashe stuffed the ends unceremoniously back into his shirt and stood up, offering her his hand. Bel ignored it, stood up and swept across the room, knowing her cheeks were scarlet. As she passed Lady Throckington's table the old woman gave a cackle of laughter, but she kept her eyes straight ahead.

The lobby was, unfortunately, empty. Bel had hoped for a crowd of people to dart between. She feinted towards the stairs, then spun round and dashed for the street door. Ashe caught her before she was halfway to it, one long arm lashed around her waist, then she was thrown over his shoulder like a sack of grain.

'Ough!' Breathless, her head spinning, Bel kicked, but Ashe's arm was firm, clamping her in place as he started to climb—and then she was too afraid of being dropped to fight. 'Just you wait until I am on my feet,' she threatened, her mouth muffled against the back of his coat.

No response. There was an awkward moment while he shuffled his hand into his pocket for the key, then he had shouldered the door open and they were inside.

Bel staggered as Ashe set her down, too dizzy while the blood went back towards her feet to do more than grip the bedpost. He was locking the door, she saw, then he threw the key out of the window with a flick of his wrist.

'How are we going to get out now?' Bel demanded.

'When we are ready—eventually—we will ring and someone will come and I will explain through the door that unfortunately I have lost the key.' Her eyes fixed on the bell pull, but he was there before her, tossing it up so that it caught high on the edge of the ornate mirror over the fireplace. She was trapped.

'Very well.' Bel walked stiff legged to the nearest chair and sat down. 'You have gone your length, I imagine.' Her heart was pounding. If he tried to make love to her again, how was she ever going to say no? She wanted him so much. So very much. Beyond all sense. 'What do you wish to say to me?'

'Tell me what you meant on the cliff top.' Ashe shrugged out of coat and waistcoat together and pulled his loose neckcloth free.

'Stop taking your clothes off,' she said shakily. 'You distract me.'

'Tell me the truth and I will stop.'

Bel searched wildly for something convincing, something that was not *I love you.*

'I am fond of you, you know that. I did not wish you hurt or in trouble.'

'I am fond of a number of people,' he countered, tossing the neckcloth aside and beginning on his shirt buttons. 'It does not break my heart if something untoward happens to them.' The fine white linen landed on the floor and he sat to tug at his Hessian boots.

'I told you I do not wish to marry again,' Bel said desperately. 'If I tell you what I meant, you will think me a hypocrite.'

Ashe pulled off both boots and sat, his head lowered as he dealt with his stockings. 'Try me,' he said at length, looking up at her.

'If I tell you, you must not think I mean to go back on what I said about us being lovers.'

'Go on.' At least he was not removing his panta-loons, she thought with shaky relief. She would lose all power of coherent thought if he did that. It was bad enough to see him sitting there, the clear marine light bathing his naked torso, highlighting the flat planes of muscle, the gilding of hair across his chest, the strong column of his neck. She dropped her gaze and the long-boned feet, flexing in the carpet, were just as distract-ing.

'I love you,' she said as though admitting to a charge in court.

'Bel!' He was on his knees at her side, her hands caught in his. It was too much, he was too close. She could smell him, the heat of him, and if she leant forward, just a little, she would be able to rest her forehead on his shoulder, kiss the satin skin over that hard muscle, taste the male saltiness of his flesh.

'I am very sorry,' she apologised. 'Right at the be-ginning, I told you that I was not—at least, I hope I made it clear that I was not looking for anything but a physical relationship. An *affaire*.'

'Yes, I was quite clear about that,' he agreed. 'Look at me, Bel.'

'No.' She shook her head. Their hands were entwined together in an elaborate love knot, her white fingers lost and enlaced in his long, strong brown ones. 'I was angry when you proposed after Aunt found us together. I hated the thought that you would be trapped into such a thing for convention, for honour.'

'And I made a mull of things, speculating about love,' he said musingly. 'I have always wanted to be honest with you, Bel. I would not have been honest if I had told you then that I loved you.'

The little glimmer of foolish hope flickered and went out. 'No, of course, I quite understand.'

'Because I did not understand what I felt. Then.' Her head came up as though he had put his hand under her chin and lifted. So close, she could see the dark flecks in his eyes, the sprinkling of darker lashes in amongst the honey blond. So close, she could drown in those eyes. 'What happened under the ash tree, Bel?'

'I realised I loved you,' she faltered. Ashe released one hand and brought it up to cup her cheek, stopping her turning her head away from him. *Go on*, his eyes said. 'And that I could no longer be your lover, because that would not be honest, not if I wanted something from you that I could not have, something that you could not give.'

'And you chide me for placing honour high?' She shook her head, puzzled. 'That is honour of a high order, Bel.' His lips found hers in a gentle salute, then he sat back on his heels, her hand still enveloped in his.

'Don't pity me.' She tried to keep her voice strong.

'I do not pity you, Bel. Do you know what I did when you vanished from London?'

Ashe watched her shake her head, her wide, strained eyes fixed on his face. She had not slept all last night worrying about him, he could see. He fought the urge to stroke away the shadows under them. 'I went to Half Moon Street and Hedges would not tell me where you were. I expected to be irritated by that, to feel frustration because I could not find you. Instead I felt lost. I felt incomplete, unable to settle or to focus. I did not understand it. I am perfectly aware of what sexual frustration feels like—you had inflicted that on me for a fortnight past.' Bel blushed deliciously and something hot and dark and possessive stirred inside him.

'No, this was something new. So I let myself into the house that night and I went to your bedroom and I sat on the bearskin rug and I thought about you. About us. In the dark, all night. And with the morning light I knew why I felt like that, Bel. I love you.'

'Oh.' Her lips parted on a soft gasp of surprise and Ashe waited, schooling himself into patience while he read on her face the questions chasing the joy into puzzlement. 'You said nothing?'

'I had to find you first. That at least was the easy part. I was planning to employ Runners—I had all kinds of stratagems and I needed none of them. Mama announced calmly at breakfast that we were all going to Margate because that nice Lady Belinda mentioned it.'

'She thinks I am nice?' Bel queried, momentarily distracted.

'She thinks you would be the perfect daughter-in-law, I can tell.' He smiled lovingly at her. 'But that can wait. I resolved to court you as though we had never been lovers, to start again. That lasted just as long as it took to see you enter that bathing machine. I wanted you with every bone in my body and I simply could not resist.'

'Neither could I,' she admitted shakily, reaching out her hand as though to lay it on his chest and then snatching it back.

'And then you were so upset, so adamant that we must never do that again. I knew something was wrong, but I could not understand what. I resolved to go back to courting you while I tried to understand, or you could come to trust me enough to tell me.'

'I trust you,' Bel said fiercely. 'I trust you as I trust nothing else in my life.' And this time she did touch him, laying her hand over his heart, her bare palm hot and strong against the beat of his love.

'I knew there was something wrong. But if I told you I loved you, you would throw emotional blackmail in my face as you had before. And I want to marry you, Bel. I want this to be for ever. I want to have children with you and grow old with you. I had to work out why you fled from me even though in my arms you were fire and passion and utter abandon.'

'Marriage?' The clear grey eyes held his, full of hope and anxiety and questions.

'I know you do not want to marry again, Bel. I will give you as long as you need if you will only think about it. I promise I will give you all the freedom you want.'

'I want nothing more than to be married to you.' The intensity of her happiness steadied her voice. 'I had no idea that feelings like this existed. I had no idea that I could ever want to belong to someone as utterly as I want to belong to you. Ashe, the day I met your sisters for the first time, before I knew who they were, I thought that Katy must be your daughter, until I worked out that the ages were wrong. I spent the day in a daze, thinking about having your children.' She smiled tenderly at him and he realised he must be staring at her like a besotted idiot. He did not care. 'And yet I didn't realise I was in love with you then,' she added. 'I think that should have been a clue.'

Ashe felt like Joshua blowing the trumpet before the gates of Jericho and then being stunned that the walls fell so easily. He should have had more faith. 'I love you.

You love me. We want to get married. If I get a licence, can we be married here? Do you mind or do you want to go back to London and do it all properly?' He felt like Joshua and he felt about seventeen again and he felt like fainting from sheer happiness. Which was impossible because what he wanted to do next was pick Bel up, lay her on that big bed and…

'May we be married from your home—from Coppergate? I want to be part of it, I want all your people around us so I can start to be part of its life. Ashe…' she stroked her hand down his chest, making him catch his breath painfully '…you have been reluctant to go home before now. Can we make it ours, together?'

'Oh, God, yes.' The breath sighed out of him as he realised why he had not felt comfortable there. It was still his parent's home and it would never be his until he brought his own bride to it. No wonder he had seen Bel everywhere he looked. Deep inside him something had known instinctively that she was the one for him. He should have listened to his heart.

'Only, it will not take too long to make the preparations, will it?' she asked anxiously. 'I wonder if Sebastian and Eva can come from Maubourg in time? I had a letter from Maubourg just before I left London and they are thinking about coming back soon.'

'We will make it as soon as you want. As soon as your family can be with us,' he assured her. Anything for Bel—he would beard the Archbishop in his palace if that was what it took. He sat looking at her, stunned that she was really his, almost afraid to touch her, the awe of it paralysing him.

Bel saw the change in Ashe and did not know whether to cry or give thanks. He had realised she was his and now he was about to set her on a pedestal, honourably determined to be the perfect gentleman.

'Ashe,' she began, letting her hand slide slowly downwards until his nipple was between her fingers. She squeezed gently. He closed his eyes. Better. 'I do not want to spend a month or so pretending that this is a suitable society marriage and that I have nothing on my mind beyond buying my trousseau. I have bought one trousseau and very boring it is.'

She lifted her other hand, bringing his with it, and bit on the knuckle of his index finger. He gasped, his eyes still closed.

'What I want is for us to make love, now, this minute and on every possible occasion. And I want to feel you inside me, not being careful, not careful at all. I want you to take me, fill me—' his eyes opened, dark as the depths and he pulled her hard into his arms '—complete me. And,' she added with a shaky smile because he was going to kiss her in a moment and it was going to be wonderful, 'we could make a start on the family.'

'Bel—' he stood and scooped her up in his arms, strode across the room and set her on her feet beside the bed '—do you realise we do not have to worry about the state we leave the bed in any longer?'

Doubt flickered through her and he laughed. 'You are just going to have to be the scandal of Margate, because I intend to demolish this bed this afternoon.'

'Oh, yes, please,' she breathed as he began to unfasten her gown. It slithered to the floor and she kicked it away, heeling off her slippers with scant regard to their fragile kid. Her petticoats and chemise followed the gown, leaving her in stockings and garters and a blush.

'Hmm,' he hummed appreciatively. 'How very pretty.' To her surprise he turned her so that she faced the bed and pushed gently until her hands rested on the counterpane. 'Oh, yes, so pretty.' His caress slid down her back, over the swell of her buttocks and he moved in close, nudging her legs apart with his knee.

Bel shivered with a mixture of shyness and wicked erotic delight. What was Ashe going to do? It did not matter, it was Ashe and he loved her and she wanted to please him. Instinctively she pushed backwards, finding the curve of her buttocks cradled against his loins. So hot, so ready for her. His hand slipped between her thighs from the back as the other one began to caress her breasts, cupping them, stroking them as he nuzzled the nape of her neck.

She was utterly open to him. 'I can't touch you,' she protested, the words breaking off on a moan as his clever fingers slid into her, filling her and tormenting her with the promise of what would follow. 'You will, *ma belle*,' Ashe promised, huskily against her nape as his other hand tormented her aching nipples into points of aching desire.

His fingers slid out of her and he surged against her, filling her more than she had ever imagined possible. With a cry Bel braced herself on her arms, her head thrown back into the angle of his neck, as his mouth worked up and down the tender flesh, driving her into screaming, shameless, writhing ecstasy.

'I love you.' His voice was a claiming in her ears as his body drove hers harder and harder to where she wanted to be.

'Ashe, please…' She did not know what more she wanted, what more she could endure.

'Yes,' he said, stroking hard into the heart of her, his hand slipping round to find the aching point of need and touching, touching until she was almost, desperately, there. 'Now, Bel?'

'Yes,' she sobbed and he took her over into bliss, into fire and light and almost unbearable pleasure and he was still with her, inside her, completing her as his voice cracked on a cry that was her name and she felt, for the first time, his love shuddering to fulfilment within her.

'I love you.' Bel woke and stirred lazily, stretching against the long, hot body beside her and remembering—Ashe telling her he loved her, Ashe murmuring words of love after his body had shown her over and over the truth of it.

'I love you too,' she whispered, mouthing the words against sweat-filmed skin. Ashe tasted delicious. Salt and male and sex and satisfied desire. Her body ached with the delicious fulfilment of their love-making and yet, deep inside, something stirred. Something wicked and needy and dark and sensual. 'Have we quite wrecked this bed yet?' she murmured, working her way up with nibbles and licks towards his ear lobe.

'Not quite,' he answered, rearing up on his elbows to survey the tangled sheets.

'Oh, good.' Bel settled down against his chest, wondering which of the infinitely delicious fantasies she had in her mind they could try next. Or which of Ashe's.

'But I suppose we have a lifetime of beds to wreck,' he said thoughtfully. 'Should we go and tell our family and friends the good news?'

'In a minute,' Bel agreed, sliding down the bed on a voyage of discovery.

'All right,' Ashe said, his diction somewhat muffled by a gasp as he grabbed for the bed head. 'In about an hour.'

* * * * *

On sale 6th June 2008

THE MAN FROM STONE CREEK
by Linda Lael Miller

There was trouble in Haven, Arizona, and Ranger Sam
O'Ballivan was the man to sort it out. Badge and gun
hidden, he arrived posing as the new schoolteacher – and
that led to a call on Maddie Chancelor, older sister of
a boy in firm need of discipline.

Maddie was a graceful woman whose prim and proper stance
battled with the fire in her eyes. Sam's job had always kept him
isolated and his heart firmly in check. But there was something
about Maddie that had him unwittingly tempted to start
down a path he'd sworn he'd never travel.

'Miller paints a brilliant portrait of the power of love
to bring light into the darkest of souls. This is western
romance at its finest.'
—*Romantic Times BOOKreviews*

Celebrate 100 years of pure reading pleasure with Mills & Boon®

To mark our centenary, each month we're publishing a special 100th Birthday Edition. These celebratory editions are packed with extra features and include a FREE bonus story.

Plus, starting in February you'll have the chance to enter a fabulous monthly prize draw. See 100th Birthday Edition books for details.

Now that's worth celebrating!

15th February 2008

Raintree: Inferno by Linda Howard
Includes FREE bonus story Loving Evangeline
A double dose of Linda Howard's heady mix of passion and adventure

4th April 2008

The Guardian's Forbidden Mistress by Miranda Lee
Includes FREE bonus story The Magnate's Mistress
Two glamorous and sensual reads from favourite author Miranda Lee!

2nd May 2008

The Last Rake in London by Nicola Cornick
Includes FREE bonus story The Notorious Lord
Lose yourself in two tales of high society and rakish seduction!

Look for Mills & Boon 100th Birthday Editions at your favourite bookseller or visit
www.millsandboon.co.uk

FREE

2 BOOKS AND A SURPRISE GIFT!

We would like to take this opportunity to thank you for reading this Mills & Boon® book by offering you the chance to take TWO more specially selected titles from the Historical series absolutely FREE! We're also making this offer to introduce you to the benefits of the Mills & Boon® Reader Service™—

- ★ **FREE home delivery**
- ★ **FREE gifts and competitions**
- ★ **FREE monthly Newsletter**
- ★ **Books available before they're in the shops**
- ★ **Exclusive Reader Service offers**

Accepting these FREE books and gift places you under no obligation to buy; you may cancel at any time, even after receiving your free shipment. Simply complete your details below and return the entire page to the address below. You don't even need a stamp!

YES! Please send me 2 free Historical books and a surprise gift. I understand that unless you hear from me, I will receive 4 superb new titles every month for just £3.69 each, postage and packing free. I am under no obligation to purchase any books and may cancel my subscription at any time. The free books and gift will be mine to keep in any case.

H8ZEE

Ms/Mrs/Miss/Mr.................................Initials ....

BLOCK CAPITALS PLEASE

Surname ....

Address ....

....

....Postcode ....

Send this whole page to:
The Reader Service, FREEPOST CN81, Croydon, CR9 3WZ